Shh!

An Oxley College Novel

STACEY NASH

Shh!

Edited by **Lauren McKellar**
Cover Art by **KILA Designs**
Interior Design by **Max Effect**

By Stacey Nash

Dedication

FOR MY CHILDREN;

may you always know

your parents' love is unconditional.

The
Rumour

Chapter 1

*S*AVANNAH WEST and I made our way down the skinny path, the lines of trees ringing the open paddock around us. None of my friends usually tagged along to hockey, but Savvy popped up at my games every now and again. We'd walked in silence for a few moments when Savvy cleared her throat. "How are things with you and Christian?"

"Fine," I said, scrunching my brows. "That's a weird question."

"It's the start of a new year, you know ..." She trailed off, leaving me wondering where the question had come from. Christian and I were pretty rocky lately, but it wasn't like I'd spoken to Savvy about it, nor was I about to.

"Are you coming tonight?" I asked in an attempt to divert the conversation.

"Of course," Savvy squealed. "I heard that Dane Beaumont is going as a bodyguard, and I'm not missing that glorious sight."

I cringed at the high pitch that shot out of her, but a smile tugged at the corner of my mouth anyway. Good lord, I loved this girl's enthusiasm.

We were almost home and I looked both ways before we crossed the road into the car park of our dorm, Oxley College. "I've got the best nurse outfit. Are you dressing up?"

"A sexy nurse, I hope." She waggled her brows.

I slid my phone out of my pocket and checked the time. "Shoot. Sorry, Savvy, I've only got ten minutes. Better run. I'll see you tonight."

"Bye." She waved her fingers as we walked through the gates of Oxley and into the back courtyard, then I peeled off toward Front and ducked into the stairwell that led up to my block. Each block was home to two floors worth of co-ed students. The dorms weren't overly fancy, but I loved living here, surrounded by friends. I also loved not being a freshman. The more senior students got the pick of the rooms and my second floor room was certainly spacious when compared to many of the others. I shoved my key in the lock, tossed my bag on the ground and ran for the floor's communal bathroom. Lucky the shower was empty.

In four minutes flat I was back in my room, twisting my long, damp hair into a bun at the nape of my neck. I slipped into the white dress and pulled my heels on, then tucked my key into my bra as I dashed out of the room and down the stairs. The costume looked pretty good, since the uniform was authentic; pocket watch and all. *Thanks, thrift store.* I ran straight to the dining hall, nodding and smiling at everyone I darted past on the way.

Voices wafting out of the back room meant the rest of the social committee had already arrived. And with words including *keg* and *goon* in the air, it sounded like they were sorting out drinks. I pushed the door open and came face to face with Christian, a keg balanced on his shoulder. Gee, he looked fine tonight, his biceps bulging through his thin t-shirt from the hefted weight.

"Hi, hon," I said, and stepped out of the way.

With the world's tightest smile, he manoeuvred around me, Dane close behind him with a second keg of beer. Sure enough, Dane was dressed security-style in black from head to toe. A two-sizes-too-small t-shirt stretched across his toned chest like he was sculptured art. He also had some kind of earpiece connecting his ear and mouth. Unlike Christian, Dane met my gaze with a wide smile and a wicked wink. Good lord, the guy was a flirt.

Tonight my job was armbands, and I needed to hop to it. It would take two of us to get everyone covered. Lucky for me Ella Parry was already there, her long auburn hair brushing over the printout in front of her. She and I had been in each other's lives forever. Our parents ran in the same social circles, so we'd been thrown together a lot over the years. When we'd both been accepted into UNE we'd somehow wound up at the same college.

"How are we looking?" I asked.

"Pretty good. There are one-hundred-ninety-eight people confirmed, which is just about everyone in Oxley. What's even better is I think we've got some ex-collegians, too. Not many though."

"Awesome. Sorry I'm late. Where are we up to?"

"You're right on time." She glanced up and pointed to a small box in the corner. "Grab the bands and we'll go set up."

I grabbed the box, and Ella stood, pushing her dead-straight hair over her shoulder. This was a courtyard party, so we'd set up registration right at the corner of Front Courtyard. It would be easy for everyone to find us and there was plenty of room for a line to form.

Ten minutes later we'd dragged a table outside, set up two chairs behind it, and were poised with highlighters, ready to verify attendees. We weren't a moment too early either. The first group stopped by on their way back from dinner, and after that people kept coming. Our task was to make sure only those who had paid actually got tagged. There'd be no free grog here tonight. It was the perfect job for me, because I got to socialise and work at the same time. Two boxes ticked; making sure everyone saw me, and fulfilling my social committee duty.

I glanced up at the person next in line and saw a face I didn't recognise. His dirty-blond hair hung over his bright blue eyes in a way that was entirely too sexy, and a tiny coating of stubble—not quite a beard, but more than one-day growth—lined his strong jaw. And his lips, smooth and pink, tipped up at the corner as if he were in on a secret ... ah, flip. I'd totally been caught checking him out.

"And you are ...?" I managed to keep my voice level.

"Logan Hays."

"You're not from here."

"No," he said. "Alumni. I lived here a few years ago, but

I've got a place in town now."

Well, that was a sad thing for the female population of Oxley.

"Loges!" Dane swaggered up to the table, baton bumping against his hip. He slapped Logan on the back, ignoring the blond hanging off his own arm. "He's cool, Livia, let him in."

I stuck my tongue into my cheek, refusing to bite. Dane knew I hated my name being shortened. The dirty flirt winked at me again. What was with him tonight? Sure he liked to banter with all the girls, but usually not with me. Christian would have his balls if knew. The fact that he was slurring and obviously half tanked wouldn't save him. The blonde leaned into his side, and my gaze flicked back to Logan. His stomach, right at my eye level, was covered with a loose-fitting shirt, but the material fell over his body in such a way it was obvious there was muscle rather than flab underneath. My gaze travelled up to meet his. He still sported that teasing half-smile, his eyebrow now raised.

"R ... right." I dipped into the box for an armband. The whole thing toppled off the table, spilling blue plastic tags all over both me and Ella.

"Flipping heck." I shoved my chair back. Staring and dropping things—I was an embarrassment tonight. Scooping the tags up, I dumped them into the box, then popped back up. Logan was still watching me, his smile full-blown.

"Flipping ... heck?"

"Yeah, she's twelve," Ella said.

"Here's your armband. Have a great night." I shoved

the thing at him. Hopefully he'd disappear into the growing crowd of partygoers before I had the chance to do anything else crazy.

"Drink?" Savannah appeared beside me, wearing next to nothing. Savvy was all of five-foot-three and had blonde hair to die for. Tonight the rich honey-coloured locks hung loose. Her skimpy black dress rode all the way up her thighs, and fit her curvy form snugly. Tonight's theme was occupations, and well, she was dressed as a stripper who was acting out every guy's cop fantasy. She shoved a plastic cup at me, its contents splashing over the side and staining the tablecloth sickly yellow.

"Thanks." I took the cup before I wore whatever was inside it. When I looked up she was gone, swallowed by the crowd.

A little while later the line finally petered out, so I grabbed my untouched drink and swept my gaze around the full courtyard. Music blared through the air, bouncing off the chocolate-coloured brick walls and people shouted over it, trying to hold conversations. A couple leaned against the wall of block A, her body pressed between him and the bricks. I averted my gaze. I had no issue with steamy PDA, but these two looked as if they were one kiss away from ripping each other's clothes off and going for gold right there in the courtyard. That was a sight I could do without. Now, where was my sexy boyfriend?

It only took a few moments to spot Christian, standing higher than the crowd. Balanced atop one of the wooden picnic tables, he pointed at Dane who stood beside him, holding a glass stein. Dane had his head tipped back and beer coursed down his cheeks as he chugged it. A thick ring of girls surrounded them, singing a drinking song at the top of their lungs. Good thing my parents had never seen this side of Christian, or they sure as heck wouldn't approve.

Someone rammed into my shoulder and I was jarred backward.

"Oh ... I'm ... I ..." The girl scooped my cup off the ground, rose and tried to shove the empty cup into my hands. "Olivia ... I didn't ..."

Her eyes were fixed on my hands. Her hair, which hung in two long plaits to her waist, when coupled with her flannel shirt gave her a cowgirl appearance. Or something. She'd lived in the room next to mine last year—super sweet girl, but not exactly socially confident. She mostly stuck to herself. I was pretty sure she was a year ahead of me and Savvy. "It's okay, honestly, I wasn't going to drink it anyway."

"I'm sorry," she said again.

"How was your summer break?" An attempt to deflect the conversation worked. She actually met my gaze, and a wide smile broke out across her pretty face.

"It was awesome. I—"

"Olivia." Dane's voice boomed across the courtyard and he swayed, dangerously close to falling on the people crowded below the table. *Holy heck.* My stomach jumped into my throat but Christian saved him from falling off the table just as Dane yelled, "Let's hook up, babe. I'll make sweet love to you aaaall night long."

"What the hell?" The curse slipped out before I had a chance to self-filter.

And Christian just stood there, doing nothing. *Double*

what the flipping hell?

I pushed through the throng of partygoers, focused on my boyfriend and his mate who both laughed while Dane's flock of admirers joined in. If they thought this was funny, if it was some kind of a joke, it was really, really, lame, and there was no way it would continue. I was not joke material. My fingers dug into the cup, crushing it in my hand.

"Livie, Livie, likes to—"

I reached up, and fisting my hand in Dane's shirt, reefed him down off his makeshift stage. Still co-ordinated, despite the drunken appearance, he landed square on his feet beside me and dropped his arm over my shoulders. The tang of his beer breath assaulted my sense of smell.

"You have exactly two seconds to remove that, Dane Beaumont." I looked up at Christian. "Do something about him before I do."

Christian just shrugged.

Dane laughed.

"Now!" I said, my hands clenching at my sides.

One of Dane's hanger-ons giggled.

"We're over, Olivia." Christian finally looked my way for the first time all night. "I can't do this anymore. You're—"

My heart stopped beating then took up again way too fast. *Over?* This joke had gone way too far. I shoved Dane off me and my glare settled on Christian as I ground out, "Inside. Now."

Christian shook his head and downed the rest of his beer. Then his gaze turned icy. "I can't compete with your sex-ploits. Not. Doing ..."—he flicked his hand between us—"this anymore."

"My ... my ... what?"

The ice was in me, curling through my veins and settling in my tummy while all sound disappeared into a dull hum. This breakup wasn't happening right now. In public.

Dane made a disgusting gesture with his fingers and tongue.

Oh my god. This can't be happening. Why in heaven's name was Christian doing this? He knew how important reputation was and now ... well, now everyone was staring.

And laughing.

Tingles swept up the back of my neck and my chest tightened. Christian loved me. He'd said so a million times. Sure he'd been cold lately, but that was something we could talk through.

There was no way I was going to let this go down in the middle of a courtyard filled with all of our friends. "Not here," I bit out.

"It's done. There's nothing more to say."

I did the only thing I could. I ducked my head and like lightning, I shot out of there, not stopping until I reached my room where I slammed the door closed and slid down it, my mind reeling as I tried to make sense of what just happened.

This night had gone from bad to catastrophic.

Chapter 2

Going to breakfast.

I WAITED FOR a few minutes after sending the text, but either Savvy wasn't awake yet, or she was already down in the dining hall without her phone. Drawing in a deep breath, I set my hand on the door handle. This was the first time I'd ventured out of the dorm since Saturday night's public break-up and my chest felt as if it were full of something unpleasant. Unfortunately my growling stomach held the upper hand, forcing me into the dining hall before I headed to classes. I grabbed my backpack, pulled my door open and swiftly jumped out of the way as a naked figure fell toward me.

My heart tried to jump right out of my chest and I braced for impact, but the body spun off me, landing on the floor half inside my room with a jolly bounce. Male laughter echoed from somewhere down the hall and the blow-up doll stared at me, its red lips open wider than a mouth should.

Again.

That stupid doll had made an appearance yesterday too. In all honesty, things had been weird since the public break-up. There had been quite a bit of knocking on my door yesterday as a direct result, but after the 'joke' visit from my friend lying on the floor here, I'd stopped answering.

I kicked Dolly out of the way and stepped over the threshold, pulling the door closed. I could do this. I would do this. I had to face them all, and better sooner than later. I marched down the stairs, through the courtyard and into the dining hall. Eight wasn't overly early or late, but the place was packed. Guess I wasn't the only one with a nine o'clock start. As I walked up to the servery, my back prickled so much my cheeks heated. It felt as if every pair of eyes in that room rested on me, burned into me, while people silently questioned Saturday night's events.

My hand quivered. My stomach churned.

My feet turned me right around and I didn't stop walking until twenty minutes later when I reached a vending machine up on campus. I fished enough coins from my purse to select the most substantial item inside the machine. It clattered to the tray and retrieving my measly breakfast, I decided to head right to class. It was a little early, but that was better than hanging out at Oxley—at least up here the people from my dorm were a minority, not the majority. I could blend into the crowd.

We were already three weeks into term and I loved Sociology; the first-year subject I chose as my elective was a nice break from all the heavy Law subjects, yet it was still relevant to my degree. I took a bite of the banana flavoured-muesli or whatever-it-was bar and picked up the pace, wanting to make sure I had plenty of time. The arts building was a little down the hill, and I strode off in that direction.

It felt good to be on campus and not floating around Oxley where all everyone was talking about were Christian and me. Just as I passed the library an ear-piercing wolf whistle sliced the cool end-of-summer morning. Not an uncommon noise, so I kept walking, but then it came.

"Olivia!"

I glanced across the perfectly mowed lawns to a group of people gathered under one of the huge gum trees.

A fresher I'd seen around college a few times beckoned me over. It looked like the whole group were all first years, so maybe they needed help with directions or something. Boy, I'd gotten lost up here during my first year. UNE was a small campus compared to the city universities, but it still felt mighty huge when you were adjusting from high school. I walked toward them, and the dude who'd called out jumped up and ambled over.

"Hey," he said, walking toward me. "I hear you're one hell of a vixen in the sack."

Every muscle in my body went rigid and I tightened my grip on my bag as I shot him the best fake smile I could muster, and said, "Then it's a pity you just blew your chances."

The laugh I forced out was just as strained as the smile, because what I really wanted to say—no, yell—was, *what*

12

is wrong with you people?

This had to stem from my public break-up with Christian. The stares in the dining hall had been horrendous this morning, but this ... this was different.

I spun away, wishing I hadn't stopped.

"C'mon, baby." He grabbed my arm.

Heat raced to my face and I tugged myself free of his slimy grip. This wasn't cool, by any stretch of the imagination. Guys didn't throw themselves at me, ever. Sure there was the odd flirt before I'd started dating Christian, but nothing as brazen as this. I held my chin steady as I walked away. It took every ounce of my strength not to run. There was no way I'd let that idiot see that he'd affected me. Maybe this was some kind of awful joke. *Let's see who can embarrass Olivia the most.* It was no secret that I was a little old-fashioned, and put too much stock in what other people thought. Maybe this was a stupid challenge for one of Oxley's boys' clubs. Whatever it was, I wasn't hanging around to find out. The group continued whistling and cat calling, but I tuned them out and kept walking until I was safely inside the glass doors and steadily moving down the stairs to my lecture theatre. Thank gosh, I was the first to arrive.

I slid into a seat in the third row, and hung my head in my hands. What a nightmare. Stares, whispers ... if there was some sort of sexual rumour going around about me, that could be the end of my hopes of getting a job at Deakin Parry Associates in Law after graduation. Reputation was everything. Well, that and a perfect academic record, and I'd worked hard to maintain both. If there was a rumour my upcoming campaign for student council president may be the only saving grace.

But rumours spread and they were sure to reach Deakin Parry, since Ella Parry's father was a senior partner. The Ella who told her mother everything, who in turn told every person who happened to cross her path. Cripes. This would surely be the beginning of the end. The end of my hope of becoming a top-tier lawyer, the end of achieving everything I'd spent my whole life chasing.

The theatre filled in around me while I tried to figure out what went wrong with Christian. He wasn't always perfect, we weren't perfect, but I thought we'd had something special. Yeah, things had been declining. It wasn't the sex; that seemed all right. We'd spent the whole night together more than a few times. But thinking about it, he'd been avoiding sleepovers lately. Making excuses to leave before we fell asleep. Whatever his reasons, the way he'd behaved on Saturday night wasn't him, and I really didn't think he'd been that drunk. Not like Dane. I wasn't all that upset. It was more like a puzzle I needed to solve.

"Mind if I join you?" A deep voice broke my thoughts and I looked up into the brightest blue eyes. They weren't a steely blue-grey, nor were they a darker navy. They were like the azure of a tropical ocean pool and they were crinkled at the corners, matching the tiny amused smile curling one side of his full lips.

I'd been staring too long. Again.

"Logan Hays," I said.

"Olivia ..."

"Wants to sit alone."

"I won't bite, promise." Logan tipped his head to the side and made those gorgeous eyes of his round and pleading. Before I could answer, he slumped into the seat beside me.

This guy was in my class and I'd never noticed him? Boy, my Christian blinkers must have been firmly on. Either way, I wasn't sure I was happy to have him sitting right next to me. Nausea had been curling inside me since Saturday night and I felt kind of like a violin strung too tight.

"You studying human nature?" he asked.

"Arts, Law major. And I haven't seen you in this class before."

"I've seen you." A knowing smile stretched across his full lips and the way he held my gaze made those strings tighten and warm. The warmth collected in the pit of my belly.

Stop it, Olivia. You're not going there. I shuffled to the far side of my seat. I needed way more space than the tiny bit between us. Couldn't he leave a spare spot like normal strangers did? I pulled out my tablet and attached the keyboard, but his gaze remained on me. I could feel it prickling my back as I set the device up on my table.

"Often."

I flinched and pulled my bag into my lap to search for some imaginary item I really, really, needed right now. Anything to avoid looking at the sexy-as-hell guy who just owned up to watching me. Often. Oh my gosh, he was totally flirting. Heat rushed to my cheeks.

Logan chuckled, a deep throaty sound, and then it hit me. He was just doing the same thing as the fresher outside; coming onto me because of a dumb game, a stupid rumour, or whatever. He was a friend of Dane's after all.

"You should go sit somewhere else. I'm not interested."

Logan pulled a lecture pad out of his bag and slapped it onto his desk.

"Nope."

"Excuse me?"

"I'm not moving."

I scooped up my tablet and grabbed my bag. There was no way I'd sit there for his amusement. I stood up and took a step, but was tugged back into my seat by a firm hand on my waist.

I froze.

Tingles shot through my entire body like little earth-quakes and the place his hand sat? That was the gosh darn epicentre. Or maybe it was centred somewhere south of the pit of my tummy. Our gazes remained locked and his blue eyes softened.

"If you really want to be alone, I'll go." Logan's voice was dead serious—all traces of teasing gone. I dropped my gaze, ashamed of the right royal bitch inside me.

"Don't bother," I said. "I just ..."

The lecturer chose that moment to finally arrive, saving me as he bustled down the aisle and took his place at the lectern. I kept my eyes on the front of the room for the entire hour, not once glancing away from the balding man speaking in a boring monotone. Not even when I could practically feel the strange tension in the few centimetres of air that filled the space between me and Logan. Tension because I'd been mean, and now things were weird. Definitely not because he was attractive. No-freaking-way.

The professor must have wound up, because people began moving, yet I still sat there facing the front, watching the space where he no longer was. I had no idea what the lecture topic had even been. My mind was a blank haze.

"I usually sit up the back. Last to arrive, first to leave."

I jumped at the sound of Logan's low voice for the second time that day. "So you're not a stalker then."

What the heck, Olivia? I had no idea where that stupid declaration had come from. A hot guy like him wouldn't stalk me. Stalk anyone. Surely he wasn't short on attention from girls. Logan seemed to think it was funny though; it scored another one of his delicious chuckles.

"Not a stalker," he said.

"So it appears." I packed up my tablet and shoved it into my bag which I then slung over my shoulder. I needed to get out of there before I embarrassed myself again. This guy sure brought out the stupid in me. "Bye, Logan."

I strode up the aisle. I'd have to move fast to make it across to Business Law. I mapped out the long route in my mind—around the back of arts, through the carparks, all the way around the back of campus to the other carpark, then up through one of the other dorms. A bypass of the science faculty and I'd be there. I didn't want to risk running into that loser fresher again.

"Olivia ..."

I spun around. My hand landing on the door steadied me.

"What's your last name?" Logan asked.

Strange question; why did it matter what my surname was? We were barely on a first-name basis.

"That's the type of question a stalker would ask."

And with that I slipped out of the lecture theatre.

AT FIVE p.m I was starving. After just the muesli bar for breakfast, I'd skipped lunch to avoid a potential repeat of this morning, which meant my stomach had jumped into full riot mode. Nervous about facing my fellow students, I pulled my big girl panties up and marched myself to the dining hall. It was early, so I wasn't all that brave, if I were being totally honest with myself. The place should have been near empty.

There were half a dozen people in the common room, watching some crappy reality television show. I scooted around the back of the seats and up into the dining hall. Dinner smelled delicious—burgers—if my senses served me right.

Twirling my meal card around my fingers, I strolled right up to the servery and stood in line. The girl in front of me turned and I tossed a confident smile her way. She smiled back. The line wasn't moving yet as dinner hadn't officially started, but people began flowing in, increasing the number of voices in the room. I swiped my clammy hands on my jeans. This was the first time in more than a year that I'd come down to dinner alone. Generally I came with Christian and being alone was a little daunting. It was all cool, though. Savvy should turn up soon, then I wouldn't look like a loner. She never responded to this morning's text and I hadn't seen her since Saturday night, but that wasn't uncommon if she'd hooked up with a guy. Especially with how busy I'd be this year. She knew my Sundays were reserved for study, so she didn't usually bother me then, and today we'd been at classes. Still it was a little weird. She could have at least called to chat about Christian, surely she knew like everyone else.

My tummy grumbled like a truck moving at high speed. I glanced up at the clock; it read fivea thirty p.m. The line started moving, thank the lord. I glanced over my shoulder, and surprisingly the line curled all the way around the edge of the hall. Everyone had to be famished tonight, not just me.

I kept my eyes to the front and walked through the servery where I built my own burger: meat, egg, tomato, beetroot, no lettuce, and a slathering of tomato sauce—perfect. As I emerged out the other side, my gaze slid over the line, looking for someone who might join me, and the weirdest thing happened. Not a soul met my gaze. It was like they all deliberately looked the other way, or were engrossed in such deep conversation that they didn't see me.

I'd never had problems with friends. People just ... well ... they liked me. It had always been that way. I liked everyone, and they all liked me back.

My tummy churned for reasons not associated with hunger. What the heck had I done wrong? I walked over to one of the many empty tables and set my tray down, then flicked my phone out of my pocket and pretended to check my texts. Savvy had replied and I'd missed it.

Sorry I missed breakfast.
Catch you at dinner.

A string of girls who I knew—we'd all been freshers together last year—walked right past me, talking softly as if they thought I couldn't hear, but when people are talking about you, it's not hard to tell. And those girls were most definitely doing just that. The glances my way every few seconds were a dead giveaway when everyone else in the room was deliberately avoiding my gaze.

I ducked my head, and studied my phone again. Whatever was going on, it was weird. I was the captain of Oxley's hockey team, netball team, in the social committee, and even campaigning for the university's student council. I had lots of friends.

Savannah's giggle sounded like it came from somewhere behind me. Thank gosh. I really needed to talk to her and figure out what was happening. The whispers and stares, the fresher at uni this morning, Dane on Saturday night, *sexploits*—Oh my gosh. Christian. I swung around and glanced over my shoulder, raising my hand to call Savvy over, but my heart dropped into my stomach.

Savvy was attached to Dane's hip. Her arm hung around his waist and his rested on her shoulders. Christian walked in step with them and the two guys wore massive grins. I hadn't seen Christian that happy since … well, since I couldn't remember. I suppose now that I thought about it, lately he'd been kind of cranky and tired. Always tired.

I swung back around in my seat, hoping they hadn't seen me, and there someone had sat in the chair opposite me: the tool from this morning. He stared like I was some porn star he'd just paid to watch. And he smelled like a brewery; not to mention his eyes looked a little glassy.

Shh!

Those same eyes locked on my mine and he placed his flattened palm on his chest like he was about to dive head-first into a heartfelt apology. Which frankly, he owed me. His hand circled over his left pec, going for his heart, but then it moved to the other side and—*ohmygod did he just tweak his nipple?* My heart pounded a little faster and I glanced away. The entire dining hall looked at us. But he was like a train wreck. I couldn't stop my gaze sliding back. His hand trailed down his chest and disappeared under the table in the general direction of his groin. He moaned, then his arm started moving slow at first and increasing in speed, all the while his dark eyes held my gaze. Then the crazy guy rolled his eyes back in his head and yelled, "Yes. Aaa—aa—ash. Yes!"

Someone clapped.

He arched his back. What in hell's name was this freak doing? It was like that old nineties movie where the chick faked an orgasm in the middle of a café, except this was some dude in the centre of the Oxley College dining hall and I wasn't entirely sure he was faking it.

Spent, he flopped in the seat, his arms hanging beside it, then snapped his head forward again and his face split in a stupid grin as he pushed his chair back, placed an arm across his waist, and freaking bowed.

Everyone laughed.

The whole room full of people thought this idiot was funny.

I couldn't move. It was as if the air had frozen around me and I was a statue unable to even blink.

"My impersonation of the one and only Olivia Dean," he shouted, loud enough for the whole room to hear.

Couldn't the ground just open up and swallow me already? My cheeks burned so hot they should have caught fire. Blood rushed past my ears so loud that I couldn't hear another thing; my stomach lurched.

I was going to throw up.

I needed to get out of there, right now. Whatever held me in place snapped free. I shot to my feet and high-tailed it out of the dining hall, past a million staring faces. The common room was no more than fuzz at the edge of my periphery, Front Courtyard much the same. I cut across the back of block F and made a beeline for K, then darted up the stairs and into my room.

Whatever was going down, it looked like I was the centre of a joke I didn't find funny or nice.

A soft tap sounded at my door. I ignored it. They could all go to hell. I flung myself on my bed, totally humiliated. Why was this happening? I didn't sleep around. I wasn't a tease. I was just me, plain old Olivia Grace Dean. Was this because of Christian? He'd said sexploits, and there must be sexy rumour with my name slapped on it. I needed to pull myself together and talk to him. Talk this out like we should have on Saturday night.

Yes, that's what I'd do. Tomorrow. Right now, I couldn't move at all. My legs felt all wobbly, and my stomach still threatened to bring up all the food I hadn't eaten today. Good thing I kept a stash of snacks in my top cupboard. Somehow managing to climb to my feet, I threw the cupboard open and my heart sank. It was just about bare. I scavenged some dried fruit from the very back and sat at my desk, busting the packet open.

I flicked my computer on, and when it booted up, went

straight to email. Four new messages. Mum, Student Services, Savannah, and lhays14@une.com. *Hmm, not an address I know.* Savvy's message was date stamped yesterday, 16:09.

> *I'm so sorry about Christian. The guy's a jerk and revenge will be sweet. Knocked on your door once or twice today to plan said revenge, but you didn't answer. I won't let you get away with solitude for long.*

I clicked to open the other message from an unknown sender.

> *Olivia Wants-To-Sit-Alone,*
>
> *Your screen was noticeably blank at the end of today's lecture. Thought you might appreciate a re-cap.*
> *You're welcome.*
>
> *Stalker Boy*

Ohmygod. I snapped the offending laptop closed and jumped away from it. Lhays14 had to be Logan. How in the heck did he get my email and why was he being nice?

He *so* wanted in because of those damn rumours. Whatever they were.

Chapter 3

I WASN'T GAME to show my face around college until I got to the bottom of this mess. At least not in crowded places like the dining hall, which meant I needed food, which meant a trip into town. Luckily, I had no early classes on Tuesdays. My first lecture was at eleven, so I had time to nick in and back out before I needed to head up the hill to campus.

After a quick shower, and pulling on my jeans and tee, I grabbed my purse and headed out. With nerves churning my tummy yet again, I took the long way around the back of the dorm and to the street, then over to the bus stop. Not walking through college was self-preservation, not cowardice. Maybe. While I waited for it to arrive, I tipped my head back and peered up at the dappled light passing through the massive elm trees.

Town, then uni, then tonight I'd talk to Christian.

A lump formed in my throat. We'd had a good thing and it was over. I had no idea why or even if it was my fault. He and Dad had gotten on so well when he'd come to visit me over the summer break that my parents would be disappointed. Christian came from a good family that was well connected. I sighed. Who broke up with someone without even discussing the reasons? And publicly? It all seemed really ... high school.

"Livia!"

I cringed at the sound of my not-name being hollered from the opposite side of the road, but it was just Savannah, looking like a giant strawberry in a bright trench coat and matching crimson boots. She waved like a lunatic, glanced both ways far too quickly and darted across the road to join me. Her arms swooped around me as she pulled me in tight. I almost melted into her embrace, for the first time in days feeling a little less alone.

"Where have you been? I've called by a dozen times and you never answer, then you're not at meals either, or answering emails. I've been worried about you, and I'm so sorry about Christian."

"It's been weird. Everyone's been weird." I swallowed the pain in my throat.

She pushed me back at arm's length and her gaze rolled over me from head to toe.

"You look terrible. Where's all your style ... and your ... your makeup?"

A rumble made me bring my gaze back to the road in time to see the bus pull up. I would have rathered stay here with my best friend, but there wasn't time.

"That's me. I've got to go, but I need to talk to you, tonight?"

"I've gotta talk to you, too."

I pushed away, fished a handful of coins out of my purse and handed them to the driver as I climbed on the bus. There were a few people sitting up back, but mostly it was empty which suited me just fine. I slid into a vacant seat near the middle and rested my head against the window.

I look terrible.

Something smacked into the glass and I glanced outside where Savvy waved her arms around like an airport landing marshal. When she realised she'd caught my attention, she shook her head and pouted. Was that a no, she couldn't talk tonight? The bus pulled away before I could figure out her wild gestures.

I just about upended my purse searching for my compact, my mother's voice admonishing me even when she wasn't here; *always look your best, Olivia. It doesn't matter if you're out to lunch with the queen or just lazing around the house.* She'd hate to see me in jeans, not a skirt or dress pants. At least my hair was styled perfectly and not pulled up in a messy ponytail. Most of the contents of my bag rested on my lap and my fingers scraped the bottom lining. It wasn't there. I shoved everything back in and took to staring out the window. No point wallowing over what I couldn't change.

We finally pulled up at my stop and I got off. My stomach rumbled like I hadn't eaten in three days, which I kind of hadn't. Not a proper meal anyway. There was enough money in my account that I could splurge on breakfast. That was an awesome idea. Bacon, eggs, sausages ... I needed all of those and by the sound my stomach just made it sure seemed to agree.

I headed into the mall. An almost empty cafe caught my attention. Privacy was just what I needed, so I waltzed in, eyeing off all four booths and less than a dozen rickety tables. No one I knew was about, so I pulled out a wooden seat just inside the door, placing my back to the mall and any passers-by. Laminated menus rested against the salt and pepper shakers. Grabbing one, I gave it a quick once over. Wow, those were some pretty steep prices. No doubt the reason this place wasn't teeming with college kids like most other cafes in town.

I scanned the menu more thoroughly. *Pancake stack served with your choice of maple syrup and double cream or a fresh fruit compote.*

Hmm not bad.

Fried bacon, mushrooms, tomato, hashbrown, eggs cooked to your liking. Served with two slices of deliciously thick toast.

My mouth flooded. My tummy grumbled. The food called my name.

"Well, if it isn't Olivia Wants-To-Sit-Alone."

I flinched at the sound of Logan's smooth voice. What the flip was he doing here? My hand hit my purse which scooted across the table, knocking over a jug of water that wasn't there a moment ago. Liquid pooled on the wooden surface and seeped toward its edges. Shoving my chair back, I grabbed the only napkin in the otherwise empty holder and tried to soak up the mess. My war was futile though—water cascaded down the sides of the table while Logan chuckled. He swept a cloth over the wooden surface, and soaked up my mess, yet bubbles of water remained on the shiny surface. I'd made such a mess even his towel sized cloth couldn't absorb it all. What was wrong with me? Every time I was around this guy I turned into a clumsy fool.

"I'm such a disaster," I muttered as my cheeks began to burn.

"Hey." Logan's large eyes captured mine. "It's just a little water, no big deal."

Maybe it was a build up of the past few days, or maybe it was the tenderness in his voice, but for a split second I lost all my inhibitions, all sense of what was important and how I should behave. I slumped back into the chair and didn't fight the painful lump in my throat or the burning behind my eyes.

It was a big deal. Everything was a big deal.

"Olivia ..." Logan's voice was soft, warm. "If you're a disaster, then I'm a fucking tornado hot on the heels of a tsunami that was caused by an earthquake."

I couldn't help the smile that crept onto my lips. I glanced up at him, only he wasn't all the way up there; his face was level with mine, his blond hair catching on his stubbled cheek as he leaned in. He'd pulled another chair over and sat so close his jean-covered knees bumped mine.

"What about the flash flood?" I bit my tongue, because I was the flash flood. The proof was right in front of us, in a puddle on the floor.

A smile crept onto his lips and he leaned further in until his face was right up in mine. "I'm the fire that burned so intense it evaporated."

His gaze burned as hot as his words and heat radiated off every part of me, too. Sweat trickled down my back. He was too close, way too close, but I couldn't move and I wasn't sure I really wanted to.

I must have stopped breathing, because when he pulled back I sucked in a huge breath.

"Do you like music?" Logan asked.

"I ... I ..." Something had severed the pathways between my brain and mouth. Logan watched me while I looked at him. He tucked the chin-length strand of hair behind his ear; his eyes still held the same heat.

"Perfect," he said, standing up. "There's an awesome band playing up at the university bar next Friday."

Was that? Did he ... my heart leapt into my throat, filling the space between with a delicious warmth. Logan Hays wanted me to go ...

No, no, no. I wasn't going on a date with him. With anyone. No matter how hot his smile was, those eyes, his ridiculously toned biceps ... Darn it. He was too hot, which meant this had to be just another huge joke. I needed to toughen up, before he faked an orgasm. In a real cafe this time. I shook my head, but Logan had already turned around and was walking away with a notepad sticking out of his back pocket.

He returned a moment later with a fresh jug of water. "Now, what can I get for you?"

"Umm ... I ... ahh ..."

"Breakfast? Cake? Really early lunch?"

I still wasn't, couldn't, go out with him. I just ... how did I know he was genuine? I didn't. Besides I wasn't attracted to him ... not really.

"About next Friday—"

"Pancakes, eggs, toast, fruit salad. What would you like?"

"I ... big breakfast, please, but I can't—"

"Coffee, tea, OJ?"

"OJ. I'm not going out with you."

"Did I ask you out?" Logan tucked his pen behind his ear, and his gaze flashed away from mine. "I thought I told you about a gig you should check out."

Foot. Mine was firmly planted in my mouth, and I couldn't form a coherent sentence. Again. Logan turned and walked toward the counter, but not before I caught the tiny smile tugging at his lips.

THE REST of my day was uneventful. There was no one from Oxley in any of my Tuesday classes, and I managed not to bump into anyone on campus. I even made it back to my room having only passed a small group of people who sat in the courtyard. Some jerk wolf whistled, but I kept my chin high and didn't stop. I needed to keep myself grounded, so I didn't lose the nerve to confront Christian.

After heating one of those ordinary-tasting packaged meals in the microwave which sat in our block's tiny kitchen, I headed back to my room and flicked the laptop on. I didn't bother pulling out any text books, because I knew I wouldn't be able to concentrate. I'd been trapped in my own head all day, thinking about Christian, my future, my presidential campaign, but mostly thinking about Logan.

Settling at the wooden desk, with my creamy chicken pasta balanced on the edge, I hovered over the Facebook icon on my favourites bar. Nope. Instead, I opened my inbox and there it was. How did I forget all about Stalker Boy's email when I saw him at the cafe? I should have asked how in the heck he got my email address, and why he was emailing me in the first place. Sure it was kind of sweet that he noticed my lack of notes and thought to offer his, but it was also kind of weird that he had somehow procured my contact information.

I scanned his email again and shook my head, then clicked on an email from Savvy I'd somehow missed yesterday. It was time stamped ten-o-nine Sunday morning.

> *Babe! What happened to you last night? You*
> *just up and disappeared. I know it's study day,*
> *but WE HAVE TO TALK.*
> *Let me know what time's cool or I'll come by*
> *when it's not.*

My stomach flipped. She knew what this was about and if I had have checked my emails on Sunday—or hell, even answered my door—instead of lying on my bed staring at the ceiling, this could have been dealt with sooner. Stupid, mopey past self. Busy or not, maybe I should try and track her down before I talked to Christian.

I finished off my pasta, and went to look for Savvy to find out what she knew. It was half seven, so she should be done with dinner. I doubted she'd be in her room since she said she was busy, but it was the first place I headed anyway. A quick dash across the courtyard and up her staircase, then I raised my fist to rap on her door. No answer. The little whiteboard attached to the front read *BBL*. I sighed; fat lot of info that gave me. Knowing Savvy, later could mean anytime between now and Thursday.

The quiet girl from last year opened a door and stepped out into the hallway. Molly was in flannelette PJs that were as daggy as her unbrushed bed-hair. Her gaze flicked from her big bird slippers to me.

"Hi, Olivia," she mumbled as she shuffled past.

"Molly," I called. "Do you know where Savannah is?"

"Ah, no. But ..." She glanced back toward the door she just came out of. "Are you okay?"

Wow, even Molly had heard about Saturday night.

"Yeah, I'm fine."

"I don't believe them."

"Pardon me?"

"The rumours about you. I don't believe them."

"Gee, thanks Molly." I ran a hand across the back of my neck. "That means a lot."

She smiled as she disappeared into her room. And there it was; further proof there were rumours flying around about me. Just freaking great. I could say goodbye to the job at Ella's father's firm Dad had lined up if it was anything damaging. Lawyers have to live up to a certain standard and if my reputation was ruined, there'd be no hope of recovering. Deakin Parry Associates was my dream. Curling my arms across my roiling stomach, I turned on my heel and went straight down the stairs. Once in the courtyard, my gaze flicked up to Christian's window, and sure enough the light was on. He owed me an explanation and he was going to give it to me.

I marched up the stairs, past the middle floor and all the way to the top floor of block L. A fat beam of light fell into the hall from Christian's open doorway. I walked right up to it and went inside without knocking.

There were people everywhere. Or so it felt, because for the first time ever I was uncomfortable in the crowd; the huge room seemed tiny. They all sat in a rough circle on the floor playing cards. Probably poker.

My gaze focused on my ex-boyfriend. "We need to talk, and don't give me any of that 'not now' crap. It's happening. Now."

"Dude, I think you better talk to her." Dane climbed to his feet, the Celtic disc on his surfer necklace slapping against his chest as he tossed a handful of playing cards onto the floor. My gaze never wavered from Christian, whose shoulders dropped. I rocked back and forth on my heels, my arms clinging to my tummy while his friends filed out. Their absence revealing *my* friend, hanging behind Dane.

My jaw tightened. She was here, with them. That was why she was busy. Savannah mouthed something as she slipped away, but I didn't bother trying to make it out; I was too upset. I'd needed her, but she was hanging out with the guys who'd started the rumour which caused all the ruin Olivia moments of the past few days.

Christian sighed and ran a hand through his chocolatey hair. "I'm sorry about Saturday night. It shouldn't have gone down like that. I was—"

"Drunk, Christian. But you weren't that drunk."

"Yeah, I was ..."

He glanced toward the door where Savvy, Dane and the other guys had disappeared.

Christian pushed himself off the floor without bothering to gather up the discarded cards. He walked across the room, and closed the door softly. He looked just as good as always, in cargos and polo-shirt.

"Olivia ..."

I met his gaze, and his brow furrowed, his lips pressed into a thin line. "We're not right together."

I took a deep breath, and he dropped onto the edge of his bed. A bed we'd shared only a week ago. Things had seemed right enough for him then when he was getting his kicks. "What did you say about our sex life?"

His head snapped up. "Nothing."

Yeah, right. The laugh that tore from me was bitter. Of course he'd lied.

"Then why is every guy in college either hitting on or harassing me?"

He shrugged, his shoulders rising and falling in such a carefree motion that I wanted to grab them and shake him. The liar had said something—he just wouldn't own it. His gaze slipped away from me again.

"Stop lying, Christian."

His gaze flashed to mine, his eyes angry. "Fine. You want a reason? I'll give you the goddamn reason."

I opened my mouth, then thought better and snapped it shut so he'd keep talking.

"This is my final year, Olivia. It's all right for you, second year's not the be all and end all. This is important shit. I can't cope with the lack of sleep anymore. It's screwing with my head, with my grades, and my future. Just lying there awake while you rub yourself all fucking night long, then every time I try to touch you, you push me away like I'm a filthy pervert—it's killing me."

My jaw dropped. What was he saying? I'd never do that, or had done anything like it. *Rub myself?*

"What are you talking about?"

"You know exactly what I'm talking about. You're obviously not that into me, and I don't give a shit anymore."

I'd never pushed him away. Whenever he'd wanted sex I'd been into it. Into him. Sure, initially we'd taken it slow, but he'd never once pushed the point, and I'd never once turned him down. It was an unspoken agreement between us, and we'd both agreed. Hadn't we? When we'd started having sex last November just before the end of year break, it was good.

"Not into you? I don't freaking rub myself, and I have never pushed you away."

Christian laughed, cold and bitter as the air outside. Then he slowly shook his head. "Who's a liar now? Always perfect, aren't you?"

I didn't understand why he was lying. Why lie about something like that? *Unless he ...*

"If you didn't love me, you could have just said so. No need for stupid stories."

He scoffed and stood, pushing past me and yanking his door open. I looked from it to him. This was it? He was done? Well, I was done too. Done with this conversation, done with him, done with his blatant lies.

"That's bullcrap." I walked out of his room.

I **TRIED GOING** down to the dining room again, but knowing that the whispers and stares were because people thought I masturbated inappropriately was just too much. Then there were the guys who thought they were funny, or the ones who thought it was a turn on. Those were the worst.

Friday rolled around and I'd eaten through the stash of food in my mini fridge, so I ordered a pizza. They said it would arrive in thirty minutes, so exactly twenty-nine minutes later I shot downstairs and to the front car park. The pizza boy wasn't there yet. Great.

I tapped my purse on my thigh and waited while the odd car drove past as I tried to ignore the noise that carried from inside: music, voices, laughter, probably people enjoying a few drinks before they went out later.

With any luck, the partiers would stay inside until I

was safely back in my room. No doubt I would be an even bigger joke than normal after a few beers. That freaking dumb rumour still hadn't settled.

Voices moved closer, headed for the car park. I pulled my coat around me and shuffled from foot to foot. *Come on, Pizza Dude, hurry up.*

"Olivia?"

My stomach dropped. Just great; I'd been seen. Now there'd be no slipping back inside without any embarrassing moments. Plastering on a smile, I turned to the sound of the voice. Three silhouettes trudged over the small arched bridge that led into Oxley. Making out the faces was near impossible; they were definitely all girls though.

"What are you doing out here alone?"

Thank gosh it was just Molly. She peeled away from two of her friends and walked toward me.

A little car with a tacky pizza box attached to its roof chose just that moment to zip into the parking lot, and I waved my hand in its general direction. "You know, just got a pizza. Curry night sucks."

"It's pasta night."

Sprung.

"Oh ... well, that sucks too."

Molly turned to her friends. "I'll catch up with you later."

The other girls nodded and continued walking. What was she playing at?

"I really feel like some pizza." Molly smiled at me. "If you've got enough to share."

The pizza guy strolled over, carrying one of those red packs that keep food hot. Opening it, he said, "Ham and

Pineapple, pan base?"

"Yes, thanks." I unzipped my purse and handed over a twenty. The guy passed off the pizza box, and fished in his pocket for some change which he dropped in my outstretched hand.

"Have a good night," he said as he turned and walked toward his car.

Molly was looking at me expectantly. I'd never eat the whole thing, so of course I could share it with her. "I'll pop some on a plate and you can take the rest."

"I haven't seen your new room. I thought maybe we could eat together?"

Warmth spread inside me. It felt kind of nice that Molly wanted to hang out, and somehow I trusted that she wasn't in this for anything more than greasy food. "Um, okay, sure."

We walked in total silence until we were inside my room with the pizza box sitting on the desk that spanned wall to wall under my window. Molly closed the door behind us then blurted out, "I meant it when I said I don't believe that rumour, and even if it was true, who cares? It's no one else's business anyway. You're a great girl, Olivia, and that's what matters."

I stopped dead, my hand hovering above the plates stored inside my food-stash cupboard. My heart hammered in my ears as a lump formed in my throat. Molly was too freaking nice, and it was a pity her words weren't true. It did matter, more than she'd ever know. It mattered so damn much, and if being a great person was the be all and end all, then how come she was the only one who'd been nice to me all week? Stalker Boy excluded.

"You've been hiding, but you shouldn't let them push you away like that. Who cares what that dumbass ex of yours said? Hold your head high, Olivia. You're way better than every single of one those guys."

With that my eyes welled, and I still didn't turn around. I just let my hand drop to my side and for the first time since this all started, I cried.

Humiliation is an awful thing. It shatters all your thoughts, all your hopes, all your belief in yourself, and leaves you feeling completely exposed. And that's exactly how I'd felt all week, as if I were naked and needed to hide, to run from my shame and never let it catch me. Now, I felt like it actually had.

The thing was, even if Molly thought I was better than the rumours Christian's public break-up had started, there was no way I could hide from them, and there was no way to undo them. Those rumours hadn't abated, so Ella was sure to tell her parents.

Suddenly Molly's arms were around me and her hug felt almost … comforting. Something loosened inside me.

A knock sounded on my door.

Unease speared through me, making my breath shake.

I pushed away from Molly and she raised a brow in question. I shook my head. There had been lots of knocking on that first Sunday, and more ever since. I quickly learned it wasn't worth opening the door to see who was there.

"Olivia. Open up. I know you're hiding in there; I can see your light on." The voice coming from the other side was Savannah, and anger blasted through me. I yanked the door open and pulled her inside my room then slammed the door shut.

Her eyes narrowed, her bottom lip slackened, and she took a step toward me like she was going to hug me, but I took a step back. Some friend she was. I'd thought we were pretty close, but I'd been wrong. She hadn't bothered to call by since two nights ago in Christian's room.

She pulled her hand into the sleeve of her oversized football jersey. Probably Dane's. "I'm so sorry—"

"If you were sorry, you would have stuck by me, Savannah."

"I tried—"

"No you didn't. You hooked up with Dane and nothing else mattered."

"Oh, Livia, it's not like that at all." She reached for my hand which was hanging by my side, but I took another step back. If she knew me at all she'd know I hated my name being shortened. Heaven knows, I'd told her enough times.

Molly moved to stand by me.

"Babe, the rumours aren't serious. The boys were pretty smashed at the courtyard party, and—"

"I don't care."

"Please, Olivia, hear me out."

I felt like I was shaking. The whole room could have been closing in, and the only thing I could see was Savannah's betrayal.

"Get out."

She fisted a hand on her hip. "Absolutely not. Pull your head in and listen to me, Olivia Dean. I had no idea about those rumours until just now when Dane told me, and yes I hooked up with him. If that's a crime, then I'm as guilty as a peppermint choc-chip ice cream. But that stupid rumour is just that—stupid. Who in their right mind would think you buff the beaver to tease Christian, and tell me this—what red-blooded male wouldn't love every second of that anyway? A hot chick in his bed, mining for gold? Of all the dumbass things for him to make up ... seriously, the guy's an idiot."

A flush crept onto her cheeks, and Molly shoved a hand over her mouth which did nothing to stifle her snicker.

"What?" Savvy demanded.

"Buff the beaver?"

Savannah's mouth twitched as she fought to hold in a smile. "Come on ..."

"Buff. The ..." A laugh erupted from Molly like lava bursting from a volcano. "Beaver."

And that was enough to set Savannah off, too. Soon both of them were laughing so hard they clutched their sides. Savvy wriggled her eyebrows at me and I shoved her in the arm as a giggle bubbled in my throat.

She was right; it was stupid.

THE WEEKEND passed rather quietly. Our hockey team had a bye on Saturday and I had a Law assignment worth twenty-five per cent of my total grade due the following week, so I kept my head down and studied hard. I much preferred the subjects on the arts side of my degree than the ones on Law, but I came from a long line of attorneys and Dad said arts would get me nowhere fast. Being a Dean meant I had to uphold the family values and name, so an Arts/Law degree was my compromise—at least then I could enjoy a few subjects.

As I walked across campus on Monday morning, I found myself looking forward to Sociology. Once I reached the lecture theatre, I took my usual seat and pulled out my tablet, ready for the lecture to begin. I tapped through my notes as the room filled with the buzz of voices. Funny, since Friday night with Savannah and Molly, I hadn't felt as humiliated and I'd been able to hold my head somewhat high with my friends by my side. But sitting here alone was a different story. My tummy fluttered, and I couldn't sit still in my seat. It seemed like forever until the middle-aged lecturer arrived, in his usual bustle.

"Morning, everyone." He peered over the top of his glasses. "Looks like some of you had too good a weekend, hmm?" He paused, and someone snickered up the back. "This week we're moving onto globalisation."

A wave of air hit my cheek, and out of the corner of my eye I saw Logan slide into the seat beside me. "Hey, you," he said as he pulled out his notebook.

The lecturer stopped mid-speech and once again peered over his horn-rimmed glasses, his gaze zoning in on the place where we were sitting. He cleared his throat and said, "If everyone is quite ready, Mr Hays, globalization is not just about economics ..."

His voice faded out to the usual monotone drone and my gaze slid to Logan's hand, watching it move so easily over his notepad. He was a lefty, and his long fingers gripped the pen right near the tip, dwarfing it. Tendons worked in his wrist and up his arms as he wrote on the paper, and a thick vein wove from his wrist all the way up to his bicep then disappeared under the sleeve of his grey shirt.

The pen poked into my side and I jumped, my gaze flashing to Logan's. He pointed toward the front of the room and leaned in close to my ear. "Pay attention."

Heat flushed my cheeks. Oh my gosh, I was totally checking him out. Again. And he totally caught me. Again. What in the heck was I doing? I didn't like this guy. I couldn't like him. What would people say when Christian and I'd only just broken up? I focused my attention on the lecturer, but didn't hear another word he said. Logan and Christian kept bouncing through my head like they were players in a tennis match competing for my attention. Attention I didn't want to give either one of them. There was no way I was opening myself up to the hurt again.

Finally the lesson finished, and I jumped up out of my chair, pushed past Logan, and made right for the door. I really didn't want to give him the chance to call me out on my blatant staring. There was no way I could talk myself out of that corner. Besides, I had to be at my next lecture before it started.

ECON LAW passed much slower than Sociology, and by the time we reached the end of the lecture my tummy was grumbling so loudly Ella swung around from the row in front and gave me a filthy look. Thank gosh I had an hour off between this class and the next.

I left the Law faculty and made straight for the cafeteria. It was a nice sunny day and lunch outside would warm up my freezing toes. The weather was getting cooler and the days shorter. This godforsaken town had far more cooler months than warm, so soaking up the rays while they were still about seemed like a great idea.

When I got to the outdoor section of the cafeteria, it looked like I wasn't the only one who'd had that idea. The place was crowded.

I clutched my bag to my chest and took a deep breath before walking through all the people. Then I grabbed a fresh salad roll and a bottle of mineral water and took them to the counter. As I stood in line, I glanced around, hoping to see Savannah or Molly. But neither of the girls were there, even though Molly had said she'd be having lunch on campus today and that she had a break around the same time as me. Guess I'd beat her to it. I had no idea if Savvy was even on campus, but the cafeteria was one of her constant haunts.

"Enjoy Socio today?" Logan's voice sounded right behind me, and I swear I jumped three metres in the air.

He chuckled.

I spun around, my mouth working to form words.

All serious, he nodded toward the counter. "Pay attention."

Sure enough, the serving lady was looking at me expectantly. I scrambled through my bag until I found my purse and retrieved it, making sure to hold it extra tight lest I have another clumsy moment. Once I'd fished out some money, I handed it over to the woman, who snatched it away with a frustrated grunt. Then I stepped to the side and looked around for somewhere to sit. Logan had managed to completely frazzle me yet again.

There was an empty table outside, right in direct sunshine, so I headed toward it. A pencil-thin girl with beautiful almost-black hair that hung straight to her hips swooped in at the exact same time. She looked up with a tiny smile, knowing full well she just stole my table. I placed my water on the far end anyway. I could share.

"I have friends coming," she said, her voice prissy.

Sighing, I picked up my water and looked for somewhere else to sit. There were no free tables, but Logan sat by himself at a spot that half rested in a delicious beam of golden sunlight. He shot me a smile and patted the seat beside him.

Ooo-kay. I took a deep breath to brace myself against the brain-fog being near him caused, and strode over to his table. *Don't act like a fool.*

Logan's smile doubled.

"Hey there, Stalker Boy."

"Hey back, Butterfingers."

Oh my gosh. He didn't just go there. Butter was slippery like ... well like what those rumours implied. I pulled my bag off the table and to my chest. Maybe I couldn't do this after all.

Logan's hand caught my wrist, and his gaze landed on mine "I know I smell bad, but you should hang around, you'll get used to it."

Whether I liked it or not, I had to face reality. Life was hard. People would tease me, and that wasn't the end of the world. I took a long breath and sucked in my bottom lip then sat back down on the opposite side of the table.

Seemingly satisfied I wasn't leaving, Logan opened the plastic around his bread roll and took a bite. Strange, my appetite had all but disappeared, so I snapped open the bottle of water and set my salad roll aside.

"So," Logan said, his lunch poised in his hand, "you coming to the gig on Friday night?"

"No."

"Why not?" He took another massive bite. His roll was almost gone.

"Because I don't want to."

I couldn't stand the thought of being out at the bar, amongst a crowd of people who had all, no doubt, heard the rumour. Yes, I wasn't letting it get to me, but I wasn't a glutton for punishment either. Besides, I had another paper due.

Logan's roll was gone in one last bite. He balled up the plastic and tossed it at the bin, scoring a perfect shot. "You should go," he said, then cracked open his can of soft drink and took a sip. His blond hair swung forward and he tucked it back under the funny cap he was wearing. Reminded me of a grandpa hat in the old movies; a puffy bit that was press studded to the actual cap. On old men it looked out-dated; Logan made it look sexy though. Amazing what a cheeky smirk, and gorgeous eyes could pull off.

"Suppose you'll need my Socio notes again." He looked up at me through ink-black lashes, his expression serious. "Do you routinely not take notes in class, or am I just—"

"Tell me, Stalker Boy, how did you get my email address?"

"A magician never divulges his secrets." His lips quirked then dropped, as he fought to keep them straight but failed. Logan flipped a yellow sheet of paper in his fingers, over and over.

"A magician—"

My words were cut off by a forced laugh, cold, with each *ha* pronounced individually. I looked up to see the table thief swing her leg over the bench Logan was sitting on so she straddled it, facing him. Her long hair hung forward like a black barrier as she leaned in toward him, blocking their faces both from sight.

"I heard you were back in town, hot stuff. It's great to see you."

Suddenly feeling uncomfortable, I picked at the label on my water. Maybe she was his girlfriend, and if that was the case then he was a player. More reason for me to stay well away.

Logan grunted and my gaze flew to him of its own accord.

He'd leaned back so I could see his face, and his eyes were on me.

"I'm free anytime you want to party." The girl placed a hand on Logan's forearm, and trailed a line with her fingers up to his shoulder.

"Great," he said, never breaking our eye contact.

With a huff, she pushed herself forward, so as she rose her breasts brushed against Logan's arm, then she settled her gaze on me. I didn't know this girl, but her stare made me feel like slinking under the table. Instead of being a coward, I sat up straighter, and met her glare for glare.

The girl walked around our table, her hips swaying with each step. All for Logan's benefit I was sure. Then she leaned down until her head was next to mine, and she hissed, "Don't think you stand a chance with him, finger fuck girl. No guy will ever take you seriously."

Logan pushed back out of his seat and stood so he was towering over the table. He glared down at the pretty brunette. "Get the hell out of here."

"Come on, Loges ..." She reached for him across the table and Logan tensed.

"I take her seriously," he growled.

The girl flipped her hair over her shoulder, and said, "whatever," then sashayed away.

While I was sitting there dumbfounded, trying to figure out not only how he'd heard what she'd said, but what he'd meant, Molly slipped in beside me. She gave Logan an appreciative glance and said, "Why hello, Logan Hays."

He smiled. No wonder girls like the table thief were all over him; that smile could awaken sleeping hearts. It could mend them, break them, make them, all in a single heartbeat. Not mine though. Not now, and surely not on Friday night.

"Hiya, Molly," he said, pushing the yellow slip my way. "I've got to get going, but I'll see you later, Olivia."

"Sure, later."

As he walked away Molly sighed. "I haven't seen that fine sight since first year."

"He was a freshman with you?"

"Well, yeah. He dropped out at the end of that year though. I didn't realise he was back."

I opened the paper. The guy was worse than a dog with a bone. Apparently the band playing up here on Friday night was called Quiet Renegade.

Molly leaned over my shoulder. "Is that—"

Shh!

"Just a flyer for a band." The look I shot her cut down any retort she might have ... except for a knowing smile.

Chapter 5

"**S**HUT UP and get dressed already." Savannah's voice came from inside my wardrobe as another item went flying over her head to land on my bed; my sheer red Witchery blouse. The one with ruffles down the front and tiny capped sleeves. The one in which I'd freeze my butt off.

"I'm not going."

Savannah stopped her search and swung around to pin me with a pointed look. "Yes, you are. You need this, Olivia. You need to get out, experience life, have fun. Be a college student, for goodness sake."

Yeah, right. I needed this like I needed yet another phone call from my mother asking if I was 'making a name for myself on campus'. Little did she know I was, just not in student politics. She'd be horrified if she knew the truth.

Ever since Molly saw Logan give me the flyer about the concert, there had been nothing but questions, which Savvy had overheard earlier this morning. So here we were with Savannah's head stuck in my closet, me sitting at the desk with the laptop on and my Econ Law assignment open, but decidedly lacking in words thanks to the blonde tornado tossing clothes around my room.

My door flew open and Molly barged in, dressed in a cute polka dot dress, albeit a little Minnie Mouse. Like Savvy, she didn't look as if she planned on staying in tonight. "Never fear, the drinks are ..." Her gaze shot to the mess of clothes covering my bed then followed the clothes trail to Savvy. "Sorry ... I ... ahh ... didn't realise."

Savvy spun around. Taking in the other girl's outfit, and grinned. "Did you say drinks?"

Molly held a four-pack of Cruisers, red as the sheer blouse, in one hand, and a bottle of wine in the other. "Sure did."

"I'm Savannah."

"I know. Everyone knows. I live on your floor, remember?" Plopping her cargo on my desk, Molly announced, "Wasn't sure what you felt like so I got everything."

"Right." Savvy pulled her head out of the cupboard and closed it behind her. "Excellent choice."

Sighing, I asked, "Why do I feel like you two are conspiring against me?"

"Because we are, or at least we would have if I knew I had a co-conspirator, right ... umm ..."

"Molly?" I supplied.

Savvy cackled like an evil witch and Molly joined in. "Right. And you're going to have fun tonight."

My chair started rolling away from the desk until my laptop was well out of reach and I let out an exasperated groan, which didn't stop Molly from shoving one of the red drinks in my hand. Savvy clinked hers against it. "To new beginnings."

"To new beginnings," Molly chimed in.

They both tipped their bottles up, taking the first sip of their drinks.

"Fine," I said, "to new beginnings."

The toast was kind of accurate. It was the beginning of the year, just a month late.

Maybe one drink would get them off my back so I could get this assignment done. But only one.

Turned out the drink was raspberry-flavoured and tasted divine. The liquid blazed an icy trail down my throat and Molly perched her rear on my desk. "So ..." She wriggled her eyebrows suggestively. "Logan Hays."

"It's not like that." I took another sip. This drink was mighty good. Just like eating those round, bumpy raspberry lollies. The strange warmth of the first sip of alcohol spread through me and I smiled. It was a nice feeling. "We're just in the same Sociology class."

Molly grinned around the bottle pressed to her lips. "And he wants you to go see Quiet Renegade tonight."

"Won't you two let up? It's nothing. Not a date or even an invite to meet him there. It's just one friend telling another about a rad gig. That's it."

Savvy's glance connected with Molly's; they both smiled. An all knowing 'we don't believe a word Olivia's saying' smile.

Whatever.

I took another swig of my drink. It really was delicious. Turning my gaze on Savvy, who was laying the red blouse and my black capri pants out on the bed, I said, "What's going on with you and Dane?"

Diversion; the oldest trick in the book.

Savvy rolled her eyes. "Nothing."

"That's not what I saw the other day."

"It's nothing. I'm not interested." She tossed the clothes at me. "Go get dressed, we're going out."

Groaning, I went to take another sip, but only a tiny drop trickled out. Molly shoved another bottle in my hand and whisked the empty away.

"To friends," she said.

Savvy and I both joined in the cheer. "To friends."

I was glad to have those girls by my side.

AS WE walked up top to the university bar I wasn't sure what it was about the hill, but tonight it felt like the slope was nothing, like maybe it tilted the opposite way and we were going down instead of up. Yet my legs were still kind of heavy.

"Come on," Savannah said, surging ahead. "We need to make it before The Bar's at capacity."

The Bar was our on-campus drinking hole. It was a good one, too, walking distance from the dorms, and it often had good bands or theme nights. I usually enjoyed hanging out there.

"Hurry up!" Savvy yelled.

Molly and I both groaned at picking up the pace and Savannah dropped back, grabbing each of our hands, then she proceeded to speed up, dragging us both behind her.

"It's a Vannah train," Molly said and I giggled. "I think I can ... I think I can ..."

"You both bloody well can." Savvy laughed and kept pulling us along behind her.

By the time we'd reached campus and walked through to the bar, my legs felt as if they'd completely disappeared. Whether it was the affects of the two vodka mixed drinks and who knew how many glasses of wine, or from the exercise, I had no idea, but the buzz of numbness through my limbs was welcome, exciting, and oh my gosh, funny.

I'd stopped moving. I shivered as we stood in line near the entrance. A table up ahead where they seemed to be selling tickets blocked the way, so only one person could trickle in at a time. It took forever to reach it.

Once we were inside, I scanned the crowd, but I didn't see Logan's mess of blond hair. In fact, it was hard to see much at all—the lights were dim and the support band was already playing. The place was jam packed. Didn't matter; I wasn't here for Logan anyway.

Savvy grabbed my hand and pulled me toward the bar, squishing her way between people to reach the counter. The guy she'd pushed in front of scowled down at me, and he was so thickset I gulped. Maybe Savvy should be more careful, but then his scowl morphed into a smile, making me more at ease.

We stood there for a few minutes watching the lead singer belt out a pub favourite from the eighties. No wonder Logan liked them. They were as vintage as his style.

Savannah swung around, with three drinks in her hand. She shoved a plastic cup at me and one at Molly who was right beside me, bobbing her head to the music. This band wasn't too bad. Some sort of rock/heavy guitar combination. Also raspberry-flavoured, the drink was just as sweet as the pre-mixed one I'd had earlier and all of a sudden my body started swaying to the grungy music. I downed the rest of the cup and set the empty down on a nearby table. The people who sat around it wouldn't mind.

"Let's dance!" I yelled at the girls, hoping they heard me over the ruckus of music, conversation, and general partying.

Molly nodded and Savvy followed my actions by sculling her cup of vodka raspberry—or so I assumed, since it looked the same as mine—and gliding her way through the crowd onto the dance floor. As I trailed after her, I spotted Logan standing on the opposite side of the bar to where we had been. He was chatting to a tall guy who had his back to us, and Logan's gaze caught mine. He smiled and gave me a slow nod. The other guy looked over his shoulder and my heart plummeted; it was Dane, which meant Christian wouldn't be too far away. I'd forgotten they were all friends. There was no doubt in my mind that Logan had heard the rumours and probably thought I was a nutcase. If he was friends with them, then he wasn't the guy for me. Hell, he wasn't the guy for me anyway. Not that I was looking. I couldn't afford a guy right now. Any guy. Period. Christian had been an exception that I couldn't make again. I had a hellish rumour to counteract,

I needed even better grades and my campaign was coming up.

I pulled my gaze away and followed Savvy, who'd either found or created a space for us. She swayed in time to the music. I swung my hips from side to side, threw my hands into the air and joined her, enjoying the feeling of the bass vibrating through me. Something slammed into my hip.

What the bejeebers?

I glanced that way to see a grinning Molly, who bumped my hip with hers again. I slung my arms around her neck and danced like I hadn't danced in a long time, maybe forever, totally losing myself in the rhythm and beat of the music, surrounded by my real friends, rather than a bunch of people who barely knew the real me. It felt absolutely fantastic.

I positioned myself so my back was to the stage and my gaze once again snagged Logan's through the crowd. He gave me a half-smile. There were too many people between us to see if he was still talking to Dane and I really didn't care. It wasn't like I was deliberately looking at him; my attention just kept sliding that way accidently.

We danced for song after song. Another drink found its way into my hand. Good thing too, because I was parched. Savvy leaned in toward me. "I gotta go to the ladies."

"Me too," I shouted in her ear then repeated the message to Molly who was still dancing with us, but her other friends surrounded her too. The ones from the pizza night. She nodded and pointed at the ground, which I guess meant she intended to stay right there.

Once we were out of the pulsating sway of sweaty bodies, Savvy hooked her arm through mine. "If that's Logan Hays that you've been making eyes at all night, wow, tell me how we've never met him before."

"I haven't ..." For some reason the rest of the sentence took a moment to work out. "... making eyes at anyone." I weaved through the people, my hip bumping against another girl's. Sure, I'd glanced his way a few times, but that hardly rated a mention. "Dunno. Looks like Dane's mate."

My tongue didn't want to twist around the words. Why'd they come easier in my head? The euphoria dancing had spread through me plummeted like a sinking ship at the thought of them being friends. How had we not met him last year if that was the case? Dane was a year above us like Molly, so Logan must be too.

"I've seen him around though, since school's been back. Maybe he's a fresher ..." Savvy said, while I followed the line of her gaze to the guys in question. There was a bunch of girls with them, and the table thief from earlier in the week had her arm around Logan's waist. His arm hung at his side and he faced the dance floor, his brows pinched.

"Who is that bitch?" Savannah asked.

"Table Thief."

"What? I meant the girl."

"Doesn't matter." I pushed the bathroom door open, and it didn't. He could hook up with whoever he wanted.

"Well, she better get her paws off Dane."

Off Dane? What was Savvy talking about? The table thief chick was all over Logan, not Dane. Ah, who cared? Dane was always surrounded by a harem. Neither of them mattered.

Surprisingly there was no line, so I waltzed right into a

cubicle. When I was done, and washing my hands, Savvy emerged, shoved her hands under the water and ran them over her dead-straight hair, smoothing down what was already perfect. I licked my dry lips and applied a thin sheen of gloss.

"It's so hot in here."

"Yeah, it's like they've got the heat up," Savvy said, pushing through the door.

We both headed straight to the bar like we were of one mind. I needed more fluids. Water this time, though, because everything was still buzzing.

I stood in line by the edge of the bar. They were flat out, staff packed so tight that they kept bumping into each other, but still they couldn't seem to keep up with the people draped over the counter waiting to be served.

"Great band," the guy beside me said while nodding.

"Yeah, they're awesome."

Savvy appeared out of nowhere and shoved a drink in my hand.

"Thanks." I took a long sip. Dancing sure was thirsty work. She didn't seem to hear what I said though; her gaze was firmly fixed right over my head. On Dane, no doubt.

"Talk to him," I urged.

She nodded. "Yeah. I ought to, right? I should tell him ... tell him ..." Determination boosted her confidence, and she handed me her drink. "I'm going."

With that, Savvy trotted off to get her man. She'd had a crush on Dane for as long as I'd known her. Of course she pretended not to, but if they'd finally hooked up the other night then I wasn't wrong in thinking he liked her too. I leaned against the wall, which felt nice and cool against my back. Logan hadn't said boo to me all night; maybe I should go talk to him too. Yes, that's what I'd do. Find out exactly how he came by my email address.

I downed the rest of my drink and blinked. My eyelids were made of lead. I wasn't drunk though. Nah-uh, not me. When I opened them, the guy from the bar stood before me, his black shirt hung loosely over his chest, which was right at my eye level. Some sort of tattoo snaked around his arm; maybe it was a snake, I couldn't really tell.

"Hi there," he said, moving a little closer.

Whoa, dude, personal space.

"Hey," I answered slowly, making sure my words flowed. "Do I know you?" He didn't look familiar; I was certain that I didn't know him at all.

"Would you like to?"

He was a bit cute with the whole bad boy ... *Oh, great.* That was why he was in my face. I glanced past him, trying to see Molly. "Um, I better go back to my friends."

"I know you." He slammed his palm against the wall near my shoulder, then his other one came down on the other side, trapping me between them. He leaned in so close I could smell the tang of beer on his breath. "You're the night nymph." His gaze slid along my neck to rest on my mouth. "I'd like to see that."

"You're not seeing anything." I ducked to sneak under his arm, but he was too fast and bent his elbows, his rough cheek scraping against mine.

My heart tried to pound right out of my chest; this guy was a douche, and jeez, there'd been a lot of them lately. He made a growling noise that was probably supposed to be sexy, but it sent an icy shiver right down my spine. It was dark, and seedy, and by golly, I needed to get away.

"Come on, let's go back to my—"

"Leave the lady alone." Logan's words came at the same time as the guy jerked backward, out of my space. I sucked in a huge breath.

"Back off," the dude growled. "I was just talking to sweet pea here. There's no problem, right darlin'?"

He moved toward me with his arm extended to drop it over my shoulders or box me in again. *Not on your life, buddy.* Grabbing his arm, I twisted it down and away; the guy grunted. But I ducked toward Logan. "We're done, so no problem."

His face twisted into something unpleasant, and his voice dropped to a sneer. "Go stroke your own pussy. I hear solo's your style anyway."

With a swift movement, Logan swept me behind him and lurched forward, his fist connecting with the guy's chin.

And the dirtbag came up fighting. Time felt like it crawled into slow motion as his head swung back around to face us, and his tongue glided across his split lip, pushing the pooling blood onto his chin. Then he smashed forward into Logan, shoulder first. Only he didn't make contact, because Logan stepped aside and swung his fist again, stopping the guy before he ploughed into me. Logan didn't miss his mark. The dirtbag stumbled back and Logan raised a fist once more.

Then Dane was there, saying something into Logan's ear. Logan shook his head and Dane said, "It's not worth it."

"You!" A bouncer, dressed from head to toe in black,

closed a hand over Logan's shoulder and shoved him through the ring of people who stood, mouths open, watching the fight.

Dane turned to me and shook his head, then disappeared into the swell of people.

Heart pounding and feeling like all this was my fault, I slumped against the wall. My head buzzed. If alcohol was my friend then we were having an argument. In fact my stomach and head both felt like they were arguing with the rest of me. Maybe my legs were gonna join in too.

"God, Liv." Savvy pushed through people to reach me, her face drawn and frantic. "What happened?"

I couldn't answer; maybe I was in shock, or maybe the alcohol had slowed my thoughts because I couldn't pull them together.

"This douchebag ... Logan came, and then Dane ..."

The room felt as if it were moving and my stomach churned.

"How about we go get you some fresh air?"

I nodded, and Savannah hooked her arm through mine. People blurred into a sea of indistinguishable faces as we made our way to the door while the music pounded through my body. Only it felt bad, not good. Everything echoed in my head.

The bouncer on the door looked right up and down Savvy, blatantly checking her out. "You leave, you're out, girls. I can't let anyone back in."

"Thanks." I conjured up my best smile. "Awesome night."

It wasn't really, but if we played nice maybe he'd let us back in anyway. He seemed to like the look of my friend.

The frigid night air hit me and I sucked in a breath. The air felt so much fresher. I hadn't realised how stuffy it was inside. Even though my ears rang, out here there was blessed silence. Fewer people were around; there was only a form pacing by the fountain and another stood right by it.

I squinted to make them out. Logan and Dane. Savvy stiffened where our arms were connected and I slid my arm out of hers. I wasn't certain what to think, but I needed to make sure Logan was all right. He had, after all, stood up for me.

Logan's hands curled into tight fists as he paced the length of the step while Dane watched.

"Remember who you're doing this for." Dane's words were kind of harsh, and I wondered what he meant. Who Logan was outside for? ... Was it a girlfriend ... table thief girl? Being seen defending me sure would have caused problems for him.

Logan hurled a kick at the solid base of the fountain and pulled both hands through his long hair.

"You don't want to be like him," Dane warned.

"Shut up!" Logan's head snapped up and his gaze landed on me. "I already am."

"Everything okay?" I asked, walking toward them.

"Hell no," Dane said.

Logan stopped his measured march. His blue eyes were fiery as they met mine then cut to Dane.

"Just walking it off," Dane said.

Logan blew out a long breath which fogged in the cold air. Then he dropped to sit on the step. "That asshole shouldn't have touched you."

"He didn't," I said, not sure if I should sit beside him or keep my distance. To be perfectly honest, part of me was flattered he'd jumped in to defend me, but the other part was a bit scared of what that might mean.

Dane looked past me to watch Savannah staring at her phone from a safe distance away.

"Shouldn't have said the crap he did either." Logan glared toward the wall of glass that was The Bar.

I winced, covering my face with my hands. It was an attempt to stop my head from spinning, but nothing could stop my stomach from dropping with a feeling of dread. I hadn't felt embarrassed about those damn rumours in days, but knowing Logan had heard what that guy had said made me want to fade into the darkness.

Warmth under my elbow tugged my hand from my face. "Hey." Logan's voice was soft. "The guy was a jerk."

Suddenly mute, I just nodded.

"Shh." Logan's hand curled around my head, and he pulled me in toward him. "It's over."

My whole body tingled and a single shiver rippled through me. Logan smelt as divine as those raspberry drinks, maybe even better. I shifted my nose toward his wavy hair and inhaled deeply. Must have been his shampoo, or maybe it was just him, but that breezy, oceany scent was intoxicating. His chest rose against mine and his hand continued smoothing my hair. I tipped my head back to look into his face and Logan's gaze was on mine. His Adam's apple bobbed as he swallowed, and an irrepressible urge to kiss this sweet guy swamped me.

His perfect lips called to me like a siren, so I pulled back from our embrace and planted one right on them. I wasn't prepared for the heat that came with our connection, how something so soft could be hot at the same time. His lips felt like heaven and hell all at once.

With a hand on my shoulder, Logan pushed me away. "You're drunk. We need to get you home."

Ouch. The tingle jumped to my face, heating my cheeks to near boiling. What in the heck was I thinking? Logan didn't like me; had never liked me. I shook out of his hold and flung a hand toward The Bar, in Savvy's general direction. "She's way more drunk than me."

His arm swept around my waist, and Logan pulled me into his side.

I pulled away. "I don't need help to stand."

"Olivia."

I wouldn't, couldn't look at him. He'd see my burning cheeks and know that attempted kiss actually meant something to me. Wait … it meant something? My heart squeezed. Tipsy or not, this was all too much. It wouldn't have made a difference, cause coming here tonight was a bad idea.

"I'm going home."

Logan's hand snagged mine. "I'll walk you."

The Fallout

Chapter 6

TWILIGHT HOCKEY was on, and I shouldn't be here the way I felt. After sleeping until almost lunchtime, I woke up feeling like I'd crawled through the desert with no water. Black patches marred my memory of last night. That's precisely why I didn't usually drink. Losing control was bad for public image and with the upcoming student council president campaign that wasn't good. Heck, it wasn't good, period.

I was pretty sure I'd walked home with Savvy, Logan, and Dane. But after that, nothing ... I'd woken sometime in the early morning hours with my PJs twisted around me and my door wide open. Not the most graceful end to the night.

The ref's whistle blew, indicating a penalty shot.

We were in the lead, despite my terrible playing. I'd lost us a goal when mid-pass I completely fumbled my stick and nudged the ball with the curved side. Then later, I totally missed a pass, letting it roll straight into the opposition's hands. Both stupid, dumbass mistakes.

I was completely off my game.

Probably had something to do with the churning in my stomach—all I'd eaten today was a slice of toast, and only half of that. Maybe it also had something to do with the half-memory I had that I'd made a pass at Logan and he'd flat out rejected me.

I clenched my jaw and dashed after the ball along with half the field of players. I trailed my stick along the astro turf and swept it in to steal the ball out of play, then ran for all I was worth toward the goal. The goalie set her feet wide, bracing herself for the shot. The others were catching me. A green blur sped past and swung around, her stick battling with mine for possession. I fought back. Out here I felt like a different person. One who could be as rough, hard, and unguarded as she wanted. One who could fight for what she wanted.

The other player's stick crashed into my shin pad, and hooked around my ankle in a completely illegal move. I fell; my face slammed into the ground, hard. Spots burst into my vision and pain echoed through my head. A stampede pounded past me.

That cow, she'd tripped me on purpose.

I pushed onto my hands and climbed up, my head spinning. The umpire blew the whistle and yelled, "Foul." She pointed back at me. "Free shot to Oxley."

The girl who'd knocked me over stormed past, and the look she shot me could have killed a healthy ox. Well, she has another thing coming if she thought that dirty move would stop me fighting to win. The cow was going down. She slugged the ball in my direction so hard it made a loud crack as it hit my stick, and I struggled to get it under control. She kept her five-metre distance exactly, scowling while I set up the shot from the sideline.

I aimed up and held. Waited. The whistle blew.

"Ohhhhgasmicoooo … ooo … ooolivya."

I fumbled the ball, my dribble into play totally out of sync. My mind flipped, reeling to figure out what the other payer had said. She swooped in, stealing it right out from under me. *Orgasmic Olivia?* She didn't … right, that was it. The bitch was so gone. Anger surged through me, but she passed the ball off to her teammate, and the look she threw over her shoulder was nothing but gloating. "Can't hold it together on the field either, hey? Just one touch."

Lifting my stick, I ran at her. "What the hell did you say?"

She met me glare for glare. "Have a naughty night, Oliv-*oh-ah*?"

Oh, she didn't.

"Watch out; here comes the game." She turned and ran toward the stampede of players headed our way. The rumours surrounding Christian and I had spread far and wide; it seemed nowhere was off-limits. If I couldn't escape it on the hockey field then nowhere was safe.

The horn sounded for half-time and I was more than ready for a break before I got sent off for fighting.

My team all headed for the sidelines where we gathered to discuss our tactics. Once we were all there, I said, "Their wings are strong. Maddy, I think we should sub you out for Aleisha."

The brunette who was our fastest player looked at me and shook her head. "I think you need to sit this one out, Olivia. That Evan's Hall girl is obviously getting under your skin, and you're letting her. Besides, after—"

"Shh," someone cut her off. "I agree, Olivia needs a rest."

A murmur of assent spread through the circle. What was this? I was their captain, for heaven's sake. They didn't sub me out. I opened my mouth to say just that, but Maddy glared me down. "You need the break."

My team sat me out for the rest of the game. I was a failure. Those dumb rumours had spread all the way to the other dorms and they were being used against me on the field.

Just freaking great.

I TIPPED my head back and let the warm water run over my face. I hadn't seen Molly or Savannah since last night. If they felt anything like I had before hockey then they were probably still curled up in bed, swearing they'd never drink again.

Not only had last night left me feeling worse than a three-day-old cheeseburger, it was a bit of a blur. Hopefully Logan got home all right. I had no idea where he lived, but surely he'd caught a cab or something.

After rinsing out my hair, I turned the water off and grabbed my towel. Thankfully, the exercise had actually done me some good. I must have sweated it out or something, because I felt better than I had all day.

The door creaked, announcing I was no longer alone in the bathroom. Not surprising when I lived on a floor with almost a dozen people, girls *and* guys.

"Did you hear about last night?" A girl's voice; it sounded like Ella Parry, who lived on my floor, so it probably was her.

"No," another girl said. I wasn't sure who she was, but there were other girls on this floor, so it was probably one of them. I flipped my head and rubbed my wet hair with the towel, listening to their conversation.

"The noise was really loud, like she had a guy over and they were getting it on. It was about three am and I was dead tired, over the screaming. You know what it's like when you're trying to sleep. Anyway, after about half an hour of noise I couldn't stand it any longer, so I went to tell them to shut the hell up, and there she was ..."

Strange. I didn't remember hearing anything weird last night, but I more than likely passed out, and when I woke it certainly wasn't three a.m, despite feeling like it. A shudder crept through me at the memory of my door standing ajar. I'd never get that drunk again.

"Come on, don't leave me hanging. There she was ... what? Spill it."

Yeah, spill, Ella. What happened?

"There she was with her pyjamas scrunched up around her neck and her hand stuck so far inside herself, her back was arched off the bed while she moaned."

She ... what ... who? Not me. Surely, they weren't talking about me. Dread weighed down my chest, made it hard to draw breath. They were talking about me. They had to be.

71

I stepped back into the shower, my legs and arms shuddering. There were parts of last night I couldn't remember, but there was no way in hell I'd do that.

"You went in her room?"

Ella scoffed. "Why would I do that? She had the door open, like she was putting on a show. And let me tell you, I wasn't the only one watching."

That wasn't true. It couldn't be true. I didn't do that at all. I never touched myself. Ever. Just the idea of it felt kind of ... wrong. I'd come home and slept all night until eleven thirty-eight this morning, with no noise, and certainly no public displays. Heck, no touching myself of any sort. Why would Ella say something so obviously wrong? Why would anyone? Why would Christian? I understood that gossip fed conversation, and people thought it made them interesting to others, but making stuff up like that was plain hurtful.

And damaging.

Hold up. My door *had* been open. How in the name of all things holy did she know about that? My gosh, it could be true. I could have actually been doing all that she said and the entire floor of students ...

My legs felt like liquid. I slipped to the floor, my arms closing around my knees and drawing them into me while I shook all over. I closed my eyes, and all I could see were visions of me in compromising positions: on my bed, on my desk, on the floor. I pressed the heels of my palms into my eyes, but the visions wouldn't stop. It was like a waking nightmare that I couldn't escape.

A violent shiver raked through me. I had to get out of the bathroom and get dressed. I couldn't face those girls, though, not after Ella had seen me like that. True or not, I was more embarrassed than if I actually had been caught in the act.

I hadn't heard a thing since I realised the girl they were talking about was me. All I heard was the thrashing of my pulse in my ears and my ragged breaths.

Sitting here would only make me catch pneumonia. I pulled the towel around me and stood up. I dried off and tugged on my yoga pants and t-shirt. Drawing the door back a slither, I peeked out into the bathroom and thank small mercies, it was empty. I gathered up my toiletries and repeated the procedure before stepping into the hallway.

It was clear too.

Then I high-tailed it down the corridor, not stopping to see if anyone heard me, and my heart didn't slow until I was in the safety of my room with the door firmly closed. Good lord, what had I done?

ANOTHER SUNDAY spent in my room with music playing loud enough to drown out the noise from outside. It wasn't so much that I wasn't game to venture out, but more that my mind wouldn't stop. It was on a continual loop: Christian's claim that I kept him up at night, all the embarrassing moments of the past few weeks, and finally Ella's announcement that I'd been ... *doing that thing.*

When the knock came on my door, I rolled over and pulled my pillow onto my head. But it didn't muffle the hissed, "It's just me, open up."

Groaning, I rolled off the bed and dragged myself to the door to find Molly standing behind it. She strode in and I yanked it closed before anyone could see me.

"You're not eating again." She dropped a tray of what looked to be tacos on my desk.

"Didn't feel like it."

"Bullshit." Molly flopped onto my bed.

"Excuse me?"

"I said, bullshit you didn't feel like eating."

I slumped in my chair, my back to her, and started shovelling meat into the hard shell. Truth be told, I was starving.

"I've heard the talk, and you better not be letting it get to you."

I spun around so fast the taco lost its stuffing all over my yoga pants. The ones I hadn't changed out of since yesterday.

"How am I supposed to show my face down there when they're all talking about how I put on a free porn show for the whole of block K?"

"Watch it; you're making a taco shower." She bugged out her eyes like she thought this was some kind of joke.

"This isn't funny. You just don't get it, Molly, do you? How humiliating it is to walk through that dining room knowing that every single person is laughing at me?"

She huffed. "I don't get it? Me? Are you forgetting who you're talking to, Miss Perfect? I'm the girl they've spent two years laughing at because I don't conform to their social norms." She waved her hands down her matching pink tracksuit that looked like it came from Kmart. "You take the hand you have, and you work it. Who gives a crap what anyone else thinks?"

"I do," I all but shouted. "I care, because if I don't then nothing works out."

She shook her head. "Olivia, their dumbass gossip won't change a single thing."

I spun around to hide the tears that threatened to fall. It would change everything. And my humiliation level would be the least affected. Masturbating in front of the entire floor wasn't a rumour that would be soon forgotten.

"Why would they ..." I couldn't finish the rest of my sentence. "Do you think I really did what they said?"

"Of course not. I think what that dirt-bag ex of yours said was enough to start this and people are running with it. You've always been so ... popular, and perfect. People get jealous, and like to see those better than them fall."

I pressed my thumbs into my tear ducts and took a deep breath, wishing Molly was right, that this was just a case of extreme jealousy, but my gut told me otherwise.

She continued, "They'll forget it in a few days. Besides, not everyone is talking about you. We're not all a bunch of gossips, you know."

I doubted they'd ever forget.

The thing was, I wasn't sure what to believe anymore. Maybe I did do those things, but if I did, it didn't seem likely that I'd not know it. Surely I couldn't touch myself in such a way that I moaned and didn't realise, even if I was passed-out drunk. The sensations that came with that weren't exactly ones to be slept through.

"So tell me." Molly's tone had changed to upbeat, teasing. "What happened with Logan?"

Images flared into my mind: a flash of my lips on his, him pushing me away with a gentle 'no', hand holding, and Logan's fist in some guy's face. Dear lord, I wasn't sure what order they happened in, and if they were all related. Stupid drunken patchy memories. But I was certain I'd put the moves on and he'd rejected me.

"Not much ..."

"Well ..." She drew the word out like she had a secret. "That's not what this text says." Molly waved her phone in the air and I sprung from my chair to grab it, but she was too fast. She jumped onto my bed and held the phone above her, tipping her head back to read the glowing screen. "Twelve o-nine: Going home. Have fun with your friends." She glanced at me and her lips twitched. "Twelve twenty-two: Logan's perfect. Perfect smile, perfect lips, and his butt looks perfect in those jeans."

"No way!" I jumped onto the bed and leapt for her arm, but my hand snatched only air as she dived to the floor.

"One forty-five: MOLLY! I'm in love." She dropped her phone on my desk and held her hands over her heart. "That's so beautiful, Olivia."

"You're making it up," I hissed. "It's all a lie to make me spill the details."

She laughed and tossed her phone to me.

My heart fluttered like a butterfly on Red Bull as I scrolled through. Surely they weren't real. But those texts were from my phone, at those times, and with those words. With a billion drunken typos. Holy buttercup, they were legit. Heat crept into my cheeks. Stupid alcohol couldn't be trusted not to embarrass me. "I barely even know the guy."

"Livia and Logan, sitting in a tree—"

I punched her in the arm. "It's not happening. I'm not interested."

"Sure you aren't." She smirked.

"I'm not. The last thing I need is a distraction. I need to buckle down and maintain my distinction average. I've got to raise it to a high distinction, and even if it weren't for that, the last thing I want with these ridiculous rumours is a guy *friend* who's heard them."

"Sometimes we don't know what we need."

Chapter 7

I **WATCHED THE** clock on the lecture theatre's wall tick through the seconds. Five minutes until the lecture started and I felt as queasy as I had when I woke up on Saturday morning. Things were no better around Oxley than they had been when Christian first told that awful lie. They were worse. The rumours had spread like wildfire, and I regretted choosing a room that looked out over the courtyard. I couldn't even open my window without being hollered at from below, nor could I look out of it without copping an eyeful of lewd gestures. The walk through Oxley to reach the path that led up to university wasn't much better. Every guy that lived in the place thought he was funny, and every girl looked at me like I was dirty. And I felt it.

Three minutes.

The walk up this morning hadn't been too bad. The air

had been crisp and pleasant. Thankfully the arts building wasn't clear across campus, so I didn't have to face running into as many people who might have heard Ella's story. The car that crawled past with people whistling from the backseat was bad enough—actual people in front of me would have been worse. I hated that people who looked at me saw that instead of the social club president, the captain of the hockey team, the Law student that I was.

Two minutes.

Would Logan even come today? Maybe I'd made things awkward between us, which really sucked, because he seemed to be one of the few genuine friends I had. But was he really a friend? My heart dipped into my stomach. That thought made me feel broken.

One minute.

To distract my wandering mind from all its anxious thoughts, I pulled my phone out and checked my inbox. There was all of one email.

The lecturer tapped his mic and started talking, but my focus was still on my inbox. The sole email was from the academic board, which was weird, because it looked like a personalized message, not one of those emailed-to-every-student ones. The subject line read: Your Student Council Campaign.

Dear Ms Dean,

We regret to inform you that your campaign to run for student body president for the student's association has been suspended in light of recent allegations.

Keith Ramage
Academic Board

Blood stilled in my veins. Everything grew sluggish and my future flashed before me.

Campaign suspended?

Someone slid into the next seat along.

Oxley's social committee wasn't enough. No council position meant no exceptional extracurricular activities on my resume, and that equalled a mediocre CV. Nothing to set me apart meant no Deakin Parry Associates. I was already behind by not studying at one of the big city universities, so I needed an outstanding record to put me back in the game. No president position was bad. All of this would add up to not following in my father's footsteps as a renowned attorney. I drew a shaky breath that rattled on the way out.

I am a failure.

A hand closed over mine.

No job meant I was a disappointment. One my parents wouldn't want around. I'd be nothing but a small-time lawyer, relegated to settling disputes in the family law court. I could feel my future slipping away.

"Liv."

And if that happened, where would I be?

"Olivia." Something dug into my side and I flinched, turning to see Logan's concerned gaze studying mine. "You okay?"

My thoughts spun. Everything felt too tight inside me,

and surely I was going to throw up. I returned my focus to the front of the room. "Yeah."

Logan leaned in and whispered, "Follow me."

My brow tightened as Logan stood, grabbing my hand in the process. I barely had time to scoop up my tablet and bag before he lead me out of the lecture hall while Professor Monotone drawled on about who knew what.

"We can't leave," I hissed, but Logan kept a firm grip on my hand and ignored me. "We'll miss the rest of class."

"Shut up." A girl in the back row gave us both a filthy look. "Some of us are actually trying to listen."

With his free hand, Logan pushed the huge wooden door open and led me out into the hall. My drunken text was right; his butt did look mighty fine in jeans. Shaking that thought away, I stopped. Everything tumbled out of my bag onto the floor. Damn him for making me look like a klutz again.

My tablet better not be broken. It had all my lecture notes, favourite eBooks, and a ton of photos. It was precious beyond replacing. Clamping my mouth shut to stop the expletive that sat on the tip of my tongue, I bent at the knees to pick up my things.

Logan's head crashed into mine.

This guy sure made me a walking disaster.

He chuckled. "I got this, Butterfingers."

Everything was already in his hands, so I stood. "We can't leave."

Maybe he didn't hear me the first time.

He shot up and held my bag out, his sparkling eyes pinning me to the spot. "Live dangerously. You might find you like it."

A wild fluttering tickled my tummy like I was at the top of a rollercoaster waiting to fall. *No.* I shook my head. This was a bad idea. It felt all kinds of wrong. But then Logan's mouth tipped up, and he leaned so close his breath skated over my ear, making that flutter inside me free-fall. "It's just one class."

Spend time with Logan or sit through a boring lecture? The fluttering in my tummy was pretty convincing. I wanted to be near him. The feeling his presence created was better than the way I felt when he wasn't there, when failure and humiliation were running a dual dictatorship. Besides, maybe he was right. It wasn't like I'd get anything out of the lecture anyway with my head spinning the way it was. Besides, I had the text book. I could catch up later tonight, like I had after every Socio class since Logan first took the seat beside me.

"Okay," I said.

Logan's lips grazed my cheek as he pulled away and my heart tried to take flight, but I tamped it down. We couldn't have any of that, not after he'd rejected me. I drew a shaky breath and damn him, by the smirk he sported, he knew exactly what he'd done to me.

"Let's get out of here." He tossed his head toward the building's side exit.

With a small smile, I turned after him, and it looked like we were headed to the arts building car park. "So what's the plan, Stalker Boy? Where are we going?"

He grinned and made for a red Corolla. It certainly wasn't new, but it wasn't ancient either. Probably a model from when we were kids.

"It's a surprise," he said, opening the passenger door.

"You expect me to hop in? What if you actually are a stalker ... or worse?" I shook my head in feigned fear. "Never let the attacker take you to a secondary location, everybody knows that."

Logan laughed and guided me into his car with a hand on my back. "Get in the car, Butterfingers."

Smiling, I buckled myself in and settled my bag on my lap while Logan jogged around the front of the car and climbed in behind the wheel. I had no idea where he intended to take me. Impulsiveness was something I generally avoided like the measles. My life was mapped out so that every choice served a purpose. Surprises made me feel uneasy. Changing plans made me feel like I wasn't in control. Sitting in Logan's car, my palms were sweaty and my tummy swirled, but it didn't feel bad—it felt kind of exciting. Like I was at the precipice of that rollercoaster again, and this time I wanted to fall.

As he pulled out of the parking lot and away from the university, I snuck a sidelong glance at Logan. He was tapping his pointer fingers off the steering wheel and sucking in his bottom lip.

"Where are we going?" I asked for the second time.

A smile crept onto his lips, part mischievous, part genuine, and it made my tummy flip. It was so gosh-darn sexy. "To get away from it all."

Sighing, I tipped my head back and closed my eyes. "That sounds perfect."

And it really did. With everything that had happened lately I'd love nothing more than to find someplace quiet where all the embarrassing stories wouldn't follow and nor would all the stress and worry.

We rode in companionable silence as Logan drove through town. My heart beat too loudly, and although I took even breaths to try and calm it down, it was a lost cause. Thoughts of where we could be headed sent it right back to its crazy beat. Every time Logan took another turn, I shuffled in my seat. I tried so hard not to feel antsy, but it just wasn't working.

I chanced a look at him. The way the sun reflected off his jaw, making the blond stubble dance in its light was almost mesmerising. There were flecks of red in there, and brown. Who knew stubble could be more than one colour? His gaze flicked to mine, his clear eyes clouding in concern. Maybe I had imagined that rejection on Friday night. If he wasn't interested we wouldn't be heading goodness knew where to do goodness knew what.

Alone.

I swallowed the liquid pooling in my mouth. We were headed out of town, following the country road that wound off to the east. Surely, he wasn't taking me all the way to the beach; that was clear over the mountains and at least a four-hour drive. But there was nothing out here, and he'd said we were going to get away from it all.

Being friends with Dane and me being the hottest gossip this side of the latest hook-ups ... Logan full well knew what *it all* was. I shifted uncomfortably in my seat. There was a very good chance he'd heard the rumours, but I hoped he hadn't heard the latest one. Fire blazed across my chest and up my face, all the way to my hairline.

"What's up?"

I clamped my teeth to stop my squeal. We'd been quiet for so long, the sudden noise startled me. After taking a deep, calming breath I said, "It's nothing."

"By the way you were blushing, I'd say it's something." Logan's gaze felt like it could penetrate my secrets. Any minute he'd say something about my alleged public masturbation.

I sighed and readjusted my ponytail. "I was thinking about Friday night."

"Oh." He looked back to the road. "What *exactly* about Friday night were you thinking?"

Good lord, why had I said that? He probably thought I was thinking about the rumour, or worse, throwing myself at him only to be pushed away. *Deflect. Deflect. Deflect.*

"I was wondering how you know Dane. I mean, I've known him for over a year and I've never met you or seen you around campus, yet you guys seem kind of tight."

Logan sucked in his bottom lip and started tapping his fingers off the wheel again as the minutes passed. It didn't look like he was going to answer. It wasn't that hard a question, so why was he stalling?

"I took a year off."

Ahh, Molly had said that once. I waited, not wanting to jump in and interrupt lest it stopped him from talking altogether. Strange, most people took a gap year between high school and uni, not after they'd started tertiary education.

"Dane and I met in first year; the year before last. I lived in college then. I wasn't there for long though, only the first semester. We hung out a lot and partied too hard. You know how it goes."

I sure did. I saw it happen to many of the fresh wave of students each year. The party atmosphere was just too appealing when you were out of home for the first time. "Is that why you took a year off?"

Logan's grip tightened on the wheel until his knuckles turned white. There was another long pause. Eventually, he veered off the sealed road and onto a dirt track. We were well out of town and looked to be heading bush.

This was crazy.

Stupid.

Unsafe.

No one knew where I was or whom I was with. What if something went wrong? He'd watched me in class for weeks without introducing himself. He'd heard those damn rumours. He'd found my email address and he was taking me out into the middle of nowhere.

"Where in the heck are we going?" This time I expected a straight answer. I grabbed hold on the side of my seat to stop my arms from trembling.

"Hey." He reached out to place his large hand over mine. "You don't really think I brought you out here to have my way with you, do you?"

I swallowed. What if he did? Every muscle in my body went rigid.

"God, Liv, I was only joking. After that tool on Friday night and the way you looked in class this morning, I thought some time away from all the crap might be a good thing." He pulled the wheel around one-handed as the road took a sharp turn. "This is Dangarsleigh Road and we're heading out to Dangar Falls, where I promise not to get all handsy."

Logan winked and shot me one of his cheeky smiles.

I let out a long breath that turned into a laugh. Gosh, I

was paranoid. When I looked at Logan he was laughing too, so hard that the corners of his eyes crinkled, morphing him from hot to cute. How one guy could be both was a mystery, but I was starting to think Logan was all that.

"Okay," I said, very aware—in a good way—of his hand still covering mine.

"That's okay?"

"Yes."

It was kind of nice to know he was only doing this because he thought I needed to unwind. People didn't think about what I needed. Heavens, I didn't normally think about that either. Life had no time for luxury.

I glanced out the side window, and we were coming into what looked like a state forest. "I didn't even know there were waterfalls out here."

Logan raised his brow up then down quickly with one of those cheeky half-smiles I was starting to think of as his trademark. "Then you're in for a treat."

We finally reached the end of the road and Logan cut the engine. There wasn't much to see here, just bush. An abundance of gum trees with the odd ironbark scattered between them, all bedded in with thick scrub undergrowth. A few picnic tables stood in a cleared area. My door opened and Logan's hand awaited mine in a gesture I wasn't at all prepared for.

"My lady."

A grin spread across my face. Hot, cute, and gentlemanly.

Logan dipped his head. "The stunning view awaits your presence."

I placed my hand in his as I climbed out of the dust-covered Corolla. The scent of wildflowers, and gum, and an earthy smell that was entirely native to the Aussie bush hit me the second I was outside. I drew in a long breath, savouring the country.

Logan led me past the picnic area and toward what seemed to be a lookout. I walked to the edge and planted my hands on the wooden railing. Gorges and ravines so deep they looked to be carved out of the mountain range were laid out below us like a stunning picture.

A stream of water plunged over the side of a ravine, rushing down to meet a wide pool. Mist sprayed out from the clear mountain water creating a myriad of tiny rainbows and an absolutely spectacular sight.

"There's not a lot of water going over at the moment 'cause it's been dry. If you come out here after we've had rain, it's breathtaking," Logan said.

"It's stunning right now."

The sight had captured my breath with its beauty.

Logan crossed his arms atop the rail while he leaned against it, completely relaxed as he looked out at the view. I stole a glance at his hand curled over his forearm. There was something about his hands that made me stare. Defined with tendons, I could watch the muscles work with each movement. Today though, that glorious hand nursed a yellowing bruise and nasty scab right across the knuckles. Impulsively, I moved closer to Logan and I ran my thumb over the sore spot.

He tensed, his hand gripping the rail instead of resting on it.

"That bloke was a dick." A pulse ticked in his jaw as he tensed up again.

I should have thanked him for stepping in, but instead my mind took a turn back to that damn email. Maybe this was what it was about. I'd assumed it was related to the rumours, but that made no sense. Even if they were true it wouldn't be a big deal—unless I was charging for the show. I'm sure the board would have a problem with prostitution. I did hurt that guy before Logan, though. It was like a light flashed on in my mind. My hand dropped to my side.

"Suspended for violence ..." The words left my mouth on whisper.

Logan pulled back from the rail. His gaze flicking over mine, concern brewing in the inky depths. "You can't get suspended from uni."

"My presidential campaign was suspended, and I bet that's why."

"Because you pushed some guy to stop him assaulting you?"

"Maybe ..."

"That's screwed."

He leaned over the rail again. This time his boot scuffed at the pebbles covering the ground while his hands fisted. He looked kind of angry. Well, I was frustrated; of all the dumb things for me do. I should have thought before I laid a finger on that jerk. Should have used my tongue to cut him down instead of my hand. Logan was right; I was screwed.

"I need to get on the student representative council. If I don't, then everything really is messed up."

"It's just the council; why is getting on it so important?"

"Do you know how competitive Law is? This is about

the best thing I can do to improve my standing in the eyes of potential employers. Everything's screwed." Well, when combined with the rumours, but I wasn't about to bring that up with him.

"Oh, come on, Liv. Not everything's bad."

A soothing touch ran down my arm and I chewed the inside of my cheek. Well, not *everything* was bad. I was standing here by a waterfall with the sweetest guy, and good lord was he hot. The way the sun hit his hair made it look almost golden, the scruff along his jaw only made it more defined, and the deep blue of his eyes felt like it captured my soul. I couldn't breathe. The longer he held my gaze the more intense it got until it felt like he was going to pounce on me. At least, that's what I wanted. Prickles crept up my arm from the place his hand sat. They tingled all the way to my lower belly where they burned like a glowing fire.

The urge to kiss him was almost irrepressible. His teeth grazed his bottom lip and I all but moaned.

But a flash of Friday night's rejection burned through my mind, snapping the hold he had on me and I pulled my arm away from his touch, reefed my gaze away from his.

"Forget it for now," Logan said. "We're getting away from it all … C'mon, Butterfingers, let's go see the falls."

Shaken from the moment, I nodded, and Logan turned toward a dirt path, well trodden into the ground it wound downward, disappearing into trees. He led the way down the steep incline, which was fine by me. The view as he placed each step carefully was just as spectacular as the waterfall I could hear. His shoulders, legs and rear worked together magnificently as he trekked down the hillside.

Shh!

My foot slipped on a loose stone, and I almost tripped. Damn, I needed to pay attention to what I was doing or I'd have another butterfingers moment, and Logan sure didn't need any more material on me. For several hundred metres, the trail wound its way to the base of the hill and at the end stood the pool we'd seen from above. Logan walked over to a smooth patch of grass and sat under the trees facing the stunning natural landmark. I sunk to the ground beside him.

My phone dug into me, so I tipped to one side and fished it out of my jeans pocket. Logan snatched it right out of my hand.

"Hey!" I made a grab, but he rolled to the side, holding the phone out of my reach as he hit the power button, awakening the screen. I held back a cry, as I dove for it again and Logan started laughing. God lord, what if he saw the message history between Molly and me?

I made another panicked dive and my chest thumped into his solid shoulder as my hand clamped around his wrist, my arms not long enough to reach the whole length of his. "Darn it, Logan. Give it back."

"Do you ever swear properly?" He laughed while his thumb worked furiously over the screen, typing out a text. Then he hit send.

A trill sounded from near his groin, and my gaze flew there before I could stop it. He wriggled his hand into his front pocket and good lord, my next breath hissed past my teeth while tingles stole all other sensation within me. He pulled out his phone, slid it open and smiled like the cat that caught the canary.

Then he tossed my phone into my lap.

I righted myself, putting a little distance between us and flicked through my sent messages. The last one read, *thanks for your number.*

"How's college these days? The food still crap?" he asked, as if he hadn't just hijacked my phone and sensibility. As if everything was hunky dory.

"Has it ever been not crap? I mean, seriously, curry night ..." I turned a raised brow on him. "... who actually likes that slop?"

A laugh burst from Logan and he lay back on the grass, tucking his hands under his head and letting his long legs flop out in front of us. "It's a great place to live."

Recently it was anywhere but a good place to live. No way was I getting into that though. Not with Logan. Instead I said, "It's great, until you don't fit in."

"I can't imagine you not fitting in, Liv. You're perfect."

I kept my gaze on the falling water as I said, "I'm not perfect enough."

"Hey." He shot up, grabbed my arm, and twisted me to face him, the blue in his eyes blazing. "You're beautiful, and funny, and clumsy as all hell, which is adorable. Intelligent, kind, and yes, perfect."

There was a stupid lump in my throat that threatened to burst with the pain of trying to swallow around it. Heavens, this guy was nice. "If I don't make president of the student council, I can kiss my future goodbye, Logan. Anyone less than perfect won't even get an interview at Deakin Parry, let alone an internship. I just ... I can't be a failure."

I closed my eyes and leaned back to lie down. Logan's arm snuck around my shoulders as I fell, and he pulled me to him so we both landed flat on our backs with his arm underneath me. He tugged me into his side.

"Just because someone isn't what other people think is perfect doesn't make them a failure, Liv."

I nestled into him, my heart beating wildly from our closeness and my flailing dreams. "My parents ..."

In a rapid smooth movement, Logan eased his arm out from under me and rose onto his elbow so he was gazing down at my face.

"They already think I'm a failure because I didn't get into the University of Sydney, or better yet, Melbourne, the best law courses in the country."

I wasn't sure what it was about him, but all my filters just fell away. I had no idea why I was telling him this stuff that I normally didn't ever air. Dirty laundry, and all that. My mother always said you shouldn't share it.

His clear eyed-gaze trailed over my face. "Who gives a rats which uni you go to or what career path you take? Parents are supposed to love their children, regardless of that crap."

That tick near his jaw was back, and although his eyes were locked on mine, his focus seemed far away.

I was acutely aware of his chest pressed against my side, his legs almost touching mine, and his arm practically nestling my head. My heart pounded as if it were trying to reel him in closer with each beat. I'm sure what was supposed to happen next was for him to kiss me, but we didn't live in a world where everything was perfect. Parents didn't love their children unconditionally and hot guys didn't kiss girls just because we wanted them to.

"Life's full of *supposed tos*," I said on a sigh.

"Yeah, it sure is."

Logan fell back to the ground, tugging me into his side again, and the silence we fell into was comfortable. There was something about being there with him that made me feel different. It was a feeling I couldn't quite pin, but it was good. The rush of water plunging over a hundred-metre drop into the deep pool was almost as relaxing as the rise and fall of Logan's chest beneath my cheek. I hadn't slept much in the past two nights, so it was no wonder my eyes slid closed.

SOMETHING TICKLED my cheek and my hip ached. How was it morning already? The bed was rock hard and a constant *boom, boom, boom* pounded right under my ear. Like a heartbeat ...

Holy harpsical; it *was* a heartbeat. I took a sleepy breath and opened one eye to the trunk of a huge gum tree. A hand tightened against my waist and yep, my head was still resting against Logan's chest. Well, this was awkward. I'd gone and fallen asleep on him. He squeezed me closer with the arm curled around me, like he didn't care that I'd used him as a pillow. How I'd managed to fall asleep in his arms was a miracle. I guess I must have been exhausted.

I felt the brush of his lips against my head, then an amused, "Morning."

My tummy gave a crazy flutter at the feel of his lips. His kiss. "Hi."

The roar of the water as it cascaded into the pool was absolutely peaceful, despite its loudness. For the first time in weeks, maybe forever, I was entirely at ease. I should have moved away, but instead I laid there, curled against his side, not game to break this tranquil moment lest it could never be recovered.

Finally Logan said, "I suppose we should get going."

I felt as if I were floating on the walk back up to the car. Everything in the world was manageable, and it would be somehow okay. Logan cranked up the music when we climbed in his Corolla. I had no idea what time it was, but my stomach growled like I hadn't eaten all day. We didn't talk much on the ride back in to town. I guess we were lost in our own thoughts, and my thoughts were filled with him.

Chapter 8

OLLY KNOCKED on my door within minutes of me closing it. When I opened, she barged past, her dark hair a mess of wet tangles that dripped down her t-shirt, which looked to be on backwards, if the "follow your dreams" logo was anything to go by. I could have sworn the words were on the back last time she wore it.

"Where have you been?" She flicked my arm. "All. Day."

The thought of Logan tugged my mouth with a wide smile and Molly grinned in return.

"You didn't?" Her eyes widened, and the innuendo was clear.

"Gosh, no." Of course a blush hit my cheeks, totally making me look guilty when I wasn't. But we did sleep and what if the rumours were true and I touched ... no way. They were lies. "We didn't ... not that ... we did ..."

Molly waggled her eyebrows and swung herself up onto my desk with her legs dangling over it. "No point in denying it, Olivia, I just saw you climb out of a strange car, and by the lack of both you and Logey-boy at lunch, I'm guessing you two played hooky so that you could do the dirty all day long."

"Ohmygod, Molly. We did not have sex."

"So you were with Logan, then?"

"Yeah."

"And you hooked up?"

My stupid grin was back. It wasn't a hook-up, but all arrows were pointing that way for the future.

An hour later and still on a crazy high, I actually braved the dining hall with Molly, and it wasn't that bad today. Or maybe it was just that I didn't notice. Savvy sashayed up to join us while we were still in line. Gosh, that girl knew how to move her curvy figure and in the skinny jeans she was wearing, it sure turned a few heads.

Molly shielded her mouth with her hand as she placed it beside Savvy's ear. "Ask Olivia how her day was."

"I can hear you," I said.

Savvy spun to face me with the sweetest smile. "Then how was it?"

Finding it impossible to tamp down the high, I laced my arms across my chest and tried to play it cool. "It was all right."

"All right?" Molly screeched. "She skipped class to hang out with Logan."

My gaze dropped to the hardwood floor as I mumbled, "The whole of Oxley doesn't care, Molly."

Just then Dane swooped in, slinking his arm around

Savvy's waist, and I shot each of them a questioning look. I swear I couldn't keep up with whatever was going on between them. Hadn't she said she wasn't interested? They were more on and off than a flickering light bulb. Dane glanced down the line that had formed behind us and frowned. He probably just wanted to use us to push in.

"What's this about Loges?" he asked.

"Nothing," I said, at the same time as Molly spilled my secret.

"Interesting." A tiny smile curled at the corner of his mouth.

The girl in front spun round. She was a third year and like all two hundred people who lived there, I recognised her face, and she mine. She probably thought she knew things about me that weren't true, too. "Have you seen all the notches in the bench of his old room? Becoming one of Logan Hays' conquests isn't exactly difficult."

My stomach dropped, and I shot her my well-practiced smile.

"Shut it, Abigail," Dane hissed.

"Oh, come on, Dane, I'm doing her a favour."

"Stop being a jealous bitch," Molly said, using her back to block Abigail out of our circle.

"Is it true?" I directed my question at Dane.

He glanced over my head, toward the servery, as he said, "It's an old dormitory. Do you know how many people have lived in that room?"

Even though she was facing the other way now, Abigail laughed then muttered, "Says the guy with a notched desk."

"Not mine or his, baby." Dane shook his head.

But it was too late. His reaction had said it all. It felt like the happiness of today had been ripped right out from underneath me. So Logan was a player, and I shouldn't be surprised; guys as good looking as him could get any girl they wanted. And usually did. Still, I couldn't stop the hurt pulsing through me. If he was a player than why the be-jeebers hadn't he let me kiss him that night?

My friends' laughter buzzed in my ears as the line moved forward and through the servery, even though I didn't hear much of what was said. Molly's hand on my shoulder drew me out of my thoughts. "You all right?"

"Hunky dory," I responded placing my tray on the table and pulling on my carefree facade.

When I got back to my room I slunk into my swivel chair and spun in half circles while I waited for the laptop to boot up. After skipping today, I had a ton of reading to catch up on as well as the usual workload. I'd be at it all night.

My phone beeped with an incoming text, from a number with no name attached.

Meet me tomorrow at the cafeteria.

Logan. I pushed my phone to the side and flopped my head back over the chair. I wasn't sure what to say to him; 'How many notches have you racked up?' didn't quite feel fair. And to be honest, the tiny butterflies that took flight when I saw his name urged me to send back a simple *okay.* I glanced at the phone, reached for it then pulled my hand away. Today had been absolutely awesome, but ...

My fingers sped over the keypad.

> I just came out of a relationship and I'm
> not ready for another one.

Sent. It was gone.

I stared at the phone. Blinked once then again. My heart beat in my ears. Holy buttercup, what had I done?

No. Don't be stupid, Olivia. It was the right choice.

Or maybe it was wrong.

My feet began to bounce. My fingers rapped the desk.

If I were being honest here, it didn't matter that I'd just broken up with Christian. I could tell already that Logan was different. But I wasn't sure I could handle him hurting me. I tossed my phone on the desk and turned to the computer. I had a group assignment for Law that I needed to work on. Heck, it wasn't just Socio I'd skipped today. There was also Torts and Constitutional Law. I dropped my forehead on the desk with the realisation, my gaze sliding to my phone. It beeped and I grabbed it.

> Did I ask you to marry me? :P

Yeah, good point. I'd totally jumped the gun and assumed he wanted a relationship. *Way to come on too strong.* I typed out my text and hit send.

> It would have been embarrassing when I
> turned you down.

His answer came back almost instantly.

I don't think you would have. My boyish
charms are hard to resist. So how about 11
tomorrow?

The warmth of my inner smile matched the one I wore.
I could make eleven, and what did a simple catch-up mean
anyway? Nothing. Just because I meet him didn't mean I'd
become a conquest.

See you then, Stalker Boy.

Night, Butterfingers.

Chapter 9

THIS MORNING'S classes had been a disaster. I hadn't managed to catch up last night, so I was pretty lost in Torts Law. Then during my other classes, I'd daydreamed. So I had double the work to catch up on. Instead of studying last night, all I could think about was Logan's texts, and the cafeteria today. It wouldn't be an exaggeration if I said I'd read them fifty times. That guy made my head so dizzy. My thoughts bounced back and forth, trying to decide if he really was the nice guy I'd been hanging out with or if he was just the player I'd heard about, looking to add the rumoured 'sex fiend' to his list of conquests. As much as I wanted to believe the first, logic wouldn't let me—until recently, Dane was the biggest player I knew, and they were good mates—but there I was, racing clear across campus to make our meeting point on time.

Logan was sitting on the same table as the day I'd had lunch with him. Literally on it—his feet lazing where his butt should have been, and his butt was where the food generally sat. His wrists balanced on his knees.

"Bananas." The look he gave me was dead serious.

"Bananas?"

He nodded. "Bananas."

"Apples?"

"Nope, bananas. That's what this whole suspension is." He jumped down from the table, and a tiny part of me was excited he had those faded jeans on again, or another pair very much like them. He pulled his grandpa cap into place and used his head to beckon me toward the library. "Come on, we're going to do something about it."

I frowned as I watched him walk away, unsure of just what he thought he could manage. When he reached the glass doors that led through the main foyer, he stopped and turned around. "I can't do this without you, y'know."

Still rooted to the spot, I shook myself free. It was a mystery just how he thought he could fix this mess with the campaign. He shrugged at me as if to say hurry up, and I finally moved. Once we were through the building and back outside, Logan swung down to the students' association, and my gosh, the guy was a genius. I'm not sure why I hadn't thought of them straight away. They acted as a union of sorts that helped students in all ways imaginable, as well as handing out condoms, which was the extent of their services most students used. He grabbed my hand and slid his fingers between mine. "We'll fix this."

At that moment I had every faith that we somehow would. Perhaps it was because I felt all kinds of awesome—not only was he standing up for me, Logan was holding my hand like he cared about me. Having someone on my side was an amazing feeling.

He pushed the door open and we stepped inside. A student-aged girl sitting behind the information desk looked up and sure enough, huge glass bowls containing foil packets of just about every colour sat on either end of the counter. She appraised Logan with a onceover that lasted entirely too long for my liking. Even our linked hands didn't seem to stop her.

Logan released me and leaned against the counter. "We've got an appointment with the Support Officer."

"Yes ..." She glanced at her computer. "Miss Dean is it?"

"That's the one," Logan said.

"Just take a seat and Ms Sarin will be ready for you in a moment."

Logan spun around and took one of the hard plastic chairs, which stood in a line by the window. I sat on the seat next him.

"This was a brilliant idea," I said. "Thank you."

Logan smiled.

After a few minutes, a lady—much younger than I'd expected, and wearing pretty casual clothes, jeans and a cardigan—emerged from a tiny hallway. Her gaze settled on Logan and me, her brow pinching slightly. "You must be Miss Dean?"

I stood and extended my hand. "Olivia Dean."

The woman's smile was tight. "Just this way."

I went to glance back at Logan, but he was already by my side. We followed her into a small office and she closed the door behind us.

"Hi, Amrita." Logan greeted her kind of warmly, as if they knew each other. "Thanks for squeezing us in."

"It was nothing a little shuffling couldn't accommodate." She smiled at Logan and I found myself feeling uneasy at their familiarity. Was this woman—who looked barely older than us—a notch in that desk? I slid to the side of my chair.

"So, what brings Miss Dean here today?" she asked, like I wasn't even in the room.

"Liv has an issue with her presidential candidacy—"

"I am in no place to offer help in that regard. We're owned by the student association, Logan, I can't bestow any favours on candidates."

The hopes I'd only just found a few minutes ago felt dashed. Of course she couldn't. It made perfect sense. If word got out, she'd lose her job. Or if I didn't get in, the first item on the new president's agenda would be to replace her.

"It's not like that." Logan leaned forward in his chair. "Just hear us out."

Amrita steepled her fingers and leaned back in her chair. "Five minutes, Logan, and no promises."

I swear he didn't even draw a breath before jumping in. "Liv's presidential candidacy has been suspended unfairly by the board and we want them to lift it."

"I don't even know why they've suspended me," I added.

"Have you tried asking them?"

"Well, no, but ..." *But what?* How did I explain that I hadn't because I was pretty sure of the reason? I snuck a glance at Logan from the corner of my eye. He looked so sure of himself. I really didn't want to come across as un-grateful for what he'd done for me that night, but the truth of the matter was he was involved, and mentioning it might get him a name as a troublemaker. Something I re-ally didn't want to do.

I closed my eyes and sighed. "I think it's because I was involved in an incident at The Bar."

"What type of incident?"

I twisted my fingers around the hem of my blouse. "Vi-olence."

"Hmm, well the bylaws state that improper conduct equals immediate disqualification."

Logan snapped up, his back ramrod straight. "There was no improper conduct. Olivia was the victim. She shouldn't be punished because some dick got all up in her face and harassed her. Besides, she wasn't the one who hit him."

Amrita's brow furrowed. "Who did hit him?"

"Not relevant," Logan said, almost before she'd finished asking.

"Did you hit him, Logan?"

It was only for a second, but I caught Logan's gaze drop to the floor as he said, "Yeah, and what of it?"

Amrita was silent for a few moments while her gaze lingered on Logan, as if she could make him look at her out of sheer will. He didn't. Finally, her gaze slid to me, and she said, "Leave it with me." She slid a notepad and business card across the desk. "I'll need your details and any relevant correspondence."

After I scrawled down my name, student number, and phone number, she stood. Logan and I both rose to our feet and Amrita showed us to the door. Even though there were no guarantees, it was good to know she was helping. Before pulling it open, she said, "I'll be in touch soon."

I gave her a small smile. "Thank you. I appreciate the help."

She returned the gesture then her gaze slid to Logan. "Make sure you stay out of trouble. You've got too much at stake. I'll see you for our regular meeting?"

Logan walked out without saying goodbye. A little shocked by his rudeness, I said, "Thanks again," and hurried to catch up.

"What was that all about?" I asked, noting his scowl.

"I don't need any damn lectures." Logan swung his bag onto his shoulder. "I got to get to class." He leaned in, his breath on my cheek. My legs almost gave way at the near kiss, but he pulled back, his expression still stony. "I'll catch you later."

He walked toward the admin building, leaving me regretting saying what I had to the welfare officer. I shouldn't have pulled him into my issues like that. My problems were mine alone, and I'd have to deal with them. It was really nice of him to set up the meeting, but Logan didn't owe me anything.

I called out his name.

Logan spun around, and I shouted, "I'm sorry."

He brought his hand to his mouth, blew me a kiss, and smiled as he turned back around the way he was headed.

Well, that was kind of weird. He'd seemed so happy to see me, but now he couldn't get away quickly enough, which kind of stung, even though I shouldn't let it. After the day we'd spent together yesterday, I had assumed he'd want to hang out. I glanced at my watch, and realised the next class didn't start for half an hour, so Logan shouldn't have been in a hurry at all. Clearly he just didn't want to be here with me for whatever reason.

I'd skipped class to make the appointment, but it would be half over by now, so I decided to head to my next one early. Maybe I could use the time to catch up. As I walked across campus, I couldn't stop thinking about Logan's weird behaviour.

When I got to the lecture hall it was empty. It was a blessing, really, that there wasn't a class before mine. I took my usual spot in the centre of the room and pulled down the desk, then set to work. The time passed quickly and before I realised it, the hall filled with students. Ella claimed the desk beside mine, and heat rushed up neck to my cheeks. I'd successfully avoided her since overhearing that conversation in the bathroom, and she hadn't sat with me in class either. I guess our volatile friendship had always been more competitive than true anyway.

"You weren't in the tutorial yesterday." Her glare felt accusatory. "You missed the mid-term quiz that's worth ten per cent of the final grade. And where's your input for the group assignment for Torts?"

Crap. Double crap. How did I forget about the test? My heart sunk to the pit of my stomach and Ella sized me up, her green-eyed gaze flicking from the work spread out before me to what I was certain was my now pale face.

"That's due tomorrow, Olivia. We need to get it organised. What's wrong with you lately?"

The answer rolled right off my tongue. "Maybe if people would give me a break and stop spreading stupid rumours, I could concentrate on schoolwork."

"Well, maybe if you didn't keep the entire floor awake every night, people wouldn't talk about it."

Ella didn't give me a chance to respond. She stood and moved to the back of the room, as far away from me as possible. The way my stomach turned and bile rose in my throat was a sure indicator that I was going to throw up any second. Missing a compulsory test was bad. It didn't matter that it was only worth ten per cent, compulsory was compulsory. It could cause me to fail the entire class.

I drew in a slow, steady breath and let it out again as Professor Renfrew took position at the front of the room. When did Ella get so nasty? Making crap up was one thing, but claiming it happened every night ... my cheeks warmed at the thought. The days we'd been friends in high school had never felt so far gone.

The lecture started with Renfrew using a laser to point at a list projected on the screen. The topic didn't even register in my head. I'd never experienced an hour that dragged so long.

I gathered up my stuff and rushed to the front of the theatre as my classmates filed out. Professor Renfrew shoved papers and books into his satchel.

"Excuse me, Sir, do you have a moment?"

He looked up. The middle-aged professor was the toughest of my lecturers this year. With a reputation for being strict about grades, I didn't stand much of a chance, but I was determined to plead my case anyway.

He nodded for me to continue and I bit down the bundle of nerves which had just hit me. "I ... ah ... I missed my tutorial yesterday, so didn't sit the quiz. Is there—"

"Do you have a doctor's certificate?"

"No."

"Was there a death in the family?"

"No."

"Any other extenuating circumstances?"

"Umm ..." Did being kidnapped by a hot guy count?

"Well, why did you miss it?"

"I ... I ... forgot all about it." *Cringe.* His barrage of questions left me floundering, and I couldn't think straight.

"Then no, I can't give you a special exemption. A ninety per cent attendance rate is also compulsory for tutorials. I trust you'll remember that, Miss Dean." He picked up his bag and walked out.

I couldn't fail over a stupid compulsory test. That wouldn't happen. There had to be a way to make it up. Heat burned in the back of my throat and chest. My eyes began to sting, but I wouldn't cry. The door to the lecture theatre slammed as he exited and I jumped like someone had fired a shot.

It would be damn near impossible to make sure I maintained a high distinction average in this class. In just a few weeks, my whole world had gone from right on track to falling apart at the seams, and there was nothing I could do to stop the disaster.

WEDNESDAY AND Thursday came and went and I didn't hear from Logan. By Friday morning I had myself convinced that even if nothing had really happened, he'd counted me as a win and lost interest. Which made me feel like utter crap, even though I wasn't sure why. I should be grateful we'd both dodged a bullet. I needed to concentrate on my classes, and he didn't need my issues bogging him down.

At the beginning of the year, I'd worked my schedule so I had a free full day each Friday, and gee was I thankful for that. Still behind on my work, I went to the library to catch up. My mind continued swirling around what Ella had said and the conviction in her voice. She'd been nice for the past year, so the turnaround was a bit of a shock. I got my portion of the group assignment to her on Tuesday night. It was due today, and I hadn't heard boo from her or the other girl in our group.

I set myself up in one of the huge desks for a day of study. I probably should have been in the Law library, but I'd come to Dixon instead. It was easier to blend into the larger library and hide myself away amongst the books.

I flipped my laptop open and hooked into the university's Wi-Fi. First job on my to-do list was to email Ella. A bunch of new emails pinged into my inbox, but I ignored them while I concentrated on what I needed to say; instructions on where my section fitted into the assignment, and a plea to send through hers so I could mesh them together. I attached my work again for good measure, and CCed both of my group members. Hopefully they'd like what I did then we could submit with hours to spare. After it had sent, I checked out my mailbox and blow me down, there was an email from Logan. I wanted to be angry that I hadn't heard from him sooner, but my heart fluttered as I clicked it open.

Sorry about leaving in a hurry the other day.
Don't stress about the suspension, Amrita will
sort it out.

Not even so much as a 'see you soon.' I tried to ignore the disappointment that spiralled through me that there was nothing more as I flicked from my emails into my working document. Whatever game he was playing I didn't have the time or energy to be part of it, even if my heart argued otherwise.

Chapter 10

MY PHONE beeped with an incoming text. Logan's name flashed across the screen and I pushed it to the side then clicked to refresh my emails. It wasn't that I didn't care he was texting, but rather that there was still nothing from either Ella or the other girl about our Torts assignment. It was due in five hours if we submitted via the online portal, which was the last way left to submit, since we'd missed the five p.m cut off for delivering in person. The fact we were so close to deadline had me more than a little anxious. I drummed my fingers against the hardwood of my desk in my dorm room. Maybe I should just go knock on her door.

My phone trilled again, reminding me I had an unread text. Sighing, I picked it up.

What's for breakfast?

I hadn't heard from him in two days and the first thing he asked about was food. I couldn't figure this guy out. But then I hadn't responded to his email either.

> Pig snouts, lambs' livers, and black cof-
> fee.

I grinned at my inventiveness. His response was immediate.

> Not anymore. I'll pick you up at eight
>
> tomorrow morning.
>
> Can't.
>
> Why?
>
> I have hockey.
>
> Until?
>
> Until I'm done.
>
> And after that?
>
> Study. Like I'm trying to do now.
>
> If you'd just say yes, I'd leave you alone.
>
> No.

Shh!

Night then.

I sighed as I typed out my last message and pushed my phone across the desk, then refreshed my email yet again. Last thing I felt like was a showdown with Ella, but this assignment needed to go. I opened my door and strode down the hall to her room. Her door was closed, which wasn't unusual; it was often that way when she studied. I was the only one who kept my door closed all the time. Not that I ever used to. I rapped my knuckles against the wood and waited.

And waited.

I knocked again.

She wasn't in. Unfortunately, I didn't know the other girl since she didn't live at Oxley. Friends with Ella she was from one of the other dorms, and I had no way to contact her other than via email, which I'd already done at least a dozen times. Growing frustrated, I stomped back to my room and slammed the door.

Over the next hour I must have hit refresh on my email a million times. It was enough that my pointer finger started aching. I had no idea how to deal with this. I had the work I'd compiled. It was a rough draft, and I didn't want to submit without my group's input, but it was getting close to the submission deadline and it didn't look as if they'd be helping.

I tried Ella's door again and got the same result.

It was nine p.m and a lot of noise bounced off the walls of the courtyard: voices and music and laughter. I pushed my fingertips around my temples. I couldn't wait any longer. It needed to go. I'd just have to do it without them.

I opened the draft and started working to polish it up.

Another two hours and it was done. There was still no word from either of my partners and the online submission portal would close in an hour. I logged into the university intranet and took a deep breath. This was the wrong thing to do, but they'd left me with no choice.

Someone squealed in the courtyard below and I yanked my curtains closed to block out the distraction.

"Olivia!" a voice called from below, but I knew better than to respond. Especially when it was a guy. "Come down. We wanna watch you play."

Raucous laughter followed and I took a deep breath.

Ignore it.

I attached the file and clicked submit.

"Livia!"

That sounded like Dane; he could go to hell. I wasn't going out there. And he'd been so on and off with Savvy, if I did go down, I'd probably give him an earful. Not the best outcome for trying to fall back under the college gossip radar.

A fast rap sounded on my door. Just freaking great. That I ignored too.

The progress bar moved across the screen while the pounding on my door continued. "Olivia, I know you're in there."

Great. It was Christian.

"C'mon, babe, let me in."

The bitch in me wanted to have it out with him—to yell and scream, and make him hurt for how he'd hurt me. But the tone of his voice was so pleading, so pained that I had the door open before I'd had time to rationalise.

Christian leaned again the frame, his head resting on his forearm. Eyes spidered with red, he looked like utter crap and smelled like a brewery. He was unshaven which was unusual, and unlike on Logan, it didn't look sexy on him at all. It looked sloppy. His dark hair was just as bad, sticking up all over the place rather than in his normal neat style.

"I miss you." He couldn't even keep his gaze locked on my face. It kept sliding to the left. He obviously had no idea what he was saying.

My hand gripped the edge of the door tightly, holding it half closed. "I doubt that."

"I do, Livia. I miss kissing you, touching you, the way you smell. I miss holding you all night."

"You're drunk, Christian. Go to bed."

"I want to come to your bed."

"That's not going to happen."

He heaved a sigh longer than I thought was possible for one single breath. "Please, babe, I love you."

"I am not your babe, Christian, and you don't love me."

"I know you're not ..." His glassy eyes flicked to mine and actually held. "I screwed up."

I tried to close the door, but he'd wedged himself in it. Christian was the last person I felt like talking to and truth be told, I wasn't sure I could contain myself.

"Forgive me."

"Oh-my-freaking-gosh, Christian. I'm the laughing stock of Oxley thanks to you and you ... you ... want me to forgive you?" I shook my head. Unbelievable.

His fingers ran along my arm. "What you do is damn hot, Olivia."

Rage boiled within me and I rolled my shoulder to shrug his touch off. Of all the dumb things to say, he had to go there, as if he actually believed it. "For heaven's sake, Christian."

Christian jerked his head back and his lips flattened.

The second he was off my door jamb, I slammed it closed. Hopefully the jerk would fall on his way down the stairs. How dare he come up here and act all flirty while he still held onto that lie?

I dropped into my chair and jammed my iPod buds into my ears before setting the volume to blaring. Drowning out the fools in the courtyard and the niggling voice in my head that was stressed about this assignment, I turned around to the computer and woke it up from hibernation.

Submission unsuccessful.
Prior submission received.

BENCHED. HOW a team could do that to their captain was beyond my understanding. Yet here I was, sitting on the sidelines again. And this time, from the very start of the game. Maddy had taken over my usual position, ordering me off for first half, telling everyone else where to play, and when I stood up to her the rest of the team voiced their disagreement. I was off. Apparently I was volatile, which meant I could lose us the game, and this game was important—it would be the one that put us through to the quarter finals. Whatever. They wanted to see volatile, I'd show them.

"What's up, Butterfingers? You look angry."

I swung around so fast the stick in my hand almost hit the fence Logan was standing behind.

"What are you doing here?"

"Picking you up for breakfast."

"I said no."

"Is that why you're scowling? Good food in your belly makes everything better."

I clenched my teeth and swung back around to watch the game. Alisha was a waste of space today; she'd over-shot the ball three times, and now she'd let the redheaded Evan's Hall girl steal it right out from under her.

Logan jumped the fence and plonked himself on the bench beside me. One of our reserves, Rovi, huffed on my other side. "Tell your boyfriend this space is reserved for the players only."

"Not her boyfriend," Logan said. "Right, Liv?"

Ignoring his mocking tone, I kept my eyes on the field and spun my stick on its curved head, balancing the twirl-ing end with my fingers.

"Alisha! No! From the left … watch it. Watch it …" I yelled at my teammate, but she still missed the pass. "Damn it. I should be out there."

Half-time came and went, and still my team wouldn't let me on the field. Logan sat beside me the whole time, and the longer it played out the angrier I got until I jumped up, tossed my stick in my bag, and looked at Lo-gan. "Let's go get some food."

A small grin graced his wind-chapped lips. The air was icy cold this morning. He jumped over the wooden fence and held his hand out. I took it and vaulted myself over to join him. His red Corolla was parked at the sports centre and even though he didn't talk on the short walk there, I could practically feel his smile in the air. I suppose he thought he'd won. Well, it wasn't like we could go anywhere fancy with me in my hockey clothes anyway.

He opened the passenger door and I climbed in the small car, tossing my duffle bag in the back seat as he closed the door after me. Logan slid in behind the wheel and started the engine. It choked once and didn't turn over. With a look of sheer determination, he hit the ignition again and this time it started. His thigh flexed against those jeans I loved as he put it into reverse. He'd coupled them with a light-weight leather jacket and a t-shirt. Good lord, the guy had style.

"What happened back there?" he asked, pulling out of the parking lot.

"I'm tired of being treated like rubbish."

"They sat you off?"

"I am the gosh darn captain. They can't sit me off."

Logan's mouth twitched, fighting a smile. I had no idea what was so funny.

"Whatever," I huffed. "I don't want to talk about it."

As the Corolla pulled out of University Drive and headed toward town, all I could think about was the game. It felt like the stupid rumour had taken over every facet of my life; from hockey to my social life, and even academically. I was stressed as all heck about the assignment not submitting on top of the missed test, and freaking Ella was still nowhere to be found.

Logan took my not wanting to talk as a precedent, and

kept his mouth shut all the way through town until we were headed out the side, this time going south. I'd assumed we'd be going to one of the cafes in town, but I hoped to high hell we weren't headed to Tamworth. It was the closest city to our university's country town, and more than an hour's drive away. Surely that wasn't what he had in mind for breakfast. Just before we hit the highway though, he indicated to turn off the main road. The sign above the place he pulled into had a bunch of strawberries on it and read 'Berry Best'

"Corny."

"Don't pass judgement too early." Logan got out of the car.

After smoothing my hair back into its ponytail, I hopped out of the car and Logan closed the door behind me. I glanced down at my shin pads, which were a little ridiculous, but Logan strode right up to the door and pulled it open. "What are you waiting for? The best pancakes in town are just inside."

I smoothed out my shirt. "I feel underdressed."

"It's breakfast, Liv, you look fine. In fact, those socks? Hot damn!"

Chuckling, I swatted his arm. My blue knee-high sports socks were ugly, and we both knew it.

Logan placed his hand on the small of my back and guided me inside the quaint little cottage. It was the cutest place imaginable, country living met chic vintage style. Little wooden tables filled the room, and a glass counter played host to a multitude of pies and muffins and cakes. This didn't look like somewhere to have breakfast; it looked like the type of place you'd come out of with eyes glazed over from a sugar coma.

We picked a table by the huge window, which with any luck should be warmed by the morning sun. It was chilly, and I hadn't thought to bring a jacket as I'd expected to be on the field then return home while I was still warm from the game.

I picked up the menu and started reading. Logan's eyes caught mine over the top.

"You really like hockey, huh?"

"Not that much. It's all right though, I guess."

He raised a brow. "You sure seemed pretty passionate back there."

"Yeah, well ... I'm the captain. Sitting on the sidelines is not where I should have been."

"Why do you play then?"

"Huh?" It wasn't like I was benched every week. In fact, the last two games were the only times it had happened. Ever.

"If you don't love it, why do you play?"

I shrugged. "Same reason I play netball when it's in season. It's good to be involved." I glanced down at the menu. "What about you? Any favourite sports?"

"I like watching the football." Logan's mouth turned up.

"Spectator, hey?"

Just then the waitress walked over, pad in hand.

"You first." Logan nodded toward me.

My gaze slid over the menu one more time. "Can I have an English Breakfast tea and the fresh berry pancakes?"

"Thought you'd be a coffee drinker." Logan palmed his hair back from his face.

"Not me." I'd never drunk a cup of coffee in my life. I

couldn't even stand the smell of it. It was somehow bitter and tangy and green, all rolled into a smell strong enough to knock your socks off. Logan placed his own order, sans coffee, thank goodness.

"Let me guess,' he said, " you hate the stuff?"

"Even the smell's a bit much," I admitted.

We spent the morning talking about everything, from my lack of siblings to my not-so-ardent love of sports, and even touched on Logan's work. He'd worked at the cafe during his freshman year, and when he came back to town the owner was happy for him to re-join the roster. I didn't ask why he'd left, not after being fobbed off last time. He'd tell me when he was ready. The time flowed by quickly, and before I knew it the cafe had filled with people who'd come to eat lunch.

Logan reached across the table and grabbed the bill from where the waitress had placed it an hour ago. I went to take it from him, but he shook his head and approached the counter. It wasn't right to let him pay. We were just hanging out, so when he came back, I slipped a twenty out of my purse.

"Keep your money, Butterfingers. It's my shout." He walked out of the cafe before I could shove the note in his hand. I'd make sure to get it next time.

Once outside, Logan gestured toward a gate. "It's not the right season for berry picking, but let's check it out anyway."

"You can pick berries here? How'd I not know this place existed?"

Logan winked and tapped his nose, whatever that meant.

We walked between the lines of tiny strawberry plants while we continued talking. The rows were so narrow, Logan's hand brushed against mine. The boundary between friendship and romance seemed to be blurring again. Being with Logan always felt so natural; our friendship wasn't forced. There was something between us that made me relax and forget about everything else.

"So what about you?" I asked. "Any siblings?"

Logan glanced away, his jaw clenched.

My phone rang. A picture of my mother flashed onto the screen, but I flicked it to silent and shoved it into my pocket. Not even a minute later it vibrated again. The woman was nothing if not persistent. A quick glance revealed the vibration was a text from Ella.

Social Committee meeting.
Tomorrow 3pm.

Great. Nothing about the assignment. I wasn't about to ruin a nice morning with Logan, so I shoved it into my pocket a second time.

"Have you heard from Amrita?" Logan asked.

"No. I guess she can't help after all."

Logan jammed his hands in his jacket pockets. "She'll pull through."

"Gosh, I hope so." I needed her to get that exclusion lifted, because if she didn't then I was in trouble. I wouldn't be the only one stressing about the ramifications. If my mother got wind that I was out of the running for president she'd be calling the board.

After we'd done a full loop, Logan glanced at his watch, his lips pressed together. "Shit. I need to get home."

I wasn't sure what the sudden hurry was, but I didn't ask. It really wasn't any of my business. We moved through the rows of plants back toward the gate, and when we were in his Corolla, I smiled at Logan. "Thanks for breakfast. It was nice."

"Better than pigs' snouts."

I chuckled. "Much better. Who eats that crap?"

Logan laughed, and it was good to see his expression more at ease. I watched his hand work to change gears and the feel of it in mine was fresh in my mind. Heat burst through my tummy and I swear I could almost feel his touch again.

At college, we pulled up in the back car park and I didn't want our morning to end. Just like that day at the waterfall, I'd forgotten about everything and just enjoyed Logan's company. Once again, the time had moved way too fast. And now that I was on Oxley's grounds, all my troubles came tumbling back. I sighed as I reached into the back, but Logan had already beat me to it and held my hockey bag in his hands. I smiled at him across the bucket seats. "Thanks."

While I repositioned my socks, he must have jogged around the car, because my door opened. "Didn't think I was going to miss the chance to walk you in, did you?"

"Guess not," I said, climbing out of the Corolla.

I hugged my tummy as we started walking in. There would be people in the courtyard since it was Saturday afternoon and there was no way I could avoid it. I just hoped that whatever was said wouldn't be too embarrassing.

He swung my bag by his side and tossed me one of those gorgeous smiles that made his mouth totally kissable. If I just moved a little closer ...

A wolf whistle cut through the air, stopping my thoughts dead.

We'd passed the gate and were just entering Back Courtyard. And of course, as my luck would have it, the wooden picnic table was crowded. Empty wine casks and beer bottles, remnants of last night's party I'd seen this morning, were gone, but in their place were sprawled the partygoers.

I kept myself facing toward the way I needed to go and ignored the catcalls.

"Good luck sleeping, man. Taking that on."

My bag landed on my feet and Logan was across the courtyard, staring down Christian in the blink of an eye. I'd kill my ex next time he got close enough; he was such a jerk. In the next instant, Dane stepped between them, pushing Christian back, and saying something to Logan that I couldn't hear. I picked up my duffle bag and started retreating. This was just too much. I couldn't go anywhere with anyone, without there being a massive scene. Logan didn't need this. I didn't need this.

As my feet hit the stairs, I heard footsteps behind me. "Liv, wait."

I turned around to face him. "What is it, Logan?"

He reached out for me, then pulled his hand back like he'd thought better of it.

We stood there for several moments, each looking at the other. Whatever he wanted to say obviously wasn't important. Or he'd changed his mind. I sucked in a deep breath and turned back the way I was headed.

"Liv ..."

I couldn't pull enough air past my thick throat to fill my lungs. I didn't turn around. "You've got somewhere to be, Logan."

I knew he stood on those stairs and watched me leave. I could feel his eyes on my back.

He never knocked on my door.

Chapter 11

SUNDAY AFTERNOON rolled around and despite staking out the stairs by my room, I still hadn't managed to catch Ella. My heart stuttered every time I thought of that assignment. It was worth forty per cent of the total grade. So I was keen for this afternoon's social committee meeting, because I knew I'd run into my project partner there. Honestly, mine and Ella's lives seemed to connect on so many levels—family, college, class, social committee—it was no wonder we'd been close in high school. Even if sometimes that friendship was rocky. And right now, it surely was. I could have strangled her.

I grabbed a notebook, pen, and my diary, and pulled the door to my room closed. We had another function (Central Night) coming up that needed to be organised and next term to start thinking about. I wasn't looking forward to seeing Christian, but I'd just have to suck that up and remember why I was there.

As I walked into the common room, my phone rang. My mother's image flashed onto the screen. Crap. I'd forgotten to call her back after the berry farm. If I didn't answer, I'd be in trouble.

"Mum. How are you?" I leaned against the wall.

"Olivia. I hope you didn't answer my call yesterday because you were studying." Her voice was terse and clipped. I didn't have time for this.

"I'm about to duck into a social committee meeting. Can I call you back later?"

"No worries. I just wanted to confirm your arrival time."

"I'm pretty sure my flight gets in at three ten."

"I'll see you in a fortnight then."

"Bye Mum."

"Olivia ..."

"Yeah?"

"Yes, Olivia, not yeah."

I sighed. "Yes?"

"Work hard."

The line went dead. Sometimes talking to my mother felt like a chore. Taking a deep breath, I slid my phone into my jeans pocket and pushed open the door to the senior common room. It was practically empty. Ella and Christian stood by the mini fridge, chatting, and a senior girl snatched empty food packets off the table and tossed them into the bin.

I glanced at my watch, and it was smack bang on three o'clock. I even watched the second hand tick. Nope, it was working. "Wow. Everyone's running late."

Ella giggled and Christian said, "Ah, nope. Just you."

My gaze slid to the senior, then back to Ella and finally Christian. "I'm right on time." I pointed to my wrist. "See."

"The meeting was at two. You missed it," said the senior as she walked out of the room.

"You said it was three." I frowned at Ella.

"Oh, did I? My bad." She tossed her cherry-red hair over her shoulder and slammed her hand against the door.

"You did that on purpose."

Ella shrugged and left the room. For heaven's sake, what was wrong with her? I pushed the door open and called out her name, but it was too late—she was already gone. Darn it, I needed to talk to her about the assignment.

"You all right?" Christian said, and it took everything I had just to shake my head. I felt like I was anything but all right lately. And why the heck was he asking anyway? It wasn't like he cared.

His hand touched my shoulder gently, and it felt as if I could crumble. My world had completely turned around. Last year I was at the centre of all these activities and now I was scraping around the edges, begging to be let in. My throat began to ache and my chest felt heavy. Crumbling was a very real prospect, but no way in hell was I going to let that happen in front of the guy who'd caused it all, so I forced a smile and said, "Of course I am."

Christian's gaze focused on mine and I knew he could see right through my facade as his cheek dimpled. He always sucked it from the inside when he thought.

"I'm really sorry about how things went down—"

"Spare me, Christian. Just don't bother." I pulled back from his touch and left the common room feeling as if I'd been muscled out of everything that mattered.

FIRST THING Monday morning I knocked on Professor Renfrew's door and was greeted with silence. Great, he wasn't in. That darn assignment not sending was a worry and I needed to sort it out. He should be able to tell me why, and maybe even allow me to submit it some other way. I knocked again. And waited. Inside was deathly silent. Great. With no choice but to come back later, I headed for my tutorial, and as I walked through the doorway my gaze landed on Ella's smug smile. Her back was ramrod straight, her shoulders square, and against my better judgement, I took the seat beside her and dropped my voice so we were the only ones to hear. "You didn't answer my emails."

"I've got better things to do than sit on a computer all day, Olivia."

"You didn't answer your door either."

"I have a life, you know. Not all of us sit in our rooms all day."

I swallowed my smart-alec retort and hissed, "The assignment wouldn't submit."

"Wouldn't it?" The tone she used was sweeter than candied honey as she twirled a pen between her fingers.

"Doesn't that bother you?"

"Why should it?"

"Because it's worth forty per cent, Ella."

"Well, good thing I submitted it then."

She freaking submitted it without consulting with me? Well, that kind of defeated the purpose of a group assignment. Heat curled in my belly and rose up to my head until it was pounding. "But we hadn't even finished it."

She tapped my chin with her pen. "Close your mouth, dear. Do you think I'd turn in anything less than perfect? Relax, Olivia. It's all good."

"You should have told me."

The professor walked in, effectively cutting off our conversation. Not that it stopped in my head. I played out so many scenarios and things I could have said—group means together, how dare you sub without us talking, you're a right royal bitch—that I made myself dizzy, and all while Ella sat there looking smug and amused. I could have killed her for putting me through all that stress.

As the tutorial wound down and my classmates filed out of the room, I caught Professor Renfrew's attention.

"Sir, I was wondering if there's another way I can make up for the test. Maybe I could write an extra paper, or—"

"Ms Dean, I've already told you. Unless you have a Doctor's Certificate or other extenuating circumstance, I can't help you."

"But surely, if—"

Professor Renfrew pursed his lips, shook his head, and left the room. I blew out a long breath and packed up, unsure of how to fix this. I couldn't just let it slide, but if he wouldn't let me make it up then I had no choice. I'd have to work extra hard to make sure I aced the next test and the one after.

"YOU'RE HIDING again." Molly's feet, crossed at the ankles, swung back and forth as she sat on the edge of my desk, casting me an accusatory glare.

"I'm not. I'm just … busy. Friday's are study days."

She raised an eyebrow. "It wasn't Friday all week."

"You know, it's almost end of term and every class has a major assignment due, if not an exam."

"And that's why you haven't eaten in the dining hall all week?"

"It's quicker and easier just to eat in my room." I let my hair fall forward as I sat on my bed with my Sociology texts spread out before me. An eraser hurtled through the air and thwacked into the side of my head.

"Liar. What is it? Those antsy-pantsy rumours or something else? I heard you were pretty pissed about the game on Saturday …"

I kept my eyes on the books.

"Is it Logan?"

"He wasn't in class on Monday." In fact, I hadn't heard from him since I'd walked away on Saturday afternoon. I didn't really have a right to care about that, nor should I want to, but that didn't stop it from sitting in my chest all ball-like.

"It is." Her voice practically bounced.

"It is not. It's just …" I sighed. "Everything, okay? Let it go."

"I will not let it go." She jumped down off the desk, landing on her toes, and tugged my keys off their plastic hanger by the door, then tossed them at me. "You need to get out of this shoe box."

"I have things to do, Molly." I flourished my hand over the bed.

"Pfft. Nothing that can't wait a few hours while we have some girl time."

"Doing what?"

"Just hanging." She tugged me up off the bed, and there was no point in resisting. Once Molly had her mind set on something there was no stopping her. Much like the Mickey Mouse sweater she was wearing. She'd decided it was cute, and no amount of persuasion could convince her otherwise. Apparently Savvy had spent close on an hour trying.

I grabbed my purse and phone, then slunk through the door that Molly held open whilst tapping her toes against the daggy nineties-style, industrial-grade carpet. She was right; I was hiding. But it wasn't because I cared what they were saying; it was because everything was spiralling out of control and I didn't know how to get it back on track.

The fresh scent of rain hit me as we descended the stairs. A soft drizzle fell from the sky, but we kept to the covered walkways as we wandered through the courtyard. A shrill voice yelled, "Livia! Molly!" I glanced up and Savannah was at her window, waving like crazy. "Wait a sec."

"Argh. How many times do I have to tell her I hate my name shortened?"

Molly chuckled and we exchanged a glance, an unspoken agreement to wait and see what Savvy wanted. The rain picked up in intensity, forcing us back against the brick wall to stay dry. Thankfully, the wait wasn't long. Savvy burst out of the door that led to block L, her blonde hair a mess of weird bendy things. "Are you guys heading to town?"

"Yep," Molly answered. "You need something to cut that crap out of your hair?"

Savvy's eyes bulged and Molly snuck a glance at me then laughed. Poor Savannah looked as if she was about to launch into a tirade of exactly where Molly could shove her suggestion.

"Do you want to come with us?"

"No, I'm trialling my hair for Central Night. Are you guys going?"

Molly rolled her eyes. "Sheesh. Keen much? It's not until next week."

"I don't think so," I said. Honestly hanging out at the Central Hotel with the rest of Oxley College didn't sound as fun as I would have found it a year ago.

Savvy held her hand out, catching drops of water on her fingers. "I can ask Dane to invite Logan."

"If I wanted to go and I wanted Logan to go, I'd invite him myself. But I don't, on either account. And right now, we need to get going or we'll miss the bus."

Savannah raised a brow. "Sure thing. See you later."

We made a mad dash to the shelter. I tried to avoid the puddles as best I could and hand over my head, I hoped it kept at least some of the light rain off. The bus pulled up just as we crossed the road. We climbed on and took a seat up the back. Once again, I found myself staring at my reflection in the window, and kicking myself for not bothering to tidy up before stepping out of my room. I had no makeup on and my hair was pulled up in a messy bun on top of my head that had turned to frizzy in the damp air. I'd have to make sure I smartened up my act before heading home to Sydney or Mum would ship me off for elocution lessons, or something equally ridiculous. It wouldn't be the first time, either.

My phone buzzed halfway to town and I slid it out of my bag. The number was unknown. Before I could answer, it stopped.

"Lover boy?" Molly asked.

"I don't know who you're talking about."

Molly chuckled. "Keep denying it, Olivia."

The phone vibrated with a chime, telling me the caller had left a message. I held the device up to my ear. "It's Amrita from Student Services ..." The message stopped abruptly. Weird.

"It was the Student Services lady." My fingers slid over the screen to call her back. Of course, my call went straight to her voicemail. I'd been hanging out to hear from her for a week, and another few minutes seemed an impossible wait. I tapped the phone against my knee. "I couldn't get through though."

My foot jigged as I waited to try and call her again. What if she couldn't help ... crap, what if she could? With voting opening in less than a week, I'd need to pull together a campaign mighty quick. We'd need flyers and notices around campus. I'd have to hang out at The Bar and the library, rallying voters. Gee, I'd lost valuable time, but maybe it could be salvaged. I ran my finger over the foggy glass.

The bus whined as it pulled into our stop.

"She'll call back," Molly said.

When we'd disembarked, Molly dragged me toward the shopping centre. The dash to the front door was enough to kick mud up my legs. "Retail therapy. You're buying, though, I'm broke."

I laughed. "And you think I'm not?"

"I know you're not." She winked. "What do you want to look at?"

"Oh, I don't know." Truth was I was never broke; not with the credit card linked to my mother's. "Maybe we can buy you an outfit for Central Night."

Molly's elbow ploughed into my ribs. What the— "And that, right there, is where we're starting." She cupped her hands around her mouth and yelled, "Oh, lover boy," dragging out the last word.

The ground needed to open up and swallow me already. Why it hadn't when I'd begged it to at least a dozen times recently was proof I had control over nothing. Or I had unrealistic expectations. Fighting the embarrassment of my insane friend, rain ruined hair, and muddy legs, I followed the line of her gaze to Logan. His grey t-shirt moved against his chest with his swinging arms as he strolled toward us. It was cold today with the rainy weather. He mustn't be able to feel it.

A younger guy walked alongside him, matching Logan's stride. He spun his baseball cap around backwards, and shoved his hands in the pockets of his jeans as his gaze skimmed over Molly and spent entirely too long on me.

"Hey," Logan said, drawing my attention away from his friend.

"Hi," I answered, a little unsure how to act. The way

we'd last parted wasn't exactly friendly. This was awkward as hell. My arms instinctively curled around my middle and I stepped back.

The other guy turned to Logan. "Dude. Are you going to introduce us?"

Logan's gaze flicked across mine and for a moment, I thought he wasn't going to. Honestly, I wouldn't blame him. Lately, I was embarrassed to be me.

"Liv, this is Jordan. Jordan ..." Logan waved his hand toward me. "Liv."

"Liv? As in, Olivia. Like *the* Olivia?"

Logan shot the other guy a pointed look.

"*The* Olivia." Molly emphasised the first word.

Logan said, "One and the same."

A low whistle came from Logan's friend as he grinned at Molly, as if the two of them shared a secret. "What are you guys up to?"

"Nothing," Molly answered. "Absolutely nothing, why don't we grab a coffee? Wait. He's allowed to call you Liv?"

"Olivia hates coffee," Logan said, his gaze still locked with mine.

"Mate ..." Jordan slapped Logan's back. "Just do it already."

"Quit it." Logan shot his friend a glare. "Not going to happen today."

"Well, *Liv* and I are headed over ..." Molly looked around "... there. To Crazy Beans to *not* have coffee. Feel free to join us."

Then she started walking away. *Gosh, girl, way to put everyone on the spot.* She'd probably made Logan feel like he had to hang out with us so he didn't look rude. "It's

okay; you guys don't have to join us. Molly's just being ob-
noxious."

"Get out!" Jordan grinned. "We're joining you."

Logan's smile started small. "If that's what Liv wants."

I shrugged. What could it hurt? If he wanted to be
there, then I guess I wanted him there. We were friends
after all, and those were a rare commodity of late.

Molly had already claimed a booth when we arrived.
Jordan slid in beside her, leaving the opposite side free.
Yeah, I was totally on to the pair of them and their little
plan. Logan gestured for me to go first, so I slid across the
vinyl and he slipped in beside me. There wasn't a lot of
room, so I squished my purse between myself and the
wall. Logan's thick thighs seemed to take up most of the
seat, but I was careful to keep a little space between us.

"It's Central Night next Thursday. You going, Logan?"
Molly cut straight to the point.

"Ah ..." He glanced toward his friend. "Don't think so."

Jordan held his hands up. "Don't let me stop you, bro. If
you wanna go bang your girl, you should do it."

"Grow the hell up, Jordan."

"I'm in high school, man. I'm supposed to act like it."

"You're in high school?" It could have been either Molly
or I who said it. It was hard to tell because I was too
stunned. I'd assumed Jordan was a first year. He had that
fresh-out-of-school look and it was Friday; school kids
should be at school.

Jordan's mouth curled up. "You thought I was older?
See, Loges, I could hit the pub with you without being
carded."

Logan shook his head at Molly's laughter. "For god's

sake, don't encourage him."

"Then how'd you guys meet?" Molly gestured between them.

"When Loges moved back up here this year, I came with him. He's a sissy like that; can't have his little brother too far away."

Logan tensed beside me and something curled around my insides and squeezed. This was Logan's bother. He had a brother? I tried to recall if he'd ever mentioned his family, but I was pretty sure he avoided answering my questions. It was probably wrong, but I felt a tad betrayed.

I smiled at Jordan. "So you're in boarding school then?"

"Nope. We're baching it up, right Loges?"

Logan drew in a noisy breath. Well, if he was annoyed then I should be doubly so; we'd been friends for weeks. I'd thought we were kind of close and he'd never mentioned that he had a sibling, let alone one who lived with him. That told me one thing: he'd definitely decided that I wasn't girlfriend material. And that there was why I hadn't heard from him all week.

A sharp pain speared my shin and my gaze shot directly across the table to where Molly smiled at me like she was expecting an answer. "Right, Liv?"

I had no idea what she was asking. Her brow raised in question. Darn it. "Yeah, I guess so," I hedged.

A silence stretched so long that if this were a movie crickets would have been chirping.

"So, what grade are you in?" Molly asked.

"What grade do you think?" Jordan challenged.

"Seven."

He barked out a laugh. "I do not look thirteen."

They bantered back and forth while my gaze shifted to a couple sitting across the way. They must have been a little older than us. It was hard to tell, but he was looking at her in that awestruck way, hanging on her every word, or maybe he wasn't hearing anything at all because he was so caught up in her. I couldn't see her face, but she'd be returning his affection for sure, and the way they looked at each other was like a knife to my stomach. Wherever Logan and I were headed, it certainly wasn't there.

Someone cleared their throat directly beside my ear, and I turned to all three of them looking at me expectantly. Again. Molly flicked her gaze up to a waitress poised at the edge of the booth with a notepad, tapping a pencil across the yellow paper. This was pure torture, but I couldn't be so rude as to up and leave, no matter how much I wanted to run away.

"Hot chocolate, thanks." I gave her what I hoped was a friendly smile.

"Twelve, it's gotta be twelve," Molly said, overly loud. "What do you reckon, Liv?"

I glanced across the table and took in Jordan's shaggy locks, much shorter than Logan's, his angular jaw, and smattering of facial hair. Once again, much thinner and shorter than his brother's. "Grade eleven."

"Eleven," Logan's confirmation echoed.

Our drinks eventually arrived and I cradled the warm cup in my hands, taking generous sips. Once I'd reached the bottom of the mug, I watched Molly's cup like a hawk, ignoring the closeness of Logan's thigh right by mine. Of course ignoring it made me think about what it would be like to rest my hand on his firm muscle. If the muscle would even be firm. It sure looked it. Gee, I needed to get a grip. But that sure wouldn't happen sitting right by him, torturing myself with what ifs when I'd never lay my hand on that leg, never trail my fingers over that thigh. I sucked back a mouthful of air too thick to reach my lungs. Right then, I couldn't care less how rude it was—I needed space, even if it was just for a few minutes.

"Excuse me." I grabbed my purse. Logan didn't move.

"Olivia?" Molly said, but I needed to leave. This whole thing had been too much.

"What happened? I say something wrong?" Jordan asked.

No doubt seeing his escape, Logan moved out of the booth.

"I'm going to the ladies," I said while pulling out a twenty. I crossed to the counter and dropped the money where the waitress was fiddling with the till. It would be more than enough to cover both mine and Molly's portion of the bill. Then I walked straight out and into the mall, my throat burning with the heat of rejection. Sure I'd made it clear that I didn't want a relationship, but part of me may have been changing her mind. I didn't understand what it was about this guy that made me feel fantastic one minute and like complete rubbish the next, but I hated it more than I hated my mother's pompous dinner parties.

Something snagged my arm; a hand around my bicep. I yanked it away, knowing exactly who it would be.

"What is it?" Logan sounded confused.

"Just leave me alone. Please."

"No, there's something not right. What is it?"

I drew in a deep breath. "It's nothing."

He sighed, but his grip tightened around my arm as I continued to stare straight ahead at the escalator I'd almost reached. If he didn't think I was important enough to mention his family to, then how I felt sure didn't matter.

When he spoke his voice was small. "Jordan being here is not something I'm proud of, okay? And this week ... it's been difficult."

I turned around, my gaze meeting his soft blue eyes. "He's your brother, and he doesn't seem like anything to be ashamed of."

"That's not what I mean."

"It's your brother, Logan—living with you. There's nothing to be ashamed of about that. It's a huge part of your life. It seems odd that you didn't tell me."

Logan ran his hand through his hair and glanced away. "You said you don't want a relationship and damn it, Liv, that's what I'm trying to do here."

I closed my eyes and concentrated on drawing my next breath then letting it go again. He was right; I wasn't his girlfriend, and I'd made it clear I didn't want to be, so I had no right to be upset he'd never told me about Jordan. In fact I had no right to feel anything. He didn't want me and I didn't want him either.

"I'm trying my best to give you time. But there's just ... there are things about me you wouldn't like."

"Right now, I don't care."

It was time to go home. But Logan spun back around, his gaze blazing as he stepped so close there was barely an inch of space between us. His huge hand snagged mine and he leaned in, his face close to mine. For a second I thought he was going to kiss me, but instead he said, "I'm sorry."

Chapter 12

S UNDAY WAS a study day. I needed to finish my major Socio assignment, study for the upcoming Torts, and Constitutional Law exams and answer my phone, since it just pinged with a text.

What are you doing?

Logan. I glanced out the window at the miserable rain and sucked in my bottom lip to stop from smiling, trying to recall the pain from yesterday. Stupid tummy had no right to be flipping happily when I was still upset with him.

Studying.

Same here. This Socio essay is hard. Do

you think increasing materialism increases the depression in a society?

I'm not answering your essay question for you.

It was worth a shot. I reckon the answer is yes. Think that'll pull a high distinction?

Nope.

Things don't replace relationships. The more things someone has, the more time they spend alone. Maybe I need more music to think properly. What are you listening to?

That last statement negates your comment about things replacing people.

:p

:p back at you.

Come here and do that.

Can't. Studying.

Hey Liv?

Shh!

Yeah?

I'm glad you met Jordan. He's a good kid. Big eater though. Just hoovered every last piece of bread in the house. Who in hell has 6 ham and egg toasties for second lunch?

For real? Six!

Guess it makes up for him not eating any fruit. Kid's all about carbs and protein.

Doesn't that build muscle?

Yep. Maybe we'll have spaghetti for dinner.With more meat than pasta.

You don't need to build muscle, Logan.

Don't I now? ;)

I'm not answering that.

You think I'm sexy.

I think you know it.

Ouch. I'm taking my sexy muscles to the shower. Then I'm cooking a delicious dinner of …

Of what?

You're thinking about me in the shower, aren't you?

Spaghetti. Cook the darn spaghetti for dinner.

The water washing over my pecs, down my abs, onto my …

Have a shower already, Logan.

☺

Chapter 13

*L*OGAN SLID into his desk at our Socio lecture on Monday morning with two disposable cups in hand. He held them both out to me. "English Breakfast or hot chocolate?"

I met his gaze with a smile. Not only had he remembered my choice of tea, but he'd noticed I had hot chocolate when we were out with Molly and Jordan.

"Whichever you don't want," I said.

Logan frowned. "Your choice."

I accepted the tea and offered him a thankful smile.

When I took a sip of my steaming drink, the warm liquid that trailed down my throat was delicious. It was raining outside, as it had been all weekend, and the dash into class had left me damp and cold. Shivering, I set up my tablet to take notes. It seemed there wasn't any time for conversation as our lecturer bustled into the room in his usual rushed fashion.

The hour passed by pretty quickly, as Sociology generally did. But Logan didn't seem to be paying much attention. By the end of the lecture, his notepad was filled with swirly drawings and patterns. Also some weird script that looked like a foreign language, maybe.

"Should I send you my notes, Stalker Boy?"

Logan bumped my shoulder with his. "If you want to email me, just do it. You don't need an excuse."

"Well, you sure don't look for one. What was with all that text spam yesterday?"

"What spam?" He sounded affronted.

"Oh, you know, the blow-by-blow account of your day."

"What? I needed your expertise on my assignment."

"And your music choice whilst studying and what you should eat for dinner."

"That's important stuff." Logan grinned. "Admit it; you love my spam and you spammed me right back"

"Sure I did." I shoved my laptop into my bag and stood to move past him.

"See you at lunch, Liv."

It didn't take long for my good mood to slip into anxiety as I rushed off to my tutorial for Constitutional Law. Along with a few lectures, it was the one tute I'd skipped the other week and I was still trying to figure out a way around the missed test. Then later I had another meeting with Student Services. Setting that up had been the purpose of the missed phone call. This day couldn't have been any more stressful than if my mother had planned it.

I walked into the tute five minutes early and got set up. It wasn't long before Ella slid into her usual seat beside me. She turned my way and offered up a plastic smile which I calmly returned.

"Fighting at The Bar and naughty night time fun." She shook her head. "That'll make my presidential campaign easier."

I spun around so fast my neck kinked. The words I was too polite to say pulsing through my mind. *You're a bitch.* Instead I said, "If that's the reason you get elected then ..." I shrugged. "Whatever."

My teeth ground together as our professor walked in and sat down. My throat burned as he started talking about a pseudo case we were examining this week. My temples throbbed as Ella answered every freaking question he asked the group in her sickly fake voice. My anger peaked when she said, "Olivia knows about assault. It happens here on campus all the time."

Longest tute ever.

It was still raining when I pulled myself together and headed to the cafeteria to grab lunch. I popped up my umbrella and made the trek across campus, careful not to ruin my favourite DKNY suede boots in the puddles. Wearing them today hadn't been the best idea, but they kept my legs warm with their velvet lining. After I grabbed a plate of hot food—it looked like some sort of stroganoff on rice—I took a table inside, and it wasn't long until Molly joined me.

"What's with the long face?" she said, glancing past me.

"Ella freaking Parry. I'm over her."

Warm hands cupped my shoulders. "Who's Ella Parry?" Logan said.

Groaning, I dropped my head back to look up at him.

"Just the meanest chick this side of Mars. Would you believe ..." I launched into a tirade of everything Ella had done in the past few weeks—excluding the overheard scene in the bathroom—while Logan's deft hands kneaded my shoulders. His thumbs worked at the knots in my muscles until I felt all gooey. By the time I had finished my speech, I felt almost lighter. As if somehow sharing all that had diminished my anger, or maybe it was the heavenly massage. Logan plopped into the seat beside me, his knee bumping against mine.

"She's a bitch. Forget about her," Molly scoffed. "So, Loges, we going to Central Night tomorrow or what?"

Logan's gaze cut to me, his eyes questioning.

"I already told you guys I'm not going."

"Why not?" Molly whined.

"I just don't want to." What I didn't say was that I had no desire to either drink or hang out with my fellow college dwellers when I'd just be the butt of all their jokes for the night. Sure the teasing had died down a little, but I was certain that given the mix of alcohol and my presence they'd start up again, and I sure as heck didn't want a repeat of the open door incident.

"Come on, Liv. It'll be awesome." Molly prodded my hands with her fork.

"No means no, Molly." Logan smirked at my friend, no doubt proud of the innuendo.

I CAME out of my last lecture of the day and Logan was

leaning against the concrete wall outside my class, his arms braided across his chest, and his blond hair curling in waves that almost brushed his shoulders. Gosh, the guy had nice hair. His gaze caught mine and his lips curled up. "You're not walking home in the rain."

I couldn't stop my smile at the surprise of seeing him for the third time that day. "You really have to stop stalking me. It's getting kind of creepy."

Logan chuckled. Maybe he knew there was no truth in my words; that I really kind of liked having him around and to be honest, I was grateful I didn't have to face what had turned into a torrential downpour.

Rain pounded against the roof and walls of the building as the crowd of students filled the hallway, clearly waiting for the deluge to abate. Logan eyed up my flimsy umbrella. "We'd better sit this out for a bit."

I rested my shoulder against the wall, facing him. "I heard back from your Student Services friend."

"Yeah?"

I slumped back, my other shoulder hitting the wall too, so I faced out toward the terrible weather. "She can't help me. The board said they won't lift it. Doesn't matter that I was the victim, they can't be seen encouraging undesirable behaviour."

"That's bullshit. The behaviour wasn't undesirable, it was self-defence."

"Doesn't matter anyway," I said, picking at my cuticle. "The vote's this Friday. It's not like I would have stood a chance anyway. Not with joining the running so late—and I'm not exactly Ms Popular around campus these days, so it would be hard to get voted in."

Logan pushed off the wall, his gaze finding mine, studying my expression. "Are you okay with that?"

"Sure," I said, even though it was a lie. Everything else I'd said was true though, so maybe it was best that I didn't go into the vote and lose abysmally. That would be far worse than not going in at all. But still, I felt as if I'd failed. As if by not even being in the running, I'd lost something important, and the lack of campus politics on my CV was a real concern. Sure I could try again next year, but with the mark on my record maybe they wouldn't let me run again. A student council position such as president was one of the few things that on its own made a massive difference.

Logan's hand snagged mine, and he pulled me off the wall. His fingers pressed their way between mine and his grip tightened as he tossed me a smile that made my heart thud. Then before I had time to respond, he tugged me out into the rain and started to run.

"Logan!" I screamed, but he didn't stop, just looked back at me with a stupid grin across his face as we jogged through the pouring rain. By the time we reached the car, we were both soaking wet, which was utterly ridiculous. Logan pulled open the passenger door and slid his free hand under the strap of my bag, removing it from my shoulder. He tossed it into the car, and we were both laughing. Water trailed down his cheeks in tiny rivers that disappeared into the stubble on his jaw and his hair was plastered to his head. His eyes, though, they looked like sparkling pools of fun.

"Hop in already," he said, because crazy me was just standing in rain staring at him.

Laughing even harder, I climbed into the Corolla. Logan jogged around the front and slid behind the wheel. We were so soaked that if the car wasn't old, I would have been seriously concerned for the upholstery. Pushing his wet hair back from his face, Logan gunned the engine.

"You're insane." I laughed.

"You love it."

I couldn't deny that running through the rain was fun, so I kept quiet as he pulled out onto University Drive. The two-minute drive home wasn't long enough. Even so, we'd both calmed down when he pulled into Oxley's car park, and that stupid grin was still stuck in place.

"Thanks for the ride." I turned to face him.

Logan reached out, sliding a clump of drowned hair from my face which he tucked behind my ear. "What time do you start tomorrow?"

"Not until ten."

"Perfect. I'll pick you up at half nine. We can grab a drink on the way to class and maybe tomorrow night we can do something?"

I smiled again as I climbed out of the Corolla. "I'd like that."

It was nice to have real friends, ones that cared about me, not just about my popularity. It wasn't until now that I realised that with the exception of Savannah I'd never been surrounded by friends, but rather by people who wanted something from me. And this was so much better.

"I'M NOT going," I told Savvy for what felt like the

hundredth time.

"You have to, it's the last function of the term," she whined then exchanged an eye roll with Molly. "And what are you going to do instead? Sit in your room and mope, I bet."

I paused while Savvy yanked open my food stash cupboard and shuffled everything around. "Haven't you got any fun snacks?"

"You ate them all and I'm not moping."

"Then what do you call it?" She flicked the doors closed and flopped back onto my bed.

"Actually ... I have plans."

"You do?" Molly's eyebrows shot into her Pollyanna fringe. "No way. It's about time."

"Yes way," I said. "So give it up, I'm not going."

"Plans with who?" Savvy fought a smile.

Molly wriggled her eyebrows suggestively. "Stalker Boy."

"Stalker Boy?" Savvy squealed. The girls had picked up my nickname for Logan and ran with it like it was an Olympic torch.

I worried the edge of my doona. "It's not like that. We're just hanging out."

Molly and Savvy exchanged a strange look then both burst out laughing.

"What? We are."

"Whatever you say, Liv." Molly dropped her voice to a deep octave when she said my name, then snickered.

"You let him call you Liv?" Savvy squealed. "Oh my, Olivia, this is serious."

"I don't let him, he just does." *And truth be told, I like it.*

My pillow thwacked into my head and Molly laughed. "What are you doing?"

"Yeah. What?" Savvy sang.

"Geez, we're just watching a movie."

"At his house."

"NO!" That was far too comfortable.

"Why not?"

"Just no, Savannah."

"Very serious." Savvy raised her eyebrows.

Molly mimicked the gesture. "Extremely serious."

"Please tell me you aren't wearing that," Savvy said, turning her attention to Molly who was dressed in loose jeans and a love heart logoed t-shirt. It was probably mean, but relief flooded through me that the attention had shifted elsewhere.

"Umm, yeah, this is what I'm wearing."

Savvy waggled her finger. "No, it's not."

"I'm not a doll, Savannah. You aren't playing dress-ups with me."

A laugh bubbled out of me as Savvy hooked her arm through Molly's and tugged the other girl out the door. Molly shot me an exasperated look and I said, "Have fun, you guys."

The door closed behind them and I went to my computer to squeeze in a little work. It seemed like there was always so much. I clicked onto my emails and deleted all the spam. I was neither a man 'wanting a bigger member', nor looking to meet 'a Siberian prince', but there was one real message and it was from my cousin Bethanie.

Hi Olivia, I sent your wedding invite to your

parents.
I've allocated you a plus one, so make sure you
bring someone exciting! Like maybe that guy
you were raving about at Christmas.
See you soon. B x

Ha. It was months away yet, and no way in hell would I bring Christian.

The courtyard noise was just starting to die down when a knock sounded on my door. Everyone must have been swarming the buses to town. The social committee would have organised one or two to ferry everyone in to the Central Hotel and back home. I wouldn't know, though, having missed the last meeting. I was still annoyed about that as I opened the door to find Logan standing in the hall with an armload of bags. He glanced past me before his gaze flicked back to mine.

"I'm not inviting you in," I said. "Let's go."

A small smile grew on his face as he stepped back to make room for me to join him in the hallway. And that's exactly why I wasn't inviting him in. We were friends, nothing more.

How was it that dressed in sweat pants he still managed to look like he'd stepped out of a catalogue?

"So, what'd you get?" I asked as we traipsed down the stairs.

Logan kept pace with me all the way to the common room. I figured we'd pretty much have it to ourselves with the whole dorm being in town at the Central. And I'd guessed right, as we walked into the small games room that doubled as another common room. I was glad to find it empty. Logan tossed his grocery bag onto one of the chairs and delved into a second bag, pulling out a stack of movies.

"I figured you'd be a chick flick kind of girl, so I got a few of them. But I also got the latest Bond, a new superhero show, and a couple of comedies. Take your pick."

"You hired seven movies, Logan? Seven?"

"Ya huh. What's it going to be?"

"Seven?"

Logan glanced up from his perusal of the back covers and blinked wide blue eyes. "Seven."

I smiled as he handed them off to me. They all looked kind of good, but I wasn't clueless to most guys' tastes, so I wouldn't make him sit through a rom-com. I held up the superhero movie. "What about this one?"

Logan shrugged. "Sure, I don't mind."

I popped it in the player, flicked off the lights, and turned to find a good position. Logan already looked at home scooched down in one of the double armchairs with his long legs propped on the chair in front that he'd spun around to face us. An assortment of junk food was strewn over a low table he'd dragged nearby. I looked around, trying to decide where to sit. If I chose one of the single chairs, I'd be a mile away, but there wasn't a lot of room to squeeze in beside him. It'd be pretty close.

As if he knew what I was thinking, Logan patted the other side of his chair and shot me one of his cheeky grins. "I don't bite, Liv. Unless you want me to."

Taking a deep breath to steel myself against the affect that being so close to him was sure to have, I plopped into the double chair. As the opening credits started, I settled down into my seat, for once feeling happy with where I was—not forced to be the life of the party when I'd rather be alone, nor hiding out in my room wondering what people were saying.

"What's Jordan up to tonight?" I asked.

"Working," Logan answered.

"Yeah, where's he work?"

"He makes pizza. I've gotta be out of here by eleven thirty to pick him up."

"On a school night?"

Logan shrugged. "We don't have a lot of choice. Thursday's the only weeknight he works. His other shifts are on the weekends."

We settled into comfortable silence, both watching the screen. After a while, Logan stretched his arm out over the back of the chair. Warmth radiated from him onto the back of my neck and prickled down my side, even though we weren't touching. I kind of wished we were. I wanted nothing more than to relax by pulling my legs up onto the seat and snuggling in. But I didn't. The boundaries needed to stay firm. We had a good friendship, and I didn't want to spoil it when he didn't want more.

No matter how hard I tired, I couldn't get into the movie. It probably had something to do with the hunk of a guy sitting next to me, sprawled out like he owned the place. Or like this didn't bother him at all. We were so close I could hear each breath he took. Was that normal? You couldn't generally hear people breathe. Could you? Cripes, maybe it wasn't his breathing, maybe it was mine. I could sure hear my heart hammering against my chest.

Darn it. I was here to watch a movie.

Kicking my feet up on the chair in front of us, I forced myself to focus on the screen. The hero was taking a whooping from some random villain and really, I had no idea what had happened in the overall story because I hadn't paid a lick of attention up until now. As he snuck up on the bad guy's lair, the music grew tense and so did I. The good guy would save the day for sure, but maybe it'd be a hard fight to get there. And his girl was in danger. The eerie glow cast through the common room from the lights being out only enhanced the atmosphere. He was almost there and the tension was palpable.

An explosion rocked the screen.

I screamed.

Logan's hand dropped onto my shoulder and he pulled me into his side, tucking me under his arm. Trembling, I let out a tiny laugh as I curled in.

"Dumb movie," I said on a shaky breath.

I felt him chuckle as I pulled my legs up and curled them to the side to watch our superhero save the world. It had been a long day, and as the movie moved into what was surely the closing scene, I started to feel tired. Logan's chest was barely an inch from my face, but I wouldn't fall asleep on him again. I couldn't. My eyes started to slide, but I caught them just in time and forced them open. Logan's arm rested warm and heavy around me and it would be a lie to say I didn't like it. The closing credits rolled onto the screen and neither of us moved. Maybe he'd fallen asleep. The way his chest rose and fell was kind of slow, sleepy.

The credits finished up and the screen flicked to blank. Still Logan didn't move. His hand rested on my hip, his arm still curled around me. He had to be asleep. It felt so good in his embrace, I let my cheek drop onto his chest. It would only be for a moment, and he'd never know. A moment wouldn't hurt anyone, right?

Logan smelled so good. A fresh ocean scent mixed with a masculine musk that made my senses tingle. All of them. My tummy fluttered in ways it shouldn't near a friend.

I nuzzled into him for one last stolen moment then went to pull away, but Logan's hold on me tightened and he mumbled something completely incomprehensible. My heart must have thought it was missing out on the party my tummy was having because it started its own weird flutter too, and good heavens, I needed space and I needed it right now.

Moving with the care of a neurosurgeon, I gently lifted Logan's hand and slipped out from his hold in a contortionist-like move that had me holding my breath as I swivelled away. Then I placed his hand on the lounge, and let go. Logan looked as peaceful as a sleeping puppy. His dark lashes fanned his cheeks, which were slightly rosy from the warmth of the room, and made his usually striking features look somehow more innocent than hot. If I just reached out and laid my hand against his cheek …

Get a grip.

I switched out the movie for one of the rom-coms. If he was sleeping anyway, it didn't really matter what I put on. There was no way I could slide back into my spot without waking him, so I sat on the floor and rested my back on the seat where I had previously sat. Logan's knee was touching my shoulder, and my waist felt cold without his arm there.

This movie proved to be almost as hard to concentrate on as the last one. If I just rested my heavy eyes for a second ...

Something startled me awake.

"Shit!" Logan cursed as he jumped over the top of me. "Shit, shit, shit!"

"What is it?" I asked, rubbing my eyes with my knuckles.

"I'm late. I gotta go."

I jumped to my feet and Logan swooped in, planting a kiss on my cheek. "See you later, Liv."

I offered him a weak smile which he returned just before he dashed out of the room. There was no point watching the rest of the movie because I had no idea what was going on after having slept through at least half of it, so I ejected the disc and packed up our mess. As I plodded up to my room with my hand pressed to my cheek, thoughts of how nice it felt cuddled into Logan's side filled my mind, no matter how hard I pushed them away.

I climbed into bed, still smiling, and pulled the covers up under my chin. If I just tried hard enough, maybe I could move past my own darn insecurities and make things with Logan work out ... somehow. The rumours, the study time, his closed off attitude ... maybe none of it really mattered.

I WOKE with a start. Each pound of my heart was so huge it slammed against my ribs.

"Wake up Oxley, it's snowing!"

Laughter followed the shout. Freaking drunk people. I bet it wasn't even cold enough to make their breaths frost.

"Shut up!" Came a reply from across the courtyard.

That only caused more laughing.

With a groan, I glanced at the glowing numbers of my digital clock. 3:09. Far out. Go to bed, people.

Then I froze.

Ohmigod.

I couldn't breathe, couldn't move, couldn't even …

My hand was on the inside of my underwear; my fingers nestled close to my body.

It was true. It was all true. Everything they'd said was true.

True.

True.

I yanked my hand away like it was poison. I clamped my thighs together and rolled onto my side, shoving the offending appendages under my pillow and crunching my head down on top. Christian, Ella, my moaning so loud I woke people up.

True.

Oh my-freaking-goodness. They'd seen me. My whole darn floor had seen me mid-act. That story about having my hand … I couldn't breathe. Ella wasn't just being a jerk, she was telling the holy truth. There's no way I'd be able to look her in the eye again. It was far too mortifying.

I gulped against a desert-dry mouth.

This couldn't be real. Tonight had to have been a once-off. Maybe I was itchy, or dreaming, or holy buttercup, anything but that. Surely it wasn't possible to do something and not realise it. Nothing made any sense.

I swallowed the tightness in my throat and squeezed my eyes shut, wishing to high heaven that I was dreaming and I'd wake any second.

I didn't.

Because I was already awake. Who was I kidding?

My stomach felt tight and so did my chest. Unable to hold it any longer, I sucked in a huge breath. I could never show my face again knowing that every time Ella or Christian or any of the guys on my floor saw me, they'd be picturing me naked. Just like they'd seen me before ...

Like that.

I just ... couldn't.

How could I ever sleep again knowing that I might do something inappropriate? I could scream, moan, or yell for everyone to hear, and oh my gosh, what about when I wasn't at college sleeping behind a locked door? When I was home for the holidays? Good lord, had I always done this? All those sleepovers with friends in high school ...

Logan.

His name seared through my mind, dropping a heaviness inside me. There could never, ever be anything more between us. I never wanted him to see me like this. *Ever.*

Chapter 14

"**W**HAT HAPPENED** with the election, Olivia? I heard you weren't voted in?"

That was my mother. No fluff, no hugs, no *happy you're home*. Just straight to the point of what mattered. I leaned against the kitchen counter, too tired to hold my posture straight, while she prepared my homecoming meal. It looked like some kind of chicken dish, maybe cacciatore. I'd been here for all of two hours and this was the first chance we'd had to talk, since she'd only returned from work ten minutes ago. I had tried to crash in that time, but it seemed being too tired to sleep was possible. I'd barely snatched a wink since discovering what I did while asleep.

"Well?"

"Not sure." I shrugged. "Guess I wasn't popular enough." With her, it was easier to lie than tell the truth.

News of the suspension would result in two weeks of her droning disappointment and lectures about my stupidity. I wasn't sure I had the strength to cope with that.

"Well, you mustn't have worked the crowds hard enough. Elouise Parry said Ella told her you've been a little absent because something happened with Christian. That's not good enough. These things take social skill, Olivia, and that's something we've taught you." She tisked. "How are you going to fix it?"

"Try harder. Do more." I sighed.

My mother's lips pressed together as she stirred the steaming tomato mix. "You know how important these things are. Your father may have secured a preliminary internship for you, but that's still dependant on you, Olivia. On your own records and standing. It would pay for you to remember that."

"Yeah, I know."

She drew in a noisy breath. "Yes, not yeah. Use your words properly, lest you sound uneducated."

"Yes, Mum." I turned to head back upstairs.

"Olivia? How are things between you and Ella? Elouise said you girls are going through a rough patch."

My phone vibrated in my pocket. "I need to use the bathroom, Mum."

As I jogged up the stairs, I whipped the phone out of my pocket and Logan's name illuminating the screen made me smile.

Are you there yet?

Yes, I'm here. Wish I was there though.

And wasn't that the truth. At least I could hide from whoever was bothering me there. Kind of. Here I had no choice but to put up with them. My phone buzzed in my hand with another text from Logan.

> Which is here and which is there? If there
> means here, then I wish you were there too.

I laughed and my response was completely unrelated, but something that had been playing on my mind since Central Night.

> Do you like living in town?

> Has its advantages. Why? You thinking of
> moving out of college?

> No reason. Just asking.

> The food's better. Company's quieter.
> Works out a little cheaper, especially if you
> share.

That was a good point. I'd spent a bucket load of money lately—buying food to cook and eat in my room or eating out—when it was money I didn't need to spend because the dorm fees covered my meals. Quietness was yet another great point. Sure we had a noise curfew at Oxley, but there was still always someone being loud in the courtyard or in the corridor, or knocking on my door. But those weren't the main reasons I was thinking of moving out. With things the way they'd been lately, I didn't exactly feel comfortable, and now that I knew those darn rumours were true, showing my face around Oxley wasn't pleasant; even walking into my own hallway set my pulse racing, let alone into the dining hall. Maybe if I moved out, people would forget all about it, and I'd just slide into being 'that girl who used to live here', not 'the finger-fuck girl' or whatever crass name they'd thought of today. The rumours and memories would die down eventually.

My phone pinged again and oops, I hadn't responded.

Wanna share? We've got a spare room.

I'm not moving into the 'bach pad'.

Why not? We cook, clean, AND put our dirty

underwear in the hamper.

Eeew, Logan.

A few minutes passed without a response, so I tossed my phone onto my bed and started unpacking. That last Thursday night at college had plagued my thoughts for the past few days. Even though evidence pointed toward everything being true there was a huge part of me that hoped maybe it was a coincidence. I plopped my laptop onto my desk and noticed a pink envelope. Slicing it open, I found a thick invitation inside. Bethanie's wedding. The almost see-through paper was really pretty, but gee, she'd gotten in early. It was only April and the wedding wasn't until October. I tossed it into my suitcase and continued unpacking my clothes. Once I'd finished, I glanced at my computer, but grabbed my tablet instead and lay down on the bed. Oh, this was divine. The beds at Oxley were pretty good, but nothing compared to the mattress I'd slept on every night for seventeen years. I turned the reader on and my phone buzzed.

Liv ...

Yeah?

I miss you.

I couldn't tell him I missed him too, or that his words made me smile. After what had happened on Central Night, I knew now more than before that Logan and I couldn't happen. So instead, I typed out;

I've been gone less than a day, Stalker Boy. Get over it.

He sent back a simple,

:P

To which I replied with a cheeky smiley of my own.

I'd only been reading for about thirty minutes when footsteps sounded on the stairs. Precisely the reason I went for a book over researching masturbation while sleeping. The type of websites that search was sure to bring up would be tricky to explain.

"Well, if it isn't my little girl."

I shot up off the bed and threw my arms around Dad's neck. He hugged me back with a simple, loose arm around my waist. "Your mother said to tell you that dinner's ready."

"Thanks." I pulled away. "How was work?"

"Busy. I had to push through a lot to get out on time."

Being home in time to eat with the family was a rarity, and the fact he'd managed it on my first night back made me feel all warm inside.

"See you downstairs." Dad disappeared down the hall and I traipsed down to the dining room.

Neither of them were there yet, but the places were laid out, as were the heat mats for the hot dishes. A bottle of Pinot Noir marked the centre of our eight-seater table, and a vase overflowing with white tulips had been pushed down the unused end. I took a seat, spreading a napkin across my lap, and waited for my parents. Mum glided into the room with her oven mitts around a square dish which she set on one of the heat mats then disappeared into the kitchen, only to return with a second dish. Dad walked into the room just as she was taking a seat directly across from me.

"How's uni?" he asked.

"It's okay."

"Are you keeping involved?"

"Of course."

Mum passed me the bowl of rice, from which I scooped

two heaped spoonfuls into my bowl before passing it on to my father. I piled the chicken sauce on top of that and started eating. The best thing about being home for the break was the food. Mum was a fabulous cook, and when at college I missed the hearty and healthy eating. If I moved out I could eat like this all the time.

"Your mother tells me that you didn't make it onto the Student Representative Council. That's a real shame, sweetheart."

Bang. There it was; that heavy feeling of guilt at being a disappointment. Thank goodness I had a mouthful of food to buy me a few moments. I nodded.

"Well, make sure you keep up with everything else. Not having the presidency on your CV will be a disadvantage."

"Yes, I know." I shovelled more food into my mouth, but it didn't ward off the conversation. Dad was happy to let his dinner go cold while he grilled me.

"I trust you're keeping up with sport, and dorm politics. Still attending the Law Society functions?"

I nodded again. Boy, nothing like cutting to the point. There was never any small talk at this table. I may as well air my moving out idea, since they knew about the presidency already. This could be the right time to float it, see what they thought. Maybe they'd warm to the concept by the time break was over.

"I'd like to move off campus."

My mother's wine glass clashed with the table as she set it down with too much force. "Absolutely not."

Dad's gaze bore into me. "Why? What benefit is there in that?"

I took a sip of the pale red to strengthen my courage.

"The food is disgusting, so I'm spending a ton of money on decent snacks. Also, I can't concentrate on my studies because of all the distractions, and Christian ..." I couldn't tell them about my social issues. The other reasons I gave were true too, but escaping the constant harassment was the only real reason I wanted out. And escaping that would help ease every other issue.

My mother shook her head. She'd started before I even began speaking. "No, Olivia. That is a ridiculous idea. You need to be in college to build relationships and if you're not involved in campus politics, then you need to be involved with the politics of the dormitory." She blew out a strained breath. "Both would have been better, but that's out of the question."

"She has no control over that now, Susan. Let it go." I could have thanked my father, but I knew his words would have no effect. "I don't think it's a good idea, sweetheart. You need to live on campus where it's close to the library and the lecture halls. If you move into town, the temptation to skip classes will be too great. All it takes is a missed bus; you can't just walk to your lectures. It will only take that to happen a few times for you to fall behind, and most people who fall too far behind wind up dropping out. So no, it's not going to happen."

"I won't, Dad. You know how studious I am. I've never missed a class in my life and I don't intend to start skipping now." The tips of my ears burned and I shook my hair down to cover it. It was almost true—I'd only ever skipped that one time with Logan, then again for the meeting with student welfare, but never before that.

My mother started stacking dishes. "You are not moving out of college while we pay for your keep."

"Fine. I'll get a job."

The glare she turned on me was final. "You will do no such thing. You have no time for work when you should be studying and building your CV. That is the end of this conversation."

I threw my napkin onto the table and stood. I was done with this conversation anyway. I was nineteen and I wasn't a child.

ALONE TIME wasn't easy to come by those first few days. I was itching to research my affliction, but had to wait. Instead I checked my email several times a day for exam results, but they still hadn't arrived. Maybe I had my dates messed up and they weren't due yet anyway. I couldn't remember if past me had opted to receive them in email form rather than via text. Today, three days into break, when I clicked my mail open there was a message from Student Services. I assumed that was what it would be.

It was just a student newsletter.

A second email was under the first, sent from my Torts professor. It would be results for the group assignment, no doubt about it. My tummy churned as I clicked to open and scanned the body of the email, but what I was looking for wasn't there. Attachments; there were two of them. I clicked on the one that had the word results in the title. A strange feeling came over me; this wasn't going to be good. We'd failed, I just knew it.

I glanced toward my phone, thinking about texting Logan, then decided better of it and drew a deep breath to steel against whatever was inside the attachment. I focused on the screen. *Fifty-two per cent.*

We'd passed, but only just.

That meant my average had dropped for that class and I was in danger of falling below a credit. Not good when I was trying to raise my all my grade averages to HDs.

This was why group assignments should be done as a group. Ella had stuffed something up pretty majorly to get us such a low mark, and if we were all working on it that would never have happened.

I pushed my chair back and jogged out of my room and downstairs. Keeping my grades up was getting harder all the time. What if I dropped below a pass? I pushed that thought away; it couldn't happen. It wasn't even a possibility.

After a few laps around the house, I realised how aimless it was and ducked into the kitchen to make a cup of tea. Some days it felt like tea made everything better. With the steaming cup in hand, I retreated back to my room.

Checking my email had become an obsession, and it didn't matter how often I looked there was always a message from Logan. I'd never admit it to him, but now that I was home for term break, I missed him like crazy. Our emails were to counter the texts which had slowed down since my mother started asking questions. Last thing I needed was for her to think I wanted to move out because of him. And god help me if she should cotton on and ask about him in particular. Logan was sure as hell the type of guy she wouldn't approve of; with the long hair and vintage style he was more mess than neat and tidy. Plus I was certain he wasn't what she'd call *of pedigree*. Not like Christian, whose parents were both surgeons.

I logged into my email and sure enough, there was a message from my Stalker Boy.

You been thinking about how good it would be to live with me and Jordan? Here are some points for the list I know you're making:

PROS
1. I have a car = free ride to and from classes
2. We have a spare room = your own space
3. Jordan brings home free pizza
4. I'm an excellent cook (when there's no pizza)
5. Living with two guys = inbuilt security team
6. You'll get to see me every day. I'm fun

CONS
1. Jordan eats all the food

I smiled as I typed out a quick reply which pretty much amounted to no. Even though the thought of moving out appealed more than ever—I was certain Ella had stuffed that assignment up on purpose, regardless of what it meant for her own grades, and distancing myself from living right on top of people like that was tempting—I wasn't moving in with Logan. That a guaranteed friendship ruining recipe, not to mention the other problem I had.

I opened up my Internet browser. Both of my parents were at work and it finally felt safe to research 'masturbation while sleeping' without the fear of someone walking in. I was a little concerned with what sort of images would pop up, and I didn't want to have to explain it to them.

With restless energy making my knees bounce, I punched the words into the search engine. I swear my insides quivered while waiting for the results to display, and it would have only been a few seconds, but it felt like the screen stayed blank for a full hour. The first few results were questions posted to forums. Things like, 'I masturbate while I sleep. Is this normal?' My gaze skimmed over those. I needed something more concrete and reliable. Near the bottom of the screen was an article titled, 'Sexomnia: More Common Than You Might Think.'

"Could be," I mumbled to myself.

As I read through the explanation, my chest tightened. It was exactly like me ... well, like what I'd heard about me. I still wasn't certain that was what was happening though. It seemed crazy that I could be doing that all night and have no memory of it. According to the webpage, *sexomniacs have sex while they're sleeping. They masturbate, fondle, initiate sex or just produce loud, sexual moaning sounds.* My stomach felt as if it were about to empty itself on my lap. This was a real thing. It happened, and the people it happened to had absolutely no recollection.

Holy cow.

I didn't want to keep reading. I'd read more than enough to make me feel like climbing under the covers to never come out again. Sure as heck, to never return to college, but it was like watching a horrific accident unfold, I had to know every tiny detail, so I kept reading. *The sex-omniac has no control over her nocturnal actions, leaving some feeling guilty, confused or ashamed over the behaviour.* The more I read, the sicker I felt. This could be my reality. Christian could have been telling the truth, and so could have Ella.

Women are more likely to masturbate and moan sexually, whereas men are more likely to fondle others and initiate sex. Well, thank the lord I was a woman. Imagine how bad it would be if I was sleeping around while I was sleeping. Then I'd be the college tramp.

I clicked through website after website until I couldn't take in anymore, then I shut the computer off and crawled onto my bed, wrapping my arms around my knees in a tight ball. It was all too much. Even though I was alone, I'd never felt more humiliated. Like every part of me had been exposed, and if I were ever to walk out in public again, I'd be completely naked. They'd all see me for what I was; a sex fiend.

Heck, they already had.

How could I go back to college knowing it was all true? There was absolutely no way I could move in with Logan and his brother.

I needed to be alone.

Chapter 15

EVEN THOUGH I wished I was back at college the whole time—horrifying as that thought was—the two-week break went pretty fast. Maybe it was the constant arguments with my parents, or maybe it was the emails from Logan, or it could have been the fact I slept like the dead knowing there was no chance anyone would hear me here, since my room was so secluded. Either way, it seemed like no time at all before I was sitting on the plane as it landed back in Armidale. I followed the line of people down the exit stairs and into the terminal. It was only a short flight from Sydney, but for some reason I felt exhausted. Possibly it was the thought of unpacking everything when I got back to college when it was nearing six pm already. No doubt the girls would be up for a long night of chatting too. Savvy had texted me this morning with warning of some 'super exciting news'. Exam results still hadn't come through, which was weird, but Savvy assured me hers weren't in either, so I guessed I must have had my dates mixed up.

I made my way to the baggage claim conveyor belt and waited for my luggage. Mine was always the last to come through. Hands covered my eyes from behind, and I sucked in a sharp breath of surprise. My heart beat hard and fast while my hands moved to pry long fingers away from my face.

A deep chuckle brushed my ear.

"Logan," I squealed as I spun around and threw my arms around his neck. He gripped my waist, scooping me up off the ground. Good lord I had missed him.

"I missed you, Liv."

"So much that you came to the airport?"

"Like I'd make you catch a cab." He set me on my feet and warmth seeped through my chest.

"That's super nice of you."

Logan shrugged, and his gaze moved to the carousel. Oops, I'd forgotten all about my bag. I waited for a few minutes just to be sure, and thankfully it came along. The only item still on there.

Logan grabbed my suitcase, leaving me with nothing more than the laptop I'd carried on as hand luggage. "This it?" he asked.

"Yes."

He shot me a grin as we walked through the airport, but something felt a little off. His eyes weren't quite right as he asked, "How was your day?"

"Oh you know, track work on the train lines to the airport, so I had to take a bus which took twice as long.

Lucky the plane was delayed though, then the guy sitting next to me ..." I glanced around to make sure the man wasn't close enough to hear "... was so huge I felt trapped between him and the window." I chuckled, and when Logan didn't I caught a glimpse of his frown. "But ... I'm here, and you came to surprise me so it's all good."

The cool air hit me like a blast of icy water when we exited the terminal. "It's freezing here!"

"Two weeks away and you've become acclimatised to warmer weather," Logan teased.

"Yeah, yeah. Where's the car?"

"This way." He power-walked toward his red Corolla. When we reached it, he placed my bag in the back while I climbed in the passenger seat, still smiling. He'd actually come to pick me up. In the whole two years I'd been travelling between home and here, no one had ever collected me at either airport. It felt kind of nice.

Logan climbed in behind the wheel and inhaled sharply, like he was about to sneeze.

"How's Jordan?" I asked.

"Barely keeping out of trouble."

Twilight had been and gone while I was disembarking, so by the time we drove to Oxley it was fully dark. Logan talked the whole way—telling me about work, and Jordan, and the massive cold snap they'd had just last week that I could feel in the air.

"You moving out of this place or what?" Logan asked as we pulled up in the car park.

"Not anytime soon, but it's certainly on my mind. My parents said I need to stay on campus to keep my finger on the pulse."

"The pulse of what?"

"Politics, sport, the social scene."

"For real?"

"They're socialites, Logan. This stuff is important to them."

"More important than their daughter's happiness?"

"I'm happy." I sighed and climbed out of the Corolla.

"Sometimes it doesn't seem like it." Logan swiped the back of his hand across his face. My nose was freezing too. Then he popped the trunk and lugged out my bag. I went to take it from him, but he shook his head and slammed the boot. I fished my keys out of my laptop bag as we traipsed into the ivy-covered brick courtyard. It was funny coming back after time away; it always felt like I'd never left. But that ivy always seemed to have claimed more of the brickwork. The courtyard was eerily quiet as we slipped through and up the stairs of my block.

Logan sneezed.

"You all right?" I asked him as I unlocked my door.

"Yeah. I'm fine." He placed my suitcase on the floor.

"You want to keep me company while I unpack?" I don't know why I'd felt so tired before; now I felt completely re-energised. Maybe it was a second wind.

He kicked his shoes off, threw himself onto my bed, and lying on his back, tucked both hands under his head then crossed his ankles.

"Make yourself right at home," I teased.

"Thanks, I already did."

Chuckling, I closed the door and as I unpacked could feel Logan watching me move around the room. I put clothes away, and since our rooms were used in the break to house other university guests, pulled all of my books and things that made the room mine out of my locked cupboard. Putting everything back in place always took the better part of a few hours, but the time moved quickly tonight with Logan's company.

A knock sounded on my door, and without thinking I crossed the space and pulled it open. A screen of Savvy's blonde hair greeted me; her head turned to look down the far end of the hall. "Grow up," she yelled then barrelled into my room, slamming the door shut with her foot.

"Livia. I had the best break. You'll never guess—" Her squeals were cut short when she spotted Logan sprawled out on my bed.

Logan grinned at her. "Hi, Savannah."

"Logan ..." She pulled her face into a weird smile-frown. "I can't figure you two out."

Logan winked at her and shuffled over on the bed, toward the wall. Savvy didn't sit in the space he'd made, though; instead she plonked herself in my swivel chair. I shifted Logan's feet and dropped to the end of the bed. "What's to figure out? We're friends. Just like me and you, or me and Molly. Nothing at all like you and Dane."

Savvy raised an eyebrow as she glanced at Logan over my shoulder then shook her head. "Don't go there."

"How was your break?" I asked her.

"Complicated." She glanced toward Logan.

"Oh, do tell."

Logan's phone rang and I felt the bed shuffle as he picked up. "Yeah ... With Liv ... now?" He blew out a long breath. "On my way."

Logan's hands landed on my shoulders and he shifted

me out of his way. "I gotta go."

"Oh." A small pang of disappointment shot through me. I stood on tiptoe, fighting the urge to hug him, but I'd just told Savvy there was nothing between us, so instead I settled for saying, "Thanks for the lift."

As I watched him slip through the door, I turned my attention on my friend. "So?"

"So, Dane—" Savvy's phone started ringing too. "Geez McCheese." She glanced at the screen, squealed, and shot out of my room. So much for her super exciting news.

I set up my laptop in its usual spot on my desk. I wasn't certain I had the sleep sex thing, but I still needed to know the stakes just in case. I hadn't researched any further at home, but back at college it all seemed more real and urgent. I flipped the computer open and powered up. My leg jigged to its own rhythm under the desk, probably something to do with the erratic beat of my heart. Well, not so much erratic as fast. Nervous. Scared to know.

This was it. Hopefully there'd be an answer. I brought up the Internet, my homepage landed on Google and I typed in 'how to cure sexomnia.'

Currently there are no approved, proven medications …

Yadda yadda yadda.

Another approach is to create a safe environment for the person affected by the condition. Sleep in a separate bedroom, lock doors, alarm the house, or even the room where the affected person sleeps in case they wander during the night.

Well that got me nowhere fast. How about 'how to treat sexomnia?'

There is no known treatment, but it is possible to in-

crease one's awareness of the sleep sex episodes.

More of the same. This didn't seem to be geared toward people who self-gratified, but rather those who had sex with other people while asleep. Thank goodness I didn't do that. I gave it one last try with a search on 'how to stop sexomnia.'

Reduce triggers such as alcohol intake, insomnia-inducing medication, and stress. Ensure the afflicted person is unable to enter other's bedrooms.

Holy buttercups. Was there nothing to help this thing I maybe had? I needed a cure-all silver bullet. One that would cut right into my traitorous body and make it normal.

MY FIRST week back was stressful. I barely slept at night, lying awake until my body gave in from exhaustion and fell asleep without my consent. Then I'd wake each morning, groggy and struggling to get out of bed when the alarm sounded. I was petrified that I'd moan in my sleep, or worse.

Then there was the college atmosphere; I was the dead opposite of the social person I'd always been. I pretty well hid in my room, not venturing to the dining hall or to hang out with friends in the courtyard. Things had died down a little, but I felt really uncomfortable—as if everyone was looking at me and thinking terrible thoughts that I knew were true. Savvy and Molly brought food up to my room every so often, but I basically lived off toast made in the tiny kitchen, and larger meals eaten on campus at lunchtime. I was more than okay with that.

I hadn't managed to see Ella yet, but I was still fuming about our result, and I had a feeling she was deliberately avoiding me. She had to be here—at college and in classes—so how I hadn't seen her yet was a mystery.

Logan hadn't been in class on Monday. In fact, I hadn't heard from him since he'd left my room on Sunday night. His silence worried me far more than it should have. I couldn't get his messy hair and unshaven face, even his clapped-out car out of my mind. Logan wasn't the sort of guy I should think about, regardless of how he made me feel. With my recent sexomnia discovery I shouldn't be thinking about any guy. Period. But here I was, unable to shift him from my mind. The fact I'd texted and called and emailed and he hadn't answered a darn one of them had me worried. It wasn't like him at all. Our friendship was easy and he'd always responded quickly.

I'd gone back through my memories of Sunday night a billion times, but couldn't find anything I'd said or done that could have caused this silence. That was why Molly and I were in town on Friday, staking out his cafe. I was pretty sure there was something wrong with me, because sane people didn't walk past other people's work places ten times. Especially when said person had been given the silent treatment by the other person for almost a week. Good thing I didn't know where he lived.

"Screw it," Molly said. "We're going in."

I took a few steps back. "Nah uh … we don't need to. He's probably hiding out the back or not even working."

"Don't be ridiculous." Molly turned on her heel and

marched right in. She didn't take a seat, but strolled up to the counter with her shoulders back and head high, like she had every right to enquire about an employee. A lady behind the coffee machine talked to Molly while she worked. The conversation looked friendly enough until Molly glanced over her shoulder at me and the woman's gaze followed, then she beckoned to me. They both turned back to their conversation.

Darn it. I walked into the cafe and joined my friend. The lady met me with a smile. "Olivia?"

Molly gestured toward the lady. "Kat here was just telling me that she sent Logan home sick on Tuesday."

"Poor kid looked like death warmed up. He'd come to work even if he was dying, that one." She shook her head.

Worry bloomed in my chest. Logan was sick, and no one had heard from him.

"Thanks," I said to her and reached for my phone as I started backing out of the shop. I had no time for the woman's stories about Logan's work ethic. I had to make sure he was okay. I flicked through my contacts and hit Logan's number again. It went straight to voicemail, so I scrolled down to Savvy's name and hit call. She picked up on the third ring.

"Hey, girl."

"Savvy, have you got Dane's number?"

"Yeah, why?"

"I need Logan's address."

"Do you now?" Screw her mocking tone. There was no time for it. "I'll forward Dane's details to you."

"Thanks." I ended the call.

"That was really rude, Liv," Molly said coming up beside me. "Kat was just being nice ..."

My phone vibrated with Savvy's message and ignoring Molly I hit the call button. It rang for a few minutes before Dane's message bank picked up. I hung up without leaving a message and grazed my fingers over the screen to type out a text instead. If he was in class, I'd probably get a quicker response that way.

> Dane, it's Olivia. Logan's sick and I need his address to make sure he's all right.

His message came back almost instantly.

> The apartments on Rawson Street. Can't remember the street number—it's about halfway along. If he's there you'll see his car out front. Everything OK?

> Not sure. I'll let you know.

I started walking toward the shopping centre's exit. If I hailed a cab, I could be there in less than ten minutes. This town wasn't big enough to take any longer, no matter where Rawson Street was.

"Where are you going?" Molly asked.

"To check on him."

"Don't you think that's overreacting?"

"Not if he's too sick to answer a simple text or phone call." I shook my head. "You don't have to come. I know you've got class soon."

"I can't let you go alone."

Molly and I were at the taxi rank in no time, but darn it, there wasn't a car in sight. I pulled out my phone and di-alled the cab company. The operator said there'd be a thirty-minute wait. To hell with that. I flicked the map app open on my phone and typed in Rawson Street. It wasn't too far away, so I started walking in that direction—which was back toward campus.

"Are you crazy?" Molly puffed behind me.

"It's not far."

A few minutes into our walk, my phone buzzed with a message. It might be Logan—maybe he was okay after all, and Dane had called to tell him I was coming over. If he'd been hiding from me, he'd have to own up and tell me I wasn't welcome. I should really look at the message, but I was scared, which was insane. It buzzed again.

"You going to get that?" Molly asked. Her messages pinged as well.

Clenching my jaw, I pulled the phone out of my pocket.

Your Results. LS231 NA LS220 C

I wasn't surprised. Not really. But the weight of dread slammed into my chest, making it hard to draw breath. A credit for Constitutional Law was bad, but a fail-incomplete for Torts? My head spun with the repercus-sions of not meeting all the unit requirements. It made me look lazy, and unorganised, and like I just didn't care. It was detrimental to my academic record.

Logan. *Logan.* Logan was sick and he needed me. I re-peated the mantra over and over as I trudged up the in-clining street.

Fail incomplete.

LOGAN.

Twenty minutes and a walk uphill in almost the same direction as campus later, we stood out the front of a two-storey block of apartments. Autumn leaves scattered around us, and just as Dane had said, Logan's Corolla was parked out front. I typed out another text to Dane.

> Found it. Which apartment is it? I can't tell from where the car's parked.

Minutes passed.

Come on Dane, hurry up. Molly puffed beside me, her hands fisted on her hips and half bent over, like she'd just run a marathon. Maybe I should recruit her for netball; the season would start soon, and she'd thank me when she noticed she'd gotten fit while playing. I tapped my foot, looking between the various apartments for any sign of which was the right one. I wasn't trying to keep my mind occupied, not at all. I wasn't sarcastic either. Never on your life.

There seemed to be six apartments in total. The top floor on the right had plants on its balcony; the other one was full of clothes-airers. Two balconies were completely empty of anything, but chairs and heck, I had no freaking idea. My phone buzzed. Thank all things holy.

> 3

Excellent. I strode up to the third apartment, and after I'd glimpsed the metal *three* attached to the sandy-coloured bricks, I rapped on the wooden door. There was no answer. Something scuttled through the shrub to my left and I flinched. A tabby cat darted away.

I rapped on the door again, louder this time, and called out Logan's name.

Still nothing.

He was inside because his car was out the front, and I could hear the TV playing.

"Logan," I yelled. "Let me in."

I glanced back at Molly, who was still standing on the street, and shrugged. A groan came from behind the door. He must still be sick. I tried the handle. It was locked. But then the door swung open and Jordan stood behind it, using the door to hold himself up. He looked terrible, his dark hair in a shaggy mess, and his face drawn.

"You guys all right?" I asked.

Jordan groaned and shuffled to a brown couch that stretched in front of the TV, which blared out crappy daytime soap operas. There wasn't much furniture in the almost bare apartment, only the essentials, but a mess was strewn all around the place. Scrunched up tissues, school bags, shoes ... I took a step inside and the musty, sick smell almost knocked me over.

"Geez, it smells like you guys are dying in here." I left the door open and shut the screen behind me. I had no idea what Molly was doing, but she'd come in if she wanted to. A large window stood to the right of the door, so I tugged the blinds back and slid the window open to let in some fresh air.

Jordan moaned something about bright lights.

His spot on the couch looked like a sick bed. An empty

water bottle toppled on its side was surrounded by a sea of tissues, speckled with empty food wrappers. A blanket scrunched up at his feet, Jordan's arm hung over the side of the couch and his tummy was flush against the fabric, his white school shirt scrunched up around his chest to expose his whole back. I bent down beside him, and Jordan's glassy-eyed gaze focused on my face.

"Leave me alone. I'm dying."

I laughed. "You're not dying. You've got the flu. Where's Logan? Is he like this too?"

"Bed," Jordan groaned.

As I stood, I spotted a hall off this room. I'd noticed a kitchen around the corner, so this had to lead to their bedrooms. Four doors opened off it and in the first one I looked there was a double bed which took up almost the entire room. Flung across it, flat on his back was Logan, not looking any better than his brother. His eyes were closed and his hair dark and damp where it was plastered against his head.

He looked terrible. If they were both sick like this, he should have called. I could have come to help—at least aired out the place for them. His sweat pants twisted all askew, the legs pushed up around his knees to show off muscled calves with a smattering of coarse hair. His t-shirt clung to his chest and tummy where it was damp with sweat. The toned muscles on display were impressive—abs that looked not only defined but rock hard.

How that could be when he claimed to be a sports *spectator* was beyond me. I bet they felt as awesome as they looked. I reached out … Good heavens, I was a creep. Here he was, sick as a dog, and I was checking him out. My gaze flew back to his face, my cheeks heating. I dropped to the bed, sitting beside him, and pushed the matted mop of hair back off his forehead. Logan's eyes rolled open; his blue irises were only a slither at the top; the rest was all white. Beads of sweat coated his forehead in a light sheen. Far out, was he okay?

"Logan," I said his name softly.

His eyes rolled forward, but he didn't focus. They kind of slid right off me. "Kay?" he said. His voice, dry and husky, broke on the word.

"It's me." I tried to reassure him by placing my hand over his.

"Kayla, I'm sorry."

I had no idea who Kayla was, but Logan wasn't well. He was burning up and I needed to cool him off. He was in a way worse state than Jordan.

"Jordan," I yelled as I rushed back into the living room. "You guys got any meds and would've Logan taken anything?"

"Kitchen. Nah, hasn't moved outta bed in days."

I rushed into the tiny kitchen, which wasn't in a much better state than the rest of the place, and threw open cupboards like a crazy person. I couldn't see anything that looked like what I wanted. Sheesh, if I had to walk back to town it'd take almost an hour round trip.

Aha! Sitting by the sink full of dirty dishes was a packet of ibuprofen. I snatched it up and filled a glass with water, then returned to Logan's room.

He didn't even register my presence. I popped two tablets from the packet and tried to pull him up, but he was a dead weight. "You need to take something to drop the fever. Sit up."

He shuffled up onto his elbows and I pressed the tablets against his lips. Logan accepted them, so I held the glass to his mouth too. He took a sip and collapsed back on the pillows.

"I should've been there ... all my fault." His words jumbled, but I could still make them out, even though I had no idea what he thought was his fault. Poor thing. His usual stubble was thicker than normal, as if he hadn't shaved all week. His damp hair had caught in it again, so I brushed it back from his face. He was so hot. A flannel, that was what we needed. There'd have to be one in the bathroom.

"Liv?" Molly's voice came from outside. "Liv ... you okay in there?"

"Yeah," I yelled out. "They're both dying of man flu."

I changed paths and headed back into the living room where Molly had her face pressed up against the screen door. "Smells like someone died in there."

"Yeah, death by flu. It's got you in its grip, right Jordan?"

A groan came from the couch and Molly snickered.

"Look," I told her, "I'm going to stay for a bit and make sure they're both all right. You've got a class to make, so head back. I'll be fine."

"You sure?"

"Yes."

"Can I get you guys anything?"

"I think we're all good."

"Okay, but make sure you text later to let me know you're all right. Maybe I can find someone to come back and pick you up."

"That'd be great. Now, shoo, get to class."

Molly nodded, then turned and walked away.

I returned to my hunt for a flannel and found a stash of clean linen in a cupboard in the hall. Running it under cool water, I returned to Logan's room and pressed it against his forehead. He moaned and squirmed against it, but didn't talk like before. At one point his eyes rolled so far back all I could see were the whites, and even though I called his name and placed my hand on his cheek he never registered I was there.

When the tablets set in and he cooled down, I sat with him for a good half hour more until finally he seemed to be asleep. His forehead wasn't as hot as it had been, and the sweat was gone from his brow, but that could have been because I'd mopped it all up with the cloth. Hopefully the meds had brought his fever down.

Now that I'd slowed and Logan wasn't so bad, it felt kind of intimate to be in his room. Band posters covered the walls, but not so many I couldn't see the cream paint. Some sort of flag hung above the bed. The bands weren't familiar to me other than Quiet Renegade.

I went to check on Jordan, and he had passed out too. They both needed to rest to recover. A quick look around the kitchen showed a very bare fridge and not much else. While they slept I should duck into town and grab some stuff. *Brilliant idea.* I called a cab and went to wait out the front.

Over an hour later I was back with supplies; more tissues—those soft aloe vera ones—another packet of pain killers, energy drinks to refuel electrolytes and fight dehydration, fresh oranges, and a bunch of packet mixes to make brothy soups.

I let myself in and Jordan was sitting on the couch, a flannel balanced on his forehead.

"How're you feeling?" I asked as I walked into the kitchen to set the shopping bags down.

"Meh."

I tossed him a bottle of drink and grabbed a second one which I took in to Logan. Jordan might be looking better, but Logan was much the same. He looked to be still sleeping, but not peacefully. The sheets had twisted around him, as if he'd fought with them. I untangled him from the damp, sweaty linen and I got some fluids into him, then switched the washcloth for a fresh one and grabbed some clean sheets for when I could make him move.

I flicked a quick text to Dane telling him both of them were sick, and I was going to take Logan to the doctor in the morning since it was nearing four p.m, and they'd all be closed soon. He responded back asking if I needed any help, and I told him I'd contact him in the morning. Next I sent a message to Savvy asking her to let the team know I wouldn't make it to hockey.

That night was long. Jordan wasn't too bad. After a nap, he got up, and even ate some soup and bread for dinner. But Logan tossed and turned and mumbled, and sweated out at least a gallon of fluids. I kept pumping them back into him, along with doses of pain meds as often as I could to keep the fever in check. When they wore off he was really bad. Morning couldn't come quick enough and at one point I thought about the ER.

But I must have fallen asleep in the beanbag I'd dragged into the corner of his room, because I woke to

Logan saying my name. He was sitting on the side of his bed, staring at me. "Liv," he croaked.

Oh my gosh. I slept. Right here. In his room.

But I couldn't think about that. Not when he was finally coherent. I leaned forward onto my knees, kneeling at the side of his bed. "How are you feeling? Hungry? Thirsty? Do you want another blanket, fresh sheets?"

"My throat is killing," he rasped out. "I feel like I swam across the Atlantic."

His face twisted, clearly in pain, as he swallowed, and his hands pushed down on the mattress either side of him. I glanced at my watch; it'd been five hours, he could have another dose of pain meds. I climbed to my feet and pulled the spare blanket I'd snuggled under around my shoulders to ward off the cold air. Logan's hand brushed against mine as I shuffled past him. His gaze held mine for a moment, then I slipped out of his room and grabbed more medicine and another bottle of sports drink.

He pulled some truly terrifying faces as he swallowed, then lay back down. "C'mere," he croaked and I moved to sit on his bed. Logan's arms swept around me, and pulled me back into him. He shuffled over to the other side of the bed, and rolled onto his side, pulling me up against him. He didn't feel scorching hot anymore, but his chest pressed against my side still felt like fire. That wasn't from his fever; I was pretty certain it had broken.

It was all me.

Logan's breathing evened out almost immediately as he dozed off to sleep. Mine didn't. I laid there concentrating on the beats of my heart, telling myself all the reasons I shouldn't like the feeling of being in his arms. Even if he was sick, and possibly still delirious, when he had asked me to climb into his bed. Eventually, I eased myself out of his hold and returned to the beanbag.

Chapter 16

*L*OGAN HAD tonsillitis. After spending the weekend nursing him and Jordan—who just had the flu and probably could have looked after himself, the big baby—it felt good to be back in my dorm room. I hadn't slept at their apartment a second time. Instead Dane had picked me up at ten on Saturday night, and I'd walked back over there at seven on Sunday morning. Logan was well enough to drive me home late on Sunday afternoon. His fever had finally gone and after two days of antibiotics he was up and about again—albeit speaking like he'd spent two days shouting and drinking nothing but tequila. He assured me he was feeling better and might even make it to classes, although he had a Doctor's Certificate for the entire week.

Wish I did.

As I rushed around packing for a day of classes, I

kicked myself that I hadn't thought to take any study over to Logan's. I was unprepared for the coming week of lectures and being a new term, I should be at the top of my game. Especially after my appalling results from earlier in the year. I shoved everything into my bag, slung it over my shoulder and headed out. Sociology was my first lecture of the day and I wasn't particularly hungry because I'd snuck down to the dining hall this morning. It turned out not many of my fellow college dwellers were up at six am. Reason enough to make a habit of rising early.

As I walked across campus my phone buzzed in my pocket, and I fished it out. The screen showed an image of my mother. Sighing, I hit accept.

"Hi Mum."

"Olivia. I heard results came in on Friday. You haven't called ..."

Dread curled in my tummy and I steeled myself against her reaction then decided better of it. "I'm on my way to class. I'll call you back after."

"Two minutes, Olivia. That's all this will take. I know you have your grades, because Ella has hers. How did you go?"

"Sorry ..." I held the phone out from my ear. "I can't hear you. Reception's shoddy."

I hit *end call*. Ella-freaking-Parry, ruining my life since the third grade. Well hopefully mum would be glad I was going to class. It wouldn't satisfy her for long, but maybe it could buy a little time, and not giving her what she wanted when she wanted? It felt good. Petty? Probably. Satisfying? Most definitely.

Walking into class, I was grateful that Socio was a year-long subject. It meant that I hadn't pulled a bad grade yet and I still had another semester to make sure I didn't. Besides, it was a good class. I actually enjoyed learning about the way society worked. My enjoyment of the subject had nothing to do with the guy who I sat with.

Good lord, I was a bad liar. Even I didn't believe me.

As I slid into my usual seat near the front of the room, my phone buzzed again. Feeling a little sick, I switched it to silent. She wouldn't give up, and my refusing to talk was a stupid move because she'd know something wasn't right. But I couldn't deal with it right now, nor could I drag up the energy to care enough to respond.

I placed the phone on my desk facedown and set up my tablet to take notes. The darn thing buzzed again, near vibrating right off the tiny table top. Inhaling a frustrated breath, I picked it up, and without even looking at her message responded with:

I'm in class, Mum.

Logan chose that moment to appear, and even though he'd said he'd come, seeing him was still a surprise. It had only been three days since he was delirious with fever. I really didn't expect him to follow through. Hopefully this wasn't too much too soon.

Despite slightly sunken cheeks, he looked so much better. There was colour in his face and his hair had its golden sheen. Even his eyes had that damn sexy twinkle, the one full of secrets I wished he would share. He frowned. "What's up?"

As if to punctuate his concern, my phone buzzed again.

I switched it off and moaned. "Parents. It seems even half a state away I can't escape them."

"Ain't that the truth." Logan sighed.

Our professor started speaking, and once again I had trouble with concentration. But it wasn't the fine specimen of a guy beside me who had my mind wandering. It was my horrible grades. A fail incomplete was disastrous, and the thought of breaking that news to my mother after class had my tummy twisting in all kinds of knots.

The blank screen of my tablet started moving with the nudge of Logan's fingertips. What in the world was he doing? I was trying to pay attention, for heaven's sake. When it was balanced on the far corner of my desk, Logan tore a sheet of paper from his notebook and slid it onto my table, then poised a pen over it and wrote. When he was finished, he dropped the pen and removed his hand.

Stop stressing. Nothing's that bad.

I took the pen and wrote, *A fail incomplete in Torts is pretty bad.*

His expression said it all. Even Logan thought that was horrendous. He simply wrote, *Ouch.*

I raised my eyebrows and shot him a pointed look. Not that bad, hey? He tapped the pen against his bottom lip then dragged his teeth across the plump surface. The fluttering in my tummy totally chased away the twisty feeling. I drew in a ragged breath.

He smiled at me, that darn twinkle even brighter, as if he knew exactly what he'd just done to my insides. Then wrote, *It's only one class. You can take it again next year.*

It will bring down my GPA.

This the cause of your parental problem?

A lump tugged at my throat. I tried to close it.

I haven't told them. Avoidance is key.

Logan's gaze met mine, and he didn't need to write his next words; they were written in his eyes. He thought I was a failure, that I should have told them, that I shouldn't have failed that class. And he was right; I shouldn't. I should be pushing up my grade point average and concentrating on building my CV, not tearing it down. Sometimes the pressure was just too much, and that was exactly how it felt. I just wanted to be one of those kids that cruised through classes, partied like an animal, and still managed to come out the other end intact and holding a degree. Yet here I was with a weird sleeping disorder, a social outcast, and failing my classes, even though I studied my butt off. I took up the pen and wrote exactly what I was feeling.

It's hard to be perfect.

Logan's hand slid over mine, his palm flush against the back of my hand. He curled his fingers around it.

My heart felt like it stopped then started again, beating way too fast. A burn grew low in my tummy and my thighs tingled. What in the world was Logan doing to me? A desire stronger than any I'd ever felt before stole over me and I wasn't sure that I could suppress my feelings for him any longer. I couldn't even remember why I wanted to. He flipped our hands over so mine was palm up, cradled in his. I think my hand trembled. A part of me just wanted to launch myself across the armrest that separated us.

Logan's gaze moved to my eyes and held as he brought the pen to my palm. He didn't smile, but his eyes spoke volumes. In that instant, I knew he wasn't holding back anymore; desire blazed in his gaze. The pen began moving on my hand and his eyes dropped to watch what he was doing. When he slid his hands away, words were scrawled across my palm.

To me you're perfect.

Something inside of me melted, causing my eyes to leak tears I hadn't even realised were building. With those four tiny words, he'd made me feel whole, made me feel good, and I didn't doubt them because when my gaze met his, the blue of his eyes was clear as a summer's day. My hands flew to either side of his rough jaw and pulled our mouths together. Our lips meshed as I kissed him over and over again.

Logan froze under my touch, completely non-responsive.

My heart froze too.

Good lord, what had I done? Kissing your best friend was a stupid move. And kissing him in the middle of a lecture was even stupider.

I started to pull back, but he looked shocked as all heck. Like he'd only just woken from the daze his hands slid up into my hair and he forced my mouth back to his, holding me in place as he kissed me back in a way I'd never been kissed before. I felt as if I were falling, whether it was falling in love or falling away from the fear I wasn't sure. As if every part of me dove from the top of that rollercoaster I'd been balanced on for so long. Logan's kiss stole my breath, my thoughts, my senses, and I kissed him back with equal zeal.

The hoots and hollers around us sent me crashing back to the reality of being in the middle of class. I'd stopped paying attention to the lecture long ago, but now I re-

membered exactly where we were and what we were doing. My cheeks burned and someone yelled, "Get a room."

Our lecturer cleared his throat, clearly not for the first
time. "I suggest you take your extracurricular activities
out of my classroom, Mr Hays. Miss Dean."

He didn't have to tell us twice. Logan grabbed my hand
and pulled me out of my seat. Together, we moved down
the aisle and right out of the door. A giggle bubbled in my
throat. This was totally insane ... who ran out in the middle of class? Not Olivia Dean, that's for sure.

Out in the corridor he turned to me with a dark gaze. I
took a step back, my laughter dying on my lips as he took
a step forward. His gaze fell to my mouth, which was suddenly dry. My tongue darted across my bottom lip, trying
to add some moisture. It was a futile action.

"I've wanted this for so long." Logan's voice was deep,
husky as he took another step forward, his nose almost
touching my cheek. There was only a slither of space between our lips but he moved fast, slamming our mouths
together again so fast that my back hit the wall and holy
bejeebers, this was sure some way to be kissed.

Logan's hand trailed down my side to rest at my waist
and I grabbed his jacket with both hands, pulling him
flush against me because I couldn't bear for there to be
any air between us. His other hand crashed into the wall
above my head, steadying his stance, and the way Logan
kissed me was like the world was about to end and we
only had this moment to show each other how we felt.

It was magic.

It was intense.

Logan's tongue slid against mine as he devoured my

mouth and I kissed him back for all I was worth, trying to tell him in this most extreme kiss of all kisses that I was his, I always had been.

Every part of him pressed against every part of me and a fiery burn sat on my waist right where his hand rested. Logan's fingers spread, their tips slipping under the hem of my blouse, and I inhaled a sharp breath as my hand slid to his nape, my fingers tangling in his hair to hold him against me and never let him go. Regardless of my death grip, his lips moved from my mouth, trailing kisses along my jaw and down my neck. He concentrated his efforts on the hollow above my shoulder. I moaned and Logan purred in response, his mouth moving more feverishly.

"Have to stop," he said between kisses. "Have to ..."

He dragged himself away and planted his palms on the wall either side of my head as he dropped his forehead to mine. His breathing was laboured, each breath dragged in over a rocky path.

"If I don't stop now, I won't be able to."

I groaned and Logan chuckled. I didn't want this to end any more than he did, but he was right. The arts building was not the place. Instead he pushed off the wall and took my hand, bringing it to his lips, and placed a tender kiss on my knuckles. Somehow the hallway had filled around us, and people moseyed on to wherever they were headed next.

My heart continued its erratic beat as Logan walked me all the way across campus to my next class, not letting my hand go until I was sitting in the lecture theatre.

Chapter 17

*L*OGAN WAITED for me outside my last class of the day, looking hotter than ever with his back against the wall and one leg bent up. His blond mess of hair was shaggier than ever, and that smile—it could melt me.

I had no idea how he'd figured out where I'd be—it was like he just instinctively knew. A quip about him being a stalker sat on the tip of my tongue, but I thought better of it and smiled instead. He was a welcome sight, and I didn't want him to think otherwise. He lifted the strap on my bag and slung it over his own shoulder.

"I tried to call, but it went right to voicemail."

I sighed just thinking about the influx of messages from my mother that would be waiting. "I haven't turned it back on."

"You're going to have to talk to them eventually, and

when you do, just remember that this is your life."

Maybe he was right. I sure felt like I could defeat the entire world. Like nothing mattered other than me and him. Us. Holy hotcakes, was there an us?

"What are you up to tonight?" Logan asked as he slipped his arm around my waist, steering me out of the Law building and toward his Corolla parked on the street.

Spending the evening with Logan was a welcome thought. My tummy flipped at the memory of the scorching kiss we'd shared earlier. I hadn't been able to think of anything else all day, and even though he'd said he'd wanted to do it for a long time, I wondered where we were now.

Now that I'd shoved all that other stuff aside and finally 'fessed up to my feelings, I wanted more. I wanted to kiss him again, but I didn't. Instead I walked along by his side, playing my own little mind game of *will he or won't he.*

"Nothing ... I mean ... I have study, but I'm not going out, and I'm not doing anything important." Good lord, that was terrible. I sounded like I was desperately waiting for him to give me a better offer, which I totally was, but I didn't want him to think that.

I climbed into the front seat before he could answer and busied myself with straightening my hair with my fingers. He hopped in the car and to ease over my desperate declaration, I blurted out, "How's Jordan?"

Logan started the engine. "Not as sick as he thinks he is. I packed him off to school this morning. He should be home again by now."

Logan drove me back to Oxley, and although the trip

was only two minutes, and we'd sat in comfortable silence for much longer than that many a time before, I filled the silence with trivial conversation. Everything felt far less than comfortable. In fact, sitting still and not fidgeting with my hair, my nails, or my bag was near impossible.

The Corolla hummed as Logan pulled it into the car park. "I was thinking we should grab some dinner tonight."

My heart jumped like a baby cheerleader on steroids. What happened this morning, it meant something to him too.

Like he could read my thoughts, Logan reached across the seats and cupped my face in his hand. His eyes searched mine, looking for what I wasn't sure, but his thumb brushed back and forth over my cheek and Logan leaned in.

He kissed me with such tenderness that it was almost like kissing someone else. The intensity from this morning had switched to a slow burn that had the exact same effect on my senses. It sent them reeling into a spiral of desire and a need to pull him in even closer. I tried to do just that, but the gear stick jammed into my thigh. Logan pulled back, and his eyes were heavily hooded, and their usual vibrant blue was much darker. He dropped his hand and I let out a tiny whimper at the loss of his touch.

Logan's mouth started turning and a slow smile built. "Let's get you upstairs."

Unable to talk in proper sentences, I settled for a simple nod. He grabbed my bag from the backseat and together, we walked into Oxley. We managed to make it all the way to my block before we ran into another soul. I almost groaned when I saw a flash of deep cherry hair and skinny jeans; Ella coming down the same stairs we were walking up.

"Ella." I gave a quick nod in greeting.

Her eyes narrowed on Logan. I cleared my throat and said, "You caused us to fail that group assignment."

She flicked her gaze back to me. "I did not."

The smirk that stole across her face made anger pound through my temples. "I got a credit in Torts because of the assignment only being a pass."

Ella tossed her hair over her shoulder. "A pass isn't a fail. Don't blame your shitty grades on me."

I knew it wasn't entirely her fault but she'd made me cranky, and the way she stood there looking all proud of the fact I'd almost failed made me hate her in a way I hadn't since we were kids and she'd called me Golly Olly – like snot.

I felt Logan's hand on my back and it had a calming effect. "Come on, Liv. It's not worth it."

With a scowl at Ella, I said, "You're right. It's not."

I heard a soft chuckle as I passed her and continued up the stairs.

You ready for dinner?

I'll meet you in the car park.

I pulled my cupboard all the way open so as to get a full

body mirror view. Black tights hugged the curves of my legs and my knit dress was just long enough to cover my thighs. My DKNY boots gave me extra height, which should make me a little closer to Logan's six feet. I ran my hands through my hair, letting it fall back around my face. Why did I feel so nervous? We'd hung out plenty of times before, yet my stomach felt so empty it was nauseous. Like a swarm of bees were trying to form a whirlpool inside me.

I gave a shaky exhale and popped my lips to even out the gloss. This was an actual date. With Logan. *My* Logan. My heart fluttered as the bees took over my whole body, as if my blood itself had sprouted a million tiny wings. An *eeeee* passed my lips and I jumped up and down then kissed my reflection.

Dinner.

With Logan.

Okay. Best not keep him waiting. I bit down on my smile and snatched my purse from the bed. I'd had to visit Savvy and ask for it back, since it was black suede and matched my shoes perfectly. Pity I'd barged in on what looked like an argument between her and Dane.

I locked up my room and headed downstairs. It was only five p.m., but already the courtyard was a highway of people going to the dining hall. I slipped out to the parking lot without seeing anyone worth talking to.

The Corolla idled in the spot closest to the footpath I strode along. Not that it was easy to stride in heels, but the second I saw Logan's little red car my feet took control. He reached across the passenger side and pushed the door open, not bothering to right himself in his seat. As I slid into the car, Logan's stubbled cheek brushed against my ear.

"Hell—"

He caught my lips in his. My bottom lip rested gently between them and those darn bees stirred low in my belly. Really low. He sucked the sensitive skin into his mouth, running his warm tongue along the plump flesh. My eyes slid closed. Logan smiled against my mouth, releasing his hold on my lip and I sighed as he pulled away, opening my eyes. Tossing his arm over the back of my seat, he looked behind us and backed out of the car space.

"Hi." My voice was entirely too breathy.

"Hi." Logan smiled.

"Hi."

"Hi." Logan's voice dropped an octave, heavy with innuendo.

I looked across and the smirk on his face made me grin.

We drove all the way into town before either of us spoke again. Every time I snuck a glance his way, Logan smiled at me. His hair looked shinier, his scruff scruffier, his eyes bluer. Even his arms looked bigger. Not that I could see them under the vintage blazer. Brown leather, it looked well worn, yet I'd never seen him wear it before. The leather was taut around his upper arms, the muscles beneath stretching the fabric. Gosh, he looked hot tonight. Forget dinner, maybe we could just find somewhere to park and I could touch his arms. Or maybe his legs ... he did have those jeans on. I sucked in a deep breath that did nothing to cool the heat that had suddenly washed over me. Boy, it was hot in here.

My tongue ran over my parched lips, and when I

peeked at Logan he winked.

Good heavens, he knew exactly how I felt.

The car suddenly stopped. I was glad he'd paid more attention to where we were going than I had. We could have still been in Oxley's parking lot for all the notice I'd given our short ride.

Logan climbed out of the car. If I didn't get a grip this dinner would be a waste of money, because I wouldn't be able to eat a blessed thing.

My door opened while I was still composing myself. Logan extended his gorgeous hand, and taking it, I stepped out of the car. He pressed a chaste kiss to my cheek. "It's nothing fancy, but the food here is great."

We stood in front of Mozzarella Pizzas.

"Family discount, huh?"

Logan smiled. "I might be cheap, but I'm not that cheap."

With our hands still twisted together, we entered the shop to the sound of the bell overhead. In my two years living in this town, I'd never been inside Mozerella's. Not owning a car made home delivery more convenient. Surprisngly, it was a tiny shop, with no tables and chairs.

A middle-aged man stood behind the counter, his round belly hung over his black pants. "Logan." He smiled. "Order's up."

"Thank, Carlos."

"Don't thank me yet. Penny made it. She's still learning the ropes. Much like young Jordan."

Carlos disappeared, only to return less than a minute later with a pizza box in hand. Logan released my fingers to extract a wallet from his back pocket. He paid Carlos, who in turn passed off the box of pizza. The olive-skinned man shot me a wide smile. "You kids have a great night."

"Will do," Logan said.

Back outside, Logan tugged open the Corolla's back door and leaned inside. *Looks like he's actually planned something.* I'd assumed we'd go to a restaurant ... but this felt almost romantic. He backed out of the car and in his hand Logan held a blanket plus a small backpack.

"Want me to take that?" I asked.

He bumped the door closed with his delicious rear end. "All good."

Hanging the bag over his shoulder, Logan shoved the blanket under his arm, balanced the pizza box on his palm and took my hand in his other one once again.

Across the road was a park I'd never really visited. Parks were something that didn't make a lot of sense for me these days. The lack of Wi-Fi made it no use to students who spent every waking moment in study time.

Logan led us across the road and onto the lush green grass that almost sponged underfoot it was so soft. The air smelled fresh and clean, like pine and grass clippings, and I drew in a long breath. We walked so far in that I could barely make out the surrounding roads. It was tranquil and quiet, as if we weren't in town at all, but rather at a beautiful landscaped garden on private property. Or maybe Sydney's Botanic Gardens less the people, since we were the only ones about. We stopped under a giant pine tree and Logan released my hand then passed me the pizza. An entirely different smell filled my nose, and made my tummy grumble.

He laid out the blanket and plopped the bag in a corner, then retrieved the pizza from me and gestured to the rug. "Dinner, my lady."

"You're such a gentleman." Smiling, I lowered myself onto the ground.

Logan sat beside me and laid the pizza between us, flicking open the box. It smelled divine and I had no idea how he knew what I liked, but it was ham and pineapple. My mouth watered as I reached for a slice.

A loud pop echoed through the air. I turned to Logan in time to see champagne flowing from the bottle he held onto the grass.

"I've always sucked at that." He poured the sparkling liquid into two glasses that no doubt came in his backpack.

"Good thing you're not planning a career in bartending."

"I dunno. I could apply sociology to handling drunks."

I laughed as I took a slice of pizza. Turned out it was just as good as it smelled. It was Mozzarella's, after all. Staff-in-training or not, they did make the best pizza in town. "Really?" I asked. "What's a degree in socio worth anyway?"

"Are you asking what I want to be when I grow up?" Logan half-smiled. "I want to work in schools or for a government organisation. Somewhere I can use my psychology degree to help people." He scooped up a slice and doubled it over, biting into the gooey cheese, which oozed out the side.

"Pysch?"

"Surprised?"

"A little ... I always assumed you were doing ... I can't

believe I never asked."

He made short work of another slice of pizza, and took a sip of bubbles. We both concentrated on eating for a while. I took a sip of my drink. The sparkling wine went straight to my head, making it a little light. I set the glass down.

"I hear pysch's a full-on degree."

"It's not too bad," he said. "I do all right."

"Just all right?"

"High-distinction average."

Good lord. I didn't mean to ask about his grades. Heat flooded my cheeks, drowned the tips of my ears.

"You ..." He tapped me on the nose. "... have no idea what I do when we're not together. I could study my guts out, for all you know."

The finger still resting on my nose trailed down the side of my cheek, over the curve of my jaw and cupped my face. Logan leaned forward and claimed my mouth again, his lips crushing into mine, his tongue sweeping over them and into my mouth. He kissed me like he had this morning, with as much need, as if I could stop him imploding. I sure felt like that was the way *I* was headed. My ears no longer burned. Instead, the fierce heat spread through my body and I wanted him closer, *needed* him closer.

As if we were of one thought, Logan shoved the pizza box away and pulled me toward him. I scooted across the soft blanket, my chest crashing into his solid mass. Logan planted a hand on the ground and gently pushed me onto my back with the force of his kiss. His hand was now by my head as he hovered above me. His tongue explored every part of my mouth, sweeping across my lips, my teeth, my tongue, exploding a need deep inside me I hadn't felt in months. There was a tingling in my tummy that drew from someplace lower and deeper.

I trailed burning fingers from his shoulders up into his soft hair, tangling them in its length, and I tugged him down until his weight rested against me, his hard chest pushed against the too-thick fabric of my dress and his knee planted between my thighs.

Logan's kisses grew softer, but I held him close with my hand at the back of his neck. I'd waited so long that I wasn't about to let him get away now. He groaned into my mouth and his lips moved, sliding over mine to place a gentle kiss on the corner of my mouth.

"Public place," he growled.

I tipped my head back and despite his declaration, his mouth moved over my cheek, his tongue gliding along my jaw. Sweet kisses dropped in its wake. Playing kids be damned—they should all be home in bed by now anyway. The daylight was pretty well gone. My back arched, my breasts ached even though they couldn't possibly be pressed closer. Logan's warm breath skated over my ear.

"I could get used to this."

"Uh-huh," I moaned. *Me too.*

Chapter 18

IT WAS Wednesday before I even entertained the thought of talking to my parents and even then, it was only because Logan convinced me that it was better to get it over and done with than wait until the issue had been blown into something huger than what it was. Of course, it was huge already, and I didn't think he truly got that, but he was right. Putting it off only made me stress about actually doing it. So, if I just bit the bullet and talked to them, hopefully I could put it behind me and the stress would be less intense.

I pulled my hands through my loose hair and yanked it up into a ponytail. I could do this.

"Liv, it's okay," Logan said from his position on my bed with his back against the wall and his legs stretched out in front of him. "I'll be here the whole time."

It still felt weird having him in my room when I'd refused to admit him so often before. Things had changed though and I hoped he'd be here often, so I tried to smile at him then glanced at my phone. There had been exactly thirty-two text messages and four missed calls since I'd hung up on my mother on Monday.

I briefly entertained the idea of sending a text instead, but that would only lead to her calling me, and it was better to do this when *I* was ready. I took a deep breath in through my nose and firmed my resolve. Then I tapped on my mother's number and held my phone to my ear. She picked up on the second ring.

"Olivia." Her voice was terse. "How dare you ignore my messages? I am one day away from booking a flight up there. Don't think I won't, young lady."

If anyone could make me feel like I was twelve years old again, it was my mother. I turned my back on Logan so he wouldn't see the guilt on my face. Best to make this quick. I'd do it like tearing off a Band-Aid—once it was done quickly, I could hang up.

"I failed Torts and got a credit in constitution."

She exhaled down the line. "What about the other subjects?"

"They're year-long."

Logan's hands slid around my waist, and he pulled me back against him, wrapping his arms around me and holding me tight as he trailed soft kisses across my shoulder. My mind reeled into a nothingness, my concentration solely on the feel of his lips against my skin. His touch sure was a welcome distraction, muddled thoughts and all.

"You're an embarrassment, Olivia. Ella Parry said ... no.

I know this is because of that boy. You listen to me, young lady, stop wasting your time dilly-dallying around with him, and get yourself back in control of this mess before it's too late to fix. If you don't improve your grades, we will cut you off. There'll be no more money to support your partying, do you hear me?"

I flinched as if I were standing in front of her with those dark eyes of hers searing my soul and making me feel two feet tall. In an effort to stop the tears coming, I clenched my teeth and said, "I'm not partying, and there is no guy distracting me. Logan—" I clamped my mouth shut before I said too much. How did she know about Logan anyway? I'd never told her who the messages where from over the break. Ella's mum ... I swear there were no secrets.

His sweet kisses stopped and he squeezed me tighter, holding me together with his strength.

"I expect better results at the end of the year." The phone was still at my ear, but the line went dead. If it weren't for Logan's arms around me, I think I would have collapsed under the weight of failure.

THE NEXT few weeks were pure bliss. I never would have thought that saying 'walking on cloud nine' was actually possible. But every time I saw Logan or even thought of him there was a bigger bounce in my step, and something felt like it floated inside of me. I'd managed to avoid any sleepovers and even though I knew I couldn't put it off forever, for now I was happy to cruise along as we were. It was hard to maintain control around him, but with the thought of Logan experiencing my sleep disorder firsthand, I managed.

We'd made it to the finals in hockey and as I shoved my shin pads in my socks and positioned them, I felt ready. This was the grand final and we'd made it, despite the team's earlier issues, and I wasn't surprised in the least that Evan's Hall was the team facing us.

I tossed Logan a smile and took my position in the centre of the field. The umpire asked me, heads or tails. "Heads," I yelled as she flipped a coin in the air. She caught it in her palm and a grin spread across her face as she called, "Heads."

"We'll take the first hit."

The game moved slowly at first, neither team achieving much at all, just wearing both our sides out as the play continually changed from one direction to the other. I had our best players on the field, but no matter what we did, we couldn't seem to pull away from them long enough to score a single goal.

When the countdown clock read 4:00 in the second half of the game, things changed in our favour. The score was 0:1 our way, and their response times seemed to be slowing. I dribbled the ball along the left wing, running as fast as I could. Both teams ran behind me, but their captain, the same girl from the now infamous 'Orgasmic Olivia' game, made a wide run down the field and she was almost in front of me when she yelled, "Hey Dean. I see you snagged Logan Hays. You must have something the rest of us don't, 'cause god only knows a ton of girls have tried to tie him down." The laugh that burst from her could only be described as a cackle. "Must be the master debate."

I put my head down, and continued dribbling the ball, all the way out. Then I sprinted past my heckler, the goal circle in sight.

"... guess he likes to watch a girl get herself off."

I fumbled. The ball slipped from the safety of my stick.

It's not worth it.

Logan's words about Ella's bitchy retorts blazed in my mind and I swung the flat side of my hockey stick around, using the end like a hook to snag the ball back into my play. I was inside the circle and their goalie feinted from side to side, her bulky gear making her look like a rocking marshmallow. And that's exactly what she was; something that was slow and soft and I could totally get this ball past her. With a high swing of my hockey stick, I slammed it against the hard ball, which glided across the astro-turf in a straight line. The goalie dove to the side, but she was too slow. The ball slipped past her fingers and slammed against the back of the goal.

The buzzer sounded and suddenly my teammates surrounded me, all squealing and shouting and holding their sticks in the air.

We did it.

We'd won the grand final, and boy it felt good. Adrenaline pounded through me, making my head buzz.

I caught Logan's gaze and he held his hands above his head in a slow clap while he grinned. Good lord, I was lucky to have such an awesome guy in my life. After shaking each of my opponents' hands, I was left with the heckler, and I'd be damned if I wasn't going to be a good sport despite her nasty scowl. I moved toward her, my hand extended and she grasped it, giving a quick shake. She dropped it just as quickly, but I didn't care. I ran to the sidelines, my duties over. Logan met me at the gate, and I threw my arms around his neck, relishing in the moment as he pulled me against his firm body.

"Congrats, Liv." He nuzzled into my neck. Then he pulled back and planted a solid kiss on my lips.

My life was almost perfect.

Chapter 19

WITH THE hockey season over, it was only a matter of weeks before netball started up. I wasn't too keen about that as it had never been a sport I'd loved, but I was the team captain last year and needed to reclaim my place. That meant I only had two Saturdays free from sport, and Logan had organised something special for this one. Not that he'd tell me where we were going or what we were doing—it was a huge surprise.

We drove through town in companionable silence. With every turn he took, I tried to guess where we were headed, but Logan just tapped his fingers on the steering wheel to the beat of the music pouring out of the speakers. Clearly, he enjoyed my every incorrect attempt.

We drove all the way to the other side of town, past the Berry Best, and through the roundabout that lead out onto the highway, at which point he pulled the car to the right and headed north. Scrunching my brows, I couldn't figure it out. There was nothing out here but the wide open plains filled with sheep farms. When we reached the second roundabout he took the exit back into town and I was completely baffled. We'd come full circle after a little scenic drive on the bypass. Logan chuckled, amused with his game.

As we pulled into his driveway I said, "What? This isn't special. It's just ... just ..."

"My place?" He grinned. "I had to make it a little fun."

"You're so crazy." I rolled my eyes, and that only made him laugh harder.

Logan jumped out of the car, but I'd be damned if I was moving my butt out of here. He'd promised fun, and I liked his little brother. Hanging out with Jordan would be enjoyable, but I'd built my hopes up for an adventure like our trip to the falls, and now I felt a little miffed. He could deliver on his promise, darn it.

Logan went inside without me. *Well, that backfired.* He'd called my bluff, and must have decided I could sit in the car. Too bad I was more stubborn than him. I shuffled until I was diagonal in the chair, kicked my feet up onto the dash, crossed them at the ankles, and scooched down in the seat with my shoulder pressed against the door, smirking. It was warm enough in the sun to take a nap.

The door fell from underneath me.

I righted myself just before I toppled out and Logan laughed then grabbed my hand. Feigning annoyance, I crossed both arms over my chest and raised my chin. It was a fight to keep from smiling. But then an arm pushed under my legs, another behind my back and Logan lifted me out of the Corolla. I squealed as he spun around and kicked the car door closed. Holding a straighter face than I could manage, Logan said, "You can either come willingly or I'll carry you."

"This isn't so bad." I snuggled in, resting my head against his firm chest.

Logan didn't move toward the front door as I'd assumed. Instead he started walking up the street with me cradled in his arms, like a bride being carried across a threshold. Just as I figured out his house wasn't our destination, the world turned upside-down and I found myself dangling over his shoulder with his arm hooked behind my knees to anchor me in place. I squealed because holy hell, surely he was going to drop me. The ground looked so close it felt as if I might slip fair over his shoulder at any second.

"Sure you don't want to walk, Butterfingers?"

Pinching my smile between my teeth, I said, "Nope. I'm good."

My body started sliding down Logan's back and I squealed again. Gosh, I was beginning to sound like a ten-year-old. My hands clamped onto his tight rear to stop my headfirst descent into the ground. I might have enjoyed the feel of his round muscles a little too much. So it was a while before I yelled, "Put me down!"

Logan laughed even harder as he did some manoeuvre that had me slipping off his shoulder from the side while his arm slid from behind my legs to my waist and he set me on my feet.

With my heart racing so fast it made me lightheaded, I

asked, "So, this is your big adventure, huh?"

"Yup." Logan put his arm around my waist and slid his hand into the back pocket of my jeans, effectively cupping my butt cheek as I did to his earlier. He gave no futher explanation, instead we fell into silence for a few minutes. "You going to miss hockey?"

"Maybe ... though, I won't have much of a chance, since netball season's about to start."

"I don't get why you play; you said once before that you didn't like it. Doesn't make any sense to spend so much time on something that doesn't make you feel good."

I pulled away from him and shoved my hands in my jacket pockets. "I wouldn't say hockey doesn't make me feel good. I like it ..." I stared at the street ahead, wondering where this walk would take us. "When I'm on the field I feel kind of alive, and like I can be whatever I want. There are no rules about how to behave or talk, or even who to be. It's very liberating."

"Sounds like you do enjoy it."

We walked along the street and it was so quiet it almost felt abandoned, except for the occasional passing car. Maybe Logan was right. I'd never really stopped to think past the responsibility of captaining the team and the fact that it was yet another thing that dragged on my time while I ensured people liked me. But being on the field was good, and I really did like the way fighting for my team felt.

"Yeah, maybe I do."

We seemed to move ever upward, and it seemed that the peak was exactly where we going; to the lookout. I'd driven past it a million times but never actually stopped for a gander. It was high on a hill at the campus end of town, surrounded by houses and streets and a beautiful park that was lined with deciduous poplars. And I could see those—they looked almost bare in their soldier-like lines with more leaves around their bases than in their branches.

"I love autumn," I said on a sigh.

Logan snagged my hand in his. "What about netball? Like it or love it?"

"Hate it."

"Then don't play."

I sighed. "I have to. Captaining the teams is just as important as being involved in student politics or on the dorm social committee, and since I lost my chance at student politics, I need to double my efforts elsewhere."

"But you hate all that too. It runs you into the ground, Liv, and makes you so darn tired and when it goes wrong ... the stress tears you apart."

Wow. I did hate it all—not always, but more and more—and I wasn't quite sure how he knew that. Sure he'd been there for me when I most needed it with the student council thing and for that I was grateful, but he was right. When things were good and I wasn't being shouldered out, it did keep me so busy I had no time for anything else. I needed to do it and that's why when it went wrong, I was horrendous. But I didn't really want to think about that. I wanted to forget it all, even if it was only for a few hours.

"It's all I know, Logan."

The leaves at our feet were so thick, I could wade

through them, and that's precisely what I did, running through the sea of crinkling colours like the happy child I wished I could be. When Logan shook his head, I gathered up an armful and tossed them at him.

"You didn't," he said, scooping up his own armful. He tossed it into the air and I dodged the raining leaves, running ahead. Out of his reach, I dragged my foot through the fallen ones like they were sand while Logan stood back watching. When I was done, there was a massive heart etched out of autumn leaves and it kind of embodied exactly how I felt. Love hearts are a happy image and childish as it was, drawing one made me feel happy. Here I was, not giving a hoot what anyone thought. All my airs and graces and pretences were stripped away, and it felt incredible.

Logan ran after me with another handful of leaves. I turned ninety degrees and made for the top of the hill. It was a steep climb, but the top was our destination anyway. My calves seared by the time I reached the lookout, and fit as I was, this was a run my muscles weren't familiar with. I flopped on the ground, puffing for breath, and it was a full two minutes, maybe more, before Logan collapsed beside me.

"You're insane," he puffed.

"Only around you."

We lay there, side by side, until we'd both caught our breaths then Logan sat up, jumped to his feet and held his hand out to me. "C'mon. We didn't run all the way up this hill not to check out the view."

"I don't know ..." I rolled my gaze up his body, settling on his chest which that t-shirt defined nicely "... the view from here's pretty darn good."

Smiling with half his mouth, Logan shook his head and grabbed my hand anyway, tugging me to my feet. He led me over to the designated lookout area and the town laid out before us was just as beautiful in its manmade glory as the waterfall had been in nature's. The steeples and spires of the city's churches were like beacons to the eye. Trails of smoke rose from a multitude of chimneys and even though autumn was drawing to a close the city was still swathed in a sea of red and yellow and orange. It was as if someone had draped a colourful blanket over patches of the town.

Logan's arms snaked around me, and he pulled my back against him, resting his chin on the top of my head. It was quite possibly the best way to be hugged.

"It's a beautiful town," I said. "And to think I was never supposed to end up here. I would have missed out on so much."

"Yeah?" He grazed his stubble along my hair then kissed the crown of my head.

"Yeah, I was supposed to go to Sydney Univeristy but my grades weren't high enough."

"They must have been darn high if you got into Law here."

"Yeah, well ... my parents weren't very impressed."

Logan's arms tightened around me. "They should have been."

"They said I was a failure."

Logan's grip on me loosened. "If we all listened to our parents, I'd still be living under my father's crappy roof and surviving off social welfare or flipping burgers, because that's about all they think I'm good for."

I spun to look at him and I'm sure the expression on my face said it all as I searched his gaze. He couldn't really think that. Logan was brilliant and clever, and he could be anything. He'd be a fabulous psychologist one day. I pressed my lips to his, and said, "You're so much more that."

"Yeah, well ..." He pulled back.

I'm not sure what came over him, but this wasn't the Logan I'd come to know. He was usually confident and self-assured. He slumped onto the park bench and pushed a hand through his hair, holding the long strands back off his face. His jaw clenched, the muscle ticking under his skin as if he were angry or trying to process a thought. I slid onto the bench beside him and placed my hand on his knee. Logan picked it up and laced our fingers together.

"To me, you're perfect." I repeated his words back to him, and Logan brought our hands to his mouth then kissed each of my knuckles.

"My parents aren't the nicest people. When someone tells you you're a little shit that will amount to nothing everyday of your life, it's hard not to believe it, and even years later when you know it's not true, the shadow lingers."

I snuggled into his side, resting my head on his shoulder. Maybe his external veneer was as forced as mine.

Logan continued, "My father may never have laid a hand on us, and my mother may have never needed to stop him, but the way they both treated us ... sometimes I think that would have been easier."

I wasn't sure what to say, and I didn't want him to stop

talking so I just sat there, curled into his side, running my hand along the length of his thigh in the hope my actions conveyed my thoughts; he was special and important.

"That's why I'm here." He sighed. "Getting an education to build a better life for me and Jordan. That kid needs to see that we can both be somebody."

"You are somebody. Somebody pretty darn awesome."

I tipped my head back to meet his gaze and Logan kissed me as if I'd just given him the world.

With each day we spent together I liked him more and more. We'd always been great friends, but this was something far deeper. There was something about Logan that pulled at the core of my soul and with each moment like this, another invisible string wove its way between his soul and mine, strengthening the bond between us.

My tummy grumbled loudly, and Logan pulled away. We'd had lunch before our drive but that was hours ago.

"Let's go home and get some dinner," he said.

I burrowed my face into his neck, inhaling his unique breezy smell, and although I was hungry, I was loathe to leave this sanctuary where we could both be our real selves.

As we traipsed down the hill hand in hand, the sun had already bled the day away and the streetlights shone. The walk back was far quieter than the one here and I couldn't speak for Logan, but I was lost in the conversations we'd had. He was right; I wasn't happy doing all of those extra-curricular things, but I couldn't see a way out of it, and that made me think about everything else too. I didn't love Law, I never had, and that's what all the other stuff cen-tred around. It made sure I kept on track for a career I wasn't particularly looking forward to.

We reached his house well before I'd realised we were even on the right street. If it weren't for Logan's hand in mine, guiding me along, perhaps I wouldn't have actually made it I was so lost in my own thoughts. I smiled at him as he unlocked the front door. I hadn't spent a lot of time at his apartment, but I'd been there often enough to feel comfortable, so I slipped my shoes off before heading inside. The smell wafting through the place was divine.

"Oh my gosh, what is Jordan cooking?"

"Not Jordan. That's all my doing and it's our dinner." Logan shot me a proud smile.

I trundled off to the bathroom and as I was washing up, a string of expletives came from the direction of the kitchen. I ran into the room looking for whatever had hurt Logan, a hot pan, a sharp knife. Instead I found him dumping a dish into the sink with oven mitts protecting his hands from the heat.

"Dumbass timer." Logan tossed the oven mitts on top of the offending dish.

I peered over his shoulder and good lord, he'd mummified a chicken. The flesh was so darkened and shrivelled it looked like it had been set out in the sun to dry in the manner of sundried tomatoes. I wasn't really sure the poor bird could be saved.

"Frigging hell." Logan tore the baking bag open and steam exploded from the confined space. The smell wasn't so divine anymore. It was more like ... burned food. Logan's shoulders slumped and despite this mess, I was touched.

"Did you cook for me, Logan Hays?" I teased.

"Not exactly."

I couldn't hide my smile. "You did so, and I love it."

"Yeah, well, it's ruined. The timer was supposed to turn the oven off, damn it."

I hooked my fingers around his waist and spun him to face me. "Well, I love the fact you thought to cook for me."

He pressed a quick kiss to my lips. "How about some pizza?"

"Sounds delicious."

Ten minutes later we were standing in Mozzarella's ordering from a blonde girl chewing gum. The way she eyed Logan over made me feel all prickly, but when she recited back the order I smiled politely and said, "Thanks." Then I slid my arm around his waist, and brushed a kiss across his lips.

She frowned and by god, it made me feel good.

Someone must have told Jordan his brother was here, because he emerged from out the back, wringing his hands on a red apron. There was a cheekiness to his expression that made it obvious he and Logan were siblings; that half-turned smile and those dancing blue eyes.

"What happened to the wining and dining?"

"I don't need it," Logan said, a little too quickly.

Jordan threw his head back and laughed. "You killed it, didn't you? You can't cook for shit, Logan."

Logan lurched forward and snapped his arm around Jordan's head, rubbing his knuckles in his brother's unruly dark hair. Jordan continued laughing and whipped his foot around Logan's leg. They scuffled back and forth until Logan had his brother in a vice-lock once again.

"Give?" Logan said.

"Never."

Logan let go anyway. "Get back to work before they fire your ass."

Jordan saluted then turned on his heel like an army cadet and marched toward the door marked *staff only*. As he reached out to grab it, he turned over his shoulder and said, "I'll cab it tonight. Don't bother dragging your girl out to pick me up."

I jumped in and said, "It's fine. I don't mind."

"Seriously, dude. I'm cool." Jordan pulled the hair net back on his head, tucking in his shaggy dark locks. Logan yanked his wallet out of his back pocket and Jordan held his hands up. "I don't need your money for a cab. It's cool." Then he shoved through the door.

"Ham and Pineapple, pan base." The gum-girl looked at Logan too closely again and fumbled with the coin she was playing with. Yeah, she needed to pay more attention to the till and stop ogling customers.

Logan and I both moved at the same time, but I grabbed the box off the counter and showed her a huge smile. One that said yep-he's-hot-and-he's-mine.

We drove back to his place and devoured the pizza, then settled into the couch to watch TV. Not that there was much on, just another reality show. The television powers that be needed to get with the program and realise everyone was over watching people make fools of themselves on-screen. Or maybe it was just me who'd rather a good drama or sitcom.

Didn't matter, though; I enjoyed being snuggled in Logan's embrace, with my legs curled around to the side, pointing away from us, and my head in the crook of his arm. My gaze was set on the TV, but my attention wandered as I trailed my fingers along his thickly-muscled thigh. Little strokes at first, just back and forth almost aimlessly while my mind ticked over our day and got stuck on what he'd said about his parents. It was the first time he'd ever mentioned them, and the thought of anyone treating him and Jordan that way made me feel icky.

Logan's chest snagged, stopping its steady rise and fall. I froze, wondering what was wrong, then noticed my fingers were almost at the inside top of his thigh. He let out a shaky breath and I trailed my fingers back down the rough jeans to his knee, then dragged them back to where they were, a slow and teasing path.

The hand that rested on my hip moved and in an instant Logan swung me up onto his lap.

This time my breath caught.

His lips slammed into mine and I'm not sure what it was about tonight, but it was different. Desperate. He grasped my hip with one hand, the other fisted in my ponytail, and our legs were in a tangle, but it wasn't enough. I needed him closer, needed to feel him. Maybe it was because all of our pretences were stripped away or just because my feelings had grown so strong.

His fingers spread over my hip, their tips reaching my waist just under my shirt. My senses rippled with his touch. His fingers glided over my skin, leaving a blazing trail in their wake and I moaned. This was exactly what I needed; Logan's skin on mine.

I moved my hand from where it caressed the soft stubble on his jaw and slid it underneath the back of his shirt, gliding my palm to the warm skin at the hollow of his back. But that still wasn't enough. I splayed my hand over the contours of his side, the dip of his waist and onto his firm stomach. The muscles felt magnificent under my palm, slight rises and dips barely there, all hard as stone.

Logan sucked in a sharp breath, breaking the lock of our lips.

"I'm not going to be able to—" Logan's warned.

"So don't," I said.

His lips came back on mine in an instant, claiming what was his. A hand edged up my back to tease the skin just below my bra. My hand curled into his chest which felt firm against me. Funny, we'd been friends all this time, and together for weeks; I'd imagined what he'd feel like but nothing compared to the hard muscles beneath my hands and the way they felt under my fingers. I could explore his perfect body for the rest of the night and still not be sated.

Which is exactly what I intended to do.

IT MUST have been after midnight when the front door opened then closed. My body still hummed from the hours of showing Logan just how I felt about him. He was breathing softly, his arms and legs tangled around me in his bed. I had no idea how I was going to get out of this, but I couldn't sleep here. It just wasn't an option when I touched myself the way I did. It was pretty late, but I'd have to brave the walk.

Gently, I picked up his wrist and moved his arm off me.

Then I used my foot to inch his leg off the top of my thigh. Untangling his limbs from mine was like unlocking one of those wooden puzzles. Just as I was sliding out of bed, Logan's gravelly voice said, "Where are you going?"

"Jordan's home and I need to go home, too."

"Stay. Jordan won't care."

I fished my bra off the floor and put it on, then shrugged into my shirt. Logan's hand caught mine and pulled me onto the bed. My back arched over his side as he laid baby kisses up my arm.

I wanted to stay, more than anything I'd ever wanted before. To lie here all night, wrapped in his embrace, and maybe start our exploration over again in the morning. The little voice in my head said that maybe nothing would happen if I did, that my sleep issue would lay dormant. Maybe it would be okay. But I wasn't prepared to risk it.

Logan meant too much, so I tore my gaze away from his. "I can't."

I'm sure he was waiting for a reason, but I didn't give one because I couldn't lie to him. Logan released my arm and swung his legs over the side of the bed, the sheet covering him strategically as he pulled on a pair of sweat pants.

He drove me back to college in complete silence.

"Good night, Logan."

The Corolla idled for a few moments while tension thickened the air. It was too much. It wasn't because of him and I needed him to see that, so I leaned over the seats and grabbed the front of Logan's jacket, using it to pull him to me. The kiss I left him with was anything but timid, but when I pulled back, he still looked a little hurt.

I despised seeing that in his eyes, but it was far better than seeing the same hatred in his gaze that I'd seen in Christian's.

Chapter 20

THINGS WERE a little weird for a few days, but they eventually evened out. Playing along as if I hadn't left in the middle of the night helped. So did not being able to keep my hands off Logan. And boy, that wasn't hard. Every kiss, every touch wanted to turn into something more. That made it near impossible to be around other people, and sitting in my room with Savvy and Logan both there, it took every ounce of my concentration to keep up with the conversation.

"Why not?" I said, leaning my back against Logan who had his long legs curled around either side of me.

Savvy jumped up and down on the spot. She'd probably come into this with an argument prepared, expecting me to say no, but it was her birthday so I couldn't decline. Besides, a night out sounded like fun.

It wasn't an Oxley function, she just wanted to hit the clubs, enjoy a night of dancing and have some fun. There was nothing too scary about that and I hadn't been out in forever. Logan's chest pushed against my back as he leaned forward and pressed his lips against the spot under my ear. His touch sent a shiver rippling down my spine to settle as tingles low in my tummy. It sure was a feeling that would never grow old.

His stubble prickled my ear and I shivered again as his voice rumbled against my skin. "Sounds like fun."

"Ooh, I need to figure out what to wear." Savvy bounded toward my door. "Let's head up at say ..." Her eyes rolled up as she probably did some sort of backward math in her head "... nine."

"Sure," I said. That would give us a couple of hours to grab dinner and get organised.

The door slammed behind her and Logan resumed kissing the most sensitive spot on my neck. It felt so good, I wasn't sure going out was the right choice. I closed my eyes and tipped my head to the side. "We'd better duck out and grab something to eat."

Logan didn't cease his attentions; instead his lips moved across my shoulder until his teeth grazed my earlobe. I moaned and he said, "Let's just stay in."

"Savvy will kill us if we don't go."

"It'll be worth it." His hand fanned across my tummy, his long fingers reaching the base of my bra and that was it. The conversation was over.

I PULLED on my black tights and slipped the red dress Savvy loved to borrow over my head, then tugged on a pair of heeled boots. Logan was still stretched out on my tiny bed, half under the covers.

"When are you going to get dressed?"

"Umm …" He puckered his lips, thinking. "When are you going to come back to bed?"

"It's already ten past nine. Come on, Romeo, we need to get moving."

He didn't move so much as a finger. "I preferred it when you called me Stalker Boy. Romeo's a little insulting; that dude married a girl he'd only known for two days. They'd kissed once."

"It was love at first sight."

Logan groaned and I scooped his jeans up off the floor and tossed them at him just as someone rapped on my door. I raised my eyebrows and widened my eyes to hurry him along, even though I would have preferred he stayed naked. Chuckling, he slid the jeans over his hips and the knock sounded again, more insistent.

"Coming," I yelled, running a brush through my long hair then reaching for the doorknob. I yanked it open and Savvy stood on the other side, glancing at her watch.

"We said nine. Oh, for Christ's sake, Logan, put a shirt on!" The grin on her face negated her disapproving words, and I smiled in response while Savvy tapped her foot impatiently. "Let's go already."

Logan pocketed a bunch of his stuff off my desk and as his keys jangled, Savvy asked, "Are you driving?"

"Sure."

My friend practically bounced down the stairs and we

followed. Maybe she'd been drinking already. When we emerged into the courtyard I was surprised to see her join a small group of people. She hadn't mentioned anything about anyone else coming, but this was Savvy—I should have known better. She gestured in our direction and Molly jogged over to join us. The way she was dressed wasn't like Molly at all ... she looked like she'd just stepped out of Savvy's wardrobe. With the exception of the Dr Martens boots which looked a little ridiculous coupled with the black and white designer dress which fell mid-thigh. Regardless, it was good she'd managed to keep a little of herself. Sometimes with Savvy that was hard.

"You're coming?" Molly asked.

Glancing over at the group which included Dane, I nodded a little apprehensively. There wasn't anyone there that I was particularly worried about, but the taunts of last term were still fresh in my mind. "It's her birthday, of course I'm coming."

Molly bumped her fist to my arm. "About time you acted like a college girl. It'll be fun."

"We're going to drive, you want a lift?"

Molly glanced back at the group and shrugged. "That'd be great."

Logan drove us into town while Savvy chattered non-stop. Apparently Dane coming tonight was a good thing. Logan had offered his mate a ride, but Dane said he'd catch the bus with everyone else and we'd meet up there. This town had a ridiculous number of drinking holes, but tonight we were heading to The Royal. It had a DJ after ten and a small dance floor, plus plenty of places to sit and chat. Perfect, according to the birthday girl.

As we walked in, Logan snagged my hand in his. The music was already playing, but only as background noise. The lights were low and the air slightly hazy. My friends made a bee-line for the bar and I led Logan toward several tables that had been dragged together that should be big enough once everyone got here.

I glanced over at the bar; a drink would be nice. I didn't want to have too much, not after the incident at The University Bar.

"What do you want to drink?" Logan asked.

"Umm," I stalled. "I'll get something in a minute."

He let his fingers drop from mine, and said, "I'll be back in a bit."

I watched him swagger up to the bar. Gosh, I was lucky; not only was he hotter than most Bonds underwear models, Logan was an awesome guy. I'd never had a male best friend before, but I sure felt as close to him as I was to Savvy or Molly. I turned around and took a seat near the end of the table.

No sooner had I sat than Savvy edged into the seat directly across from me, giggling like a silly schoolgirl as she set down three drinks she'd carried in the triangle of her hands. They were all clear, but I'd bet my last twenty they weren't water. Molly arrived next with a tray full of shot glasses that she also set on the table. Then she plopped down beside me. "Happy Birthday!" she shouted across the table, sliding a shot to the space in front of Savannah.

Savvy's grin spread wide and she squealed, "What is that?"

"It's your birthday celebration." Molly skated another drink along the table which stopped right in front of me.

"No way," I said. "I'm not doing any shots. Especially not something ... is that green?"

Molly laughed. "You'll love it."

I'd be sloshed in under ten minutes was more like it.

"Come on," Savvy pleaded. "It's my birthday, and all I want is to drink and dance with my best friend."

I pushed the green away. "Your puppy dog eyes aren't going to work on me."

Savvy lifted her cup and took a tentative sniff. "Smells like liquorice."

Molly pushed the tiny glass back onto the ring of liquid it had left right in front of me then raised her cup across the table. Savvy's eyebrow beckoned for me to follow suit, and with a sigh I picked up the sticky glass and clinked it against theirs with a, "Happy Birthday." Then I tipped my head back and drained the thing in a single gulp. My throat burned, and good lord it tasted nothing like liquorice. The stuff was a vile mix of sugar, liquid fire, and pure alcohol. I slammed the shot glass onto the table and the look on Savvy's face must have matched my own; horrified. She shoved one of the three glasses of clear liquid toward me and I grabbed it, gulping down the sweet fluid to rid my mouth of the previous horrid taste.

"You guys are wusses." Molly laughed. "That stuff is awesome."

"If you like setting your throat on fire," Savvy said.

The burning spread to my belly, but my throat wasn't right so I finished off the lemonade Savvy had given me. Logan returned and took a seat by my side, placing a cola in front of himself and something that looked suspiciously like more alcohol in front of me. "Are you guys trying to get me drunk?"

Molly choked on her drink. "Loosen up, Olivia. It's not every day Savvy says goodbye to her teens."

"Yeah," Savannah said. "Twenty's ancient. I'm like … almost an adult. Before you know it, I'll be all old and wrinkled."

"Pfft, you'll never be old," I said.

Our banter was broken by the arrival of the rest of our group. I knew all of them by name, even though we rarely spoke. Most were Savvy's teaching friends that I'd never really gotten to know beyond the surface. That's the way it was when you were a friend to everyone. There wasn't enough time to really *know* anyone. Savvy must have become friends with them through shared classes. She and I had such different courses, I sometimes wondered how we'd buddied up in O-week last year. I guess it was her epic love of socialising, and my need to be known. I smiled at that while ignoring the familiar spread of warmth through my body as the hellish shot kicked in.

Savvy's friends crowded in around her and Logan leaned closer to talk in my ear. "Enjoy yourself. I'm driving, so you don't need to worry about getting home."

"What's in the drink?" I asked and he gave me one of his crooked smiles.

"Mostly lemonade."

"And …" I coaxed him.

"Bit of this, bit of that."

"Logan," I warned, eying off the drink which was also green. "It's not the same poison Molly just made us down is it?"

"Nope." He dropped a kiss at the corner of my mouth.

"Whoa, dude. When did that happen?" Dane's voice boomed from the other end of the table. "About bloody time!"

Logan pulled my hand into his and threaded our fingers together. His answer to Dane was no more than a smile. A smile that made me feel as if he was proud of being with me, and damn, if I wasn't proud of him too. Logan was sweet, and kind, and darn sexy with his unique style. Whenever I was around him I felt like everything was right. I'd never been happier. Here I was with a hunky guy who actually cared about me. Feeling all warm and gooey, I squeezed his hand and took a tiny sip of the drink.

Good heavens, it was some sort of sweet fruity nectar of the gods. I wasn't going to get drunk though, so I'd have to sit on this one all night. If it was even alcoholic. It sure didn't taste it, but who was I kidding, he'd told me to drink up. Leaning back, I eyed up the size of the hourglass-shaped glass—what'd they call that? —I should know, Mum had always encouraged using things' proper names. My head was a little light, and I had a definite buzz going, but that was okay, I could manage it. *Hurricane.* That's what it was called, a hurricane glass. Wait ... weren't they used for cocktails?

Molly jabbed me in the ribs, and my gaze slipped to her. She gave me a massive grin. "Having fun, sweet cheeks?"

"Sweet cheeks, Molly? Sometimes you're crazy."

She nodded toward Savvy, who had a collection of glasses on her table space. "Her hand's empty. We should get her another drink."

I frowned. "No more green hellfire."

247

Molly jumped up out of her chair and beckoned me to follow, but I wasn't moving. I felt too relaxed. Logan's thumb was stroking sweet circles over the soft skin between my thumb and pointer finger, and that sensation wasn't worth leaving just to follow Molly to the bar. Besides, Savvy didn't need another drink yet. She needed to take a rest after that shot, and the several other empty glasses in front of her.

"She doesn't need another one yet. Water might be good though."

I took another sip of my heavenly green drink. I'd tasted something like this before. It was a sweet melon flavour with a hint of something cocunuty. "Midori Splice?" I asked Logan and he smiled.

"Take it slow, Liv."

A glance at the glass showed that I'd drunk less than a third, which was slow. I rolled my eyes and slunk down in my seat. Good heavens, it was comfy. Molly returned with more of those atrocious shots … only on closer inspection they weren't the same. These ones were black. She pushed one into Savvy's hands then slid one in front of me.

"Hell no," I said.

"Come on," Molly dragged it out in a plea.

"Nah-uh." I shook my head.

"What the hell," Savvy said. "I'll only turn twenty once." And she downed the dark liquid in a single gulp.

Molly clapped.

Savvy's gaze met mine across the table and she sang, "Livia," with a quirk of her brow.

No way was I touching that stuff.

"Don't call me Livia."

She said my name again, and then once more before Molly joined in and it somehow became an O-livia chant.

I sucked back a deep breath 'til my lungs felt tight.

"Leave it be," Logan said. "Liv's had enough." *My knight in shining armour.* I wanted to hug him, so I did. Tossing my arms around his neck, my chair felt a little wobbly and Logan pushed me away. My heart did a funny stop-start as my tummy dipped.

"Just stopping you from hurting yourself," he explained, pressing a hand against the corner of my chair. The leg clapped against the floor.

"Whoopsie." I licked the sweet remnants of my drink from my bottom lip.

"Party pooper," Molly said.

I could cope with that; I'd been called far worse. I bumped her with my shoulder and suddenly, music erupted out of nowhere. It was loud and poppish and thrummed through my whole body.

"Dance?" Savvy said.

I jumped to my feet and grabbed her hand across the table, singing, "I love this song!"

"Duck," Savvy warned, but Molly didn't manage in time, so our hands tangled around her and came apart. We both squealed with laughter. I tugged on Molly's arm, urging her to come with us. She didn't take any persuading, turning to join in the fun.

The three of us were amongst the first on the wooden dance floor, but it filled quickly around us. Savvy threw her hands in the air in her trademark dance style, her glittery top riding up to show off her midriff. Molly hooted.

It felt freaking awesome to move in time with the music buzzing through me. I always did like dancing, and it had been way too long. Some of Savvy's friends shimmied up beside her and I glanced back toward the table where Logan sat chatting with Dane. His gaze met mine across the room and he winked.

Good god, that man was sexy without even trying.

He turned away abruptly, and in those few seconds we'd been flirting across the room, Dane had stood up, and was talking to Christian.

Where did he come from? My ex had his hands stuffed in the pockets of his jacket, and he glanced down at Logan, who didn't bother to stand. In fact, Logan looked a little pissed off. They both did.

A forceful tap on my shoulder drew my attention around to Molly who pointed to Savvy. The birthday girl held her hands out across the circle of her dancing friends and wriggled her fingers at me. Knowing exactly what she wanted, I grabbed her hands and we came together in the centre. There was something about dancing that was almost the same feeling as being on the hockey field. Out here with my best friend, I could let my guard down and just have fun. It felt mighty good not to care, even though I probably should have. Pity my gaze kept flitting back to Logan.

What did Christian want with him?

After we'd danced so long I felt all loose and slightly wobbly, I moved back to my spot beside Molly. Glancing over my shoulder, I saw that Logan hadn't moved. He didn't look happy. Dane sat beside him, bent forward with his forearms balanced on his lap and his hands gripping one another. Whatever they were talking about seemed serious.

Molly tapped my shoulder and raised her hand to her mouth in a gesture meaning she wanted a drink. I felt kind of parched too, but dancing was good. Dancing was wonderful. I never wanted to stop dancing. So I shook my head and grinned. The music morphed from pop to an older song and our group grew smaller. They must have all needed a rest. A strobe light started flickering and Savvy jumped in and out of my vision, the sweat on her brow shining in the white light.

The beat of this song was fast and the bass thumped in time with my heart. My blood felt as if it were dancing through my veins. The room flashed to black again and my hand was caught from behind. Smiling, I pulled him in behind me, but Logan didn't give, just tugged on my hand to draw me off the dance floor.

Now who was the party pooper? In the next flash of white, Savvy's happy dance face slipped to surprised, her eyes wide and mouth slightly open.

"Can we talk?" A husky voice spoke in my ear and I spun around, tugging my hand out of his grasp.

Christian's gaze met mine, set in determination.

"What are you doing here?" I said. "You didn't come with us, just Dane. 'Cause Savvy likes him."

Oops. Did I actually just say that out load? *Filter, Olivia, find it!*

Christian's gaze rolled over me, and was he looking at my chest?

The dirty perv. I pressed my finger into his chest. "Why the hell did you tell the entire university that I touch myself in my sleep? That was a jackass thing to do, and you know what?" I waited for him to answer, but Christian didn't. Maybe his mouth wasn't working right either. Mine seemed a few seconds too fast for my thoughts, or maybe it was my thoughts that were too slow for my mouth. Either way, the words had blurted out before I could stop them. "Well?"

His gaze moved to mine. "I'm sorry. I never should have said that, no matter if it was true, but I was just so tired, Livie. So goddamn tired all the time. Sleep deprivation—"

I raised my hands and slammed them right into his chest. "Sorry is bullcrap, Christian. You ruined my life."

He stumbled back and kept talking. "I didn't mean it. I didn't mean for any of it to happen."

"Well, it did."

Christian reached for me, trapping my upper arm in his hand. His touch made my blood turn to ice. I wasn't exaggerating when I said he'd ruined my life. He had ruined my career aspirations. A few good things had come out of this mess, like our break-up, Logan, and my new friendship with Molly. I wasn't about to give him credit though.

"Please, Olivia, forgive me. We were so good together. We ..." Christian's gaze flicked behind me. He pulled me toward him, and I had too many feet. They got twisted around each other and stumbling forward, my chest crashed into his and Christian's arms wrapped around me. He smelled like musky aftershave, and scotch, and completely familiar. My body wanted to melt into his embrace. It started to, but I couldn't.

Wouldn't.

Jerking my hands into the space between us, I shoved

away from him, but Christian's hold was too strong. It didn't break. "Get your hands off me."

He didn't. He must have thought forcing me to hug him would make everything better.

"Let her go," Savvy yelled, and Christian's hold on me released slowly, reluctantly.

The jerk had held me on purpose, and my arm stung where his fingers had dug in. His gaze dropped to my chest again and without a second thought, my hand connected with his cheek in a ringing slap.

Christian reeled back then lunged forward, his hands gripping my arms again. "Livie," he pleaded.

"Get your fucking hands off her."

Logan.

Suddenly he was there, prying Christian's fingers from my left arm.

A look of pure hatred came over Christian's face, highlighted by my hand print shining on his left cheek. "Are you with him now?"

My glance caught Logan's, and Christian said, "You are."

I'm not sure how it happened but somehow his fist slammed into Logan's face and my man skidded backward a few feet. "Creep," I growled, punching Christian in the chest. My other fist followed the first, and he was like a solid brick wall, but I kept pounding into him. "It's none of your damn business who I'm with."

Someone pulled me away, and I struggled to get free. But Logan was there, punching my ex in the face when I couldn't and damn, Christian deserved it.

"Logan!" Dane's voice boomed from behind me. He

swooped in, pushing between the two guys with a hand on each of their shoulders.

But Christian shoved him away, and then neither one was paying Dane any attention. People crowded around. Logan hurled a fist that connected with Christian's chin. And my ex bounced right back, socking Logan so hard I heard a crack. A circle had formed around them as everyone on the dance floor stopped to stare. Dane grabbed Logan by his shirt and yanked him back.

Christian took the second's reprieve to make eye contact. "He's not right for you, Olivia."

The anchor on my arm fell away and I surged forward, flying at Christian in a Miss Piggy-style move. Two moments after my body slammed into his I was surrounded by iron-tight arms.

"Logan," Dane growled. "With me. Now!"

"Bastard needs—"

"Right now, damn it." Dane's voice was too close to my ear and too loud. Savvy shrank as either her or I moved further away. I didn't feel like I was moving, I felt like I was being held. I fought to get away, but my feet couldn't find purchase. They were dangling in the air. Where did the ground go?

"Logan," Dane warned, right in my ear.

They'd moved away and I couldn't see a darn thing through the crowd.

"Time to leave." A voice I didn't know.

"Come on, Logan. Let it be ... for Jordan," Dane said, his voice vibrating through my back where he'd pinned me to him.

There was another loud crack, like a fist thunking into

solid bone, and the unfamiliar voice snarled, "I'll throw you all out if I have to."

Must be a bouncer. I stopped fighting against Dane, and he growled, "For Christ's sake, Logan, if not for Jordan then for Kayla."

"Fuck," Logan growled, and he sounded different; still angry, but different.

I don't know if it was Dane's tight grip on my middle or the tension of the fight, but I felt like I needed to vomit.

"Let me go," I demanded, but Dane didn't. He tucked me into his side and started walking. Everything spun and then we were outside. A strong arm tight around me, holding me up because my legs were like liquid. Abso-freaking-lutely useless.

"Get in the car," Dane ordered and a door squeaked open. He dropped me onto the back seat and closed the door. Good lord, I was tired. Maybe if I just closed my eyes the sick feeling would disappear. Another door opened and closed.

"Logan?" I asked.

His arm curled around me while he reached for the seatbelt with his other hand and buckled me in. The car started, but how was it moving when Logan was beside me? It wasn't the future; we didn't have hover cars, yet. Didn't matter. I collapsed against his shoulder and closed my eyes.

My arm shook. A gentle nudge at first then a little more fiercely. Groaning, I opened my eyes and the world spun. Whoa, not good. I snapped them shut again.

"Wake her up. We're home." Was that Dane? What was he doing?

The cushiness of the seat fell away from underneath me. The world really was spinning. Lurching almost. A warm firmness appeared under my cheek. *Logan?* I drew in a deep breath. *Yep, Logan.* Curling into him, I left myself drift off again.

They were shouting.

Everyone was shouting.

I forced my eyes open and Logan sat on the couch across from me. His ugly brown couch at his apartment. I tried to smile, but my mouth didn't want to co-operate with my thoughts. There was blood on his face, all across his cheek which was red and swelling. He needed to ice it. I should grab him some from the freezer. As soon as I could make my tired legs work. Whatever made my thoughts connect with my actions wasn't working. Good lord, I was drunk.

"You're no better than Dad," Jordan shouted.

A door slammed and I flinched. Not physically, but mentally. Maybe I only blinked. Logan reefed his shoe off and tossed it. A loud crash sounded then another as the other shoe followed.

"Need to go home," I said, but my voice wouldn't work loud enough.

"You two need to calm the hell down," Dane said. "Put Olivia to bed, man, then get your shit together."

The front door slammed.

The room continued spinning, but my eyes were too heavy to care.

MY HEAD pounded like the beat of a bass drum. Surely each thud slammed my tender head against concrete and my mouth, good lord, it felt as if something had curled up inside it and died, sucking all moisture out in the process. I groaned and pulled myself into a tighter ball. Bad idea. My stomach lurched violently at the movement.

An arm flopped over me and my eyes sprung open to a cream wall covered with music posters rather than the white painted cement render of my college room.

I was at Logan's.

In his bed.

With him.

I'd stayed overnight.

And I'd slept.

My lungs burned. I'd stopped breathing or something. I gasped in a lungful of cold air and my eyes stung just as badly as my throat. This wasn't happening, couldn't be happening. I just couldn't.

Logan would have seen everything.

So much for a quiet night with only one drink. I was such a Cadbury. Just a glass and a half and I was plastered. How the hell had I wound up here instead of at my place? If I was so drunk I couldn't remember getting home then my little disorder no doubt would have reared its embarrassing head.

Who was I kidding all this time?

I couldn't have a relationship. I couldn't be with Logan if we couldn't share the same bed. I was broken beyond repair and there was no way that would ever be okay.

I swung my legs around and sat up. My tummy felt like a roiling ocean. *Ignore it.* I grabbed my boots off the floor and tugged them on.

I couldn't be here.

I couldn't ever be here, and I sure as hell couldn't turn around and see Logan's face. The sight of him sleeping peacefully would be too much to bear. I hugged my arms around myself and the huge t-shirt that had somehow found its way onto me, then I tiptoed to the door. My dress was slung over the back of the couch and my purse lay on the coffee table. I snatched up both.

"You can't do this to him again," Jordan said. He must have been in the kitchen.

Holding my breath to stop the ache in my throat from exploding, I didn't turn around to face him either. "I won't."

And I wouldn't. This would be the last time I walked away from Logan, ever. Just like it would be the last time I was ever in this apartment. Logan deserved so much better than the issues I brought to the table.

As I pulled the front door closed behind me, and walked down the drive, the tears came. Unable to hold them back anymore, sobs tore from somewhere near my heart and with my dress in my hand, and still wearing my shoes from the night before, I took the walk of shame back to Oxley.

The Reality

Chapter 21

THERE'S ONLY so long you can stare at the same sentence before the words in it disconnect from one another, then those words start to lose all meaning.

We need to talk about last night.

Talk was an ambiguous word. It could mean that he wanted to have a two-way discussion, or more likely he had something even shorter than that text to say. In which case, he'd be the only one talking.

Yeah, those seven words scared the life out of me.

We: there was no we anymore.

Last night: it had happened, and there was no way I could make it unhappen.

Need to talk: I sure as hell didn't want, let alone need,

to talk about it. The only things that could be said would be words like, 'I can't see you anymore' or 'What in the hell were you doing' or 'I should have believed those rumours' or maybe even 'You felt yourself up right beside me'.

People say masturbation isn't a dirty thing; it's natural, everybody does it, and it's just a part of life. I couldn't agree more. But when you have no control of over what you do to your own body and in the presence of whom, it sure as heck feels dirty. And right now, I felt dirtier than a prostitute straddling her third client of the night.

I didn't want to talk about it. We were over and that's all there was to it. I couldn't be with someone with my condition. It just wouldn't be fair to expect understanding. Expect sleeplessness. I needed to face the fact that I'd be alone forever. I'd sink everything I had into a career.

Cradling my phone in my hands, I stared at the screen for so long the words blurred. Again. He'd sent this message two hours ago—it had been almost three hours since I'd walked out, and I felt like my heart was bleeding. I hadn't responded, because I couldn't. How do you tell someone you cared about over text message that it's over?

You didn't.

That was the cowardly way out. Equal to walking out at six a.m. I wasn't ready to face him yet. Heck, the way I'd been feeling last night, I was pretty sure that I loved him, and that only made this whole thing a billion times worse. I shouldn't have let myself get into such a mess. I curled myself into a tight ball under the covers on my bed, and holding the phone to my chest, I cried.

Like the words, time blurred.

Sometime later there was a knock on my door. I'd been expecting it, but that didn't make it any easier. I pulled my head under the covers as Logan bashed on the door and said my name. I wasn't ready for his talk. I still didn't know what to say. It stopped after a few minutes and a silent sob tore from my aching throat. Then my phone rang. I stuffed it under my pillow, but it was too late.

"I know you're in there, Olivia, I can hear your phone. Please ..." Something broke inside of me, right near where my heart lived. "Let me in."

I covered my face with my hands and held my breath to keep everything inside of me. I couldn't ... I couldn't look him in the eye and share that knowledge. I'd have to eventually, but not right now.

Logan stayed out there way longer than I thought he would. He didn't knock again, but I knew he was there because I could hear him talking. At first I thought he was speaking with someone in the hallway, but when I crept to the door and slid down against it, I could hear his words more clearly. They were like a mantra.

"Please ... stop running."

I turned around and pressed my cheek against the cold wood, my palm right beside it, and I didn't try to stop my heart from tearing.

MAYBE IT was a sick obsession or maybe it was a need to know for certain; a desperate plea that maybe, possibly, there was an iota of hope that I could be with Logan.

That I wasn't really broken after all.

I twisted the computer around to point at my bed and opened up the program Google had directed me to for the job I wanted to carry out, then I clicked the appropriate buttons, switched off the lights and climbed into bed. My heart beat a nervous rhythm. There was so much relying on this single night.

That's probably why sleep didn't come easily.

I tossed and turned and tossed some more. I thought about Logan and about last night. How I was a coward for walking out on him while he slept. How I could have possibly gotten that drunk. There was the vile shot then the cocktail Logan gave me. The lemonade from Savvy must have been laced too. Heck, maybe I'd had more drinks than just those three. My memory was a little hazy after we started dancing, just flashes here and there, not a solid block from point A in time to point B. That somehow made me more nervous. I couldn't even remember how I got to his house, or why I would have suggested going there instead of coming back here.

I sat up and yanked my hair back off my face, twisting it into a braid. Maybe a glass of water would help me to settle. I tiptoed out of my room and down the hall. It was late, but there were still doors open and lights on. Thankfully none I had to pass in order to reach the kitchenette. I filled my glass from the tap and made my way back to my room. Just as I reached for the door, I saw it.

A bunch of autumn leaves pinned to my door.

My heart constricted at the message he'd left me and I pulled the door closed behind me, switched the light off and crawled back into bed, my mind torturing me with happy images of Logan. The day he'd taken me to the waterfall, the afternoon at the lookout, the first time we'd made love. The stupid giant love heart I'd drawn in the autumn leaves. All the inconsequential hours spent doing absolutely nothing special. But that was just it. Time with Logan was never not special, and I was lucky to have stolen the little bit of precious time that I had.

He'd eventually left this afternoon. I felt terrible for not letting him in, but I couldn't stand to see the look on his face when he told me what happened last night. What I'd done in his bed. Beside him.

I needed to stop thinking about him if I was going to make my mind sleep.

One hundred.

Ninety-nine.

Ninety-eight.

Ninety-seven.

Asking someone to love you when you kept them awake every night doing inappropriate things just wasn't right.

Ninety-six.

Nor was it something I could ever do.

Ninety-five.

Ninety-four.

The countdown continued.

I WOKE up slowly, then with a sudden jolt as my mind kicked into gear and I remembered the webcam pointed

265

at my bed. I shot up and pressed stop, then hovered over the program, staring at the frozen image of me reaching for the mouse. The frigid air bit through my thin PJs and my skin broke out in goose bumps. Why was it always so flipping freezing here? It only took another few seconds of hovering before I caved and dove back into the warmth of my bed. It was as if I were torn in two. Part of me was dying to watch the footage and see how the night had played out, but the other part was scared out of her mind of what she'd see.

I couldn't hide in bed forever though. Or maybe I could. Maybe if I stayed here long enough, shoved my head deep under the covers, I'd wake up and it would have all been a bad dream. Or rather, a nightmare.

Not likely.

I hauled my butt out of bed along with the top blanket, and wrapped it around my shoulders, then with a resigned sigh, plonked myself in the swivel chair and clicked play. The night vision was kind of weird. Everything was in shades of grey and even though I was a shadow, I was clearly visible. The covers made me a mound though. Hopefully they wouldn't make it too hard to see. In retrospect, I probably should have cranked up the heat and slept on top of them. With each passing minute of nothing but the dark shape that was me tossing and turning, the anticipation made my empty tummy shiver and my legs bounce. I skipped through the first hour then sat and watched for about fifteen minutes. It was worse than reality TV.

Nothing happened, and I guess that was good.

I picked up my phone and the screen was black. Dead

Flat. Sighing, I put it on to charge. Then, with the video still playing, I started moving about my day; shoving books into my bag together with my purse and a few pieces of fruit. I still felt like crap and didn't want to face a day of classes, especially not Socio, but with each passing minute the image of me peacefully sleeping remained on-screen, and my mood felt a tad brighter. Maybe Logan and I weren't doomed after all.

I picked up my brush and ran it through my long hair, untangling the knot—

I froze.

I was moving.

On-screen.

The covers almost ... were they dancing? My heart dropped into my toes and I moved closer to the computer. The me on-screen had her head tipped back, her face away from the camera and her chin pointing upwards.Her back arched like a she couldn't get enough. Sound came from the speakers, but it wasn't clear enough to make out. I swallowed against a dry throat and turned the volume up.

Moaning. And not the kind you do when you're in pain. With a shaking hand, I clicked stop and fell onto my bed.

It was true. All true.

The nightmare wouldn't end.

I couldn't wake up because this was my reality.

I touched myself when I slept, and my life had gone to crap because of it. There was no coming back. I wouldn't be begging forgiveness from Logan.

It was over. For real.

Sometime later when my phone buzzed against the

desk, I opened my eyes enough to stare at it until it faded to a black screen. Even after, I couldn't drag my gaze away. Not until it buzzed again bringing the message on-screen to remind me I hadn't seen it earlier. Time to turn that feature off. I didn't need the second buzz. Heck, I didn't want the first. I dragged myself out of bed and picked it up.

A text from Logan.

Don't skip class because of me.

I couldn't summon enough *anything* to care. I tapped on the text which took me to our message history. There were a string of texts from him to me. A lump jammed in my throat, but I was a glutton for punishment so I read them all.

8.30: Where are you?

9.45: Wanna grab us bacon and egg rolls while you're out?

10.00: Liv, this isn't funny. Where the hell are you?

10.15: Jordan saw you leave. We've got to talk.

11.15: I'm coming over. We need to talk.

11.45: Liv, are you in? I want to speak to
you about last night.

Noon: I know you're home. Answer the
damn door, Olivia.

12.24 Please, Olivia. I know I went off the
rails last night, but I'm not like that. I don't
go around punching people, no matter how
shitty they are. I'm sorry. We've got issues.
Talk to me.

13.02 OLIVIA!!!!!!!!

15.08 Don't do this, Butterfingers. Let's
chat.

And just now,

10.07: Don't skip class because of me.

Right from the first one he'd sent yesterday morning,
up until the one a few moments ago. All his messages said
the same thing; he wanted to talk. Well, the proof of what
we'd be talking about was on my computer, so I didn't
need to hear it from him.

I crawled back in bed and didn't get out.

ON TUESDAY, I hauled myself out of bed, and I did the same again every day that week, even though I didn't feel like going to class. Just because I'd let my problems get the best of me the day before wasn't any excuse to let everything else slide. I still had an end goal to meet; graduate with honours. I didn't see Logan up top, but then I kept my attention focused on what I was doing—walking, talking, breathing—just to keep going. Turned out, attending class was a waste of time because by the end of the day I had no clue what the lessons had even been about, but at least I wouldn't earn any more fail incompletes for non-attendance.

On Saturday I stood in the freezing morning on the netball courts, jigging to keep myself warm. The tiny uniform was no help against the frigid air. No matter how many times Logan's voice replayed in my head, telling me not to bother with something I hate, I'd still showed up to play for my dorm. After all, I'd been the one to scrounge a team together and register it a few weeks ago. It would be both rude and reflect badly on myself to back out.

Molly eyed me off from her position in the goal circle and her gaze felt more like my mother's; weighing, appraising, finding me lacking. I glanced away quickly, and concentrated on the girl I was defending; a short, thin blonde thing whose nails looked far longer than was permitted for the game. The look she gave back to me was a challenge and that's what I hated about this sport. It was all snatches and scratches and filthy looks. The umpire blew the whistle and I passed the ball to my Goal Attack.

The game moved fast. Overall, netball was a much quicker moving game than hockey, and twice as vicious. I managed to get out of this game with no injuries. Molly however, copped a scraped knee and red gorges down her left arm, reminiscent of cat scratches. As we picked up our stuff and started the walk back to Oxley, her weighted gaze rested on me again. I wasn't about to buy into it though, so I kept my eyes set on the path ahead and didn't mention it. I even pulled one of the balls out and bounced it against the pavement as we walked to lighten the mood, and hopefully keep her from talking.

It didn't work.

The brown-trimmed front of our college came into view and Molly seemingly couldn't hold it in any longer. She practically blurted, "What happened?"

I inhaled, slow and steady to keep the ever-present burning in my throat and eyes in check. "Nothing."

She gave me a sideways look, but I didn't engage. After a few seconds the silence felt like a physical weight, and I couldn't stand it any longer. *Time to deflect.* "How'd you like your first game of netball?"

"Hated it," she said, "but for you, I'll play. Who knows, maybe I'll get to put some catty girl on her butt."

"Molly!"

She laughed. "Good to see you smiling, girl."

I heaved a long sigh as we walked over the arched bridge and into the ivy-covered Front Courtyard. The smell of brunch—fried eggs, bacon, and those other foods that were good for the soul—wafted on the faint breeze. I didn't really feel like eating though.

"Olivia." A finger jabbed me in the side. Molly nodded back toward Front Courtyard. "You going to say hi to Savvy or what?"

"What?"

"I didn't mean it literally. She's called out to us three times. Stop snubbing her."

I glanced back, and sure enough Savannah was sunning herself on the lush grass with a spread of text books and other girls around her. I waved, yelled hello, and moved on, because sitting around with a fake smile wouldn't happen today. My heart wasn't in it.

It wasn't until I was halfway up the stairs that I realised Molly was two steps behind me. "What are you doing?" I asked.

She shot me a wide grin. "Coming up for a chat."

"I don't want to chat."

"I don't care."

I unlocked my room, and tempted as I was to slam the door in Molly's face, I didn't. She kicked her shoes off, opened up my food cupboard and tossed a block of chocolate on the bed which she proceeded to open and snap into bite-sized pieces while I stood there, gobsmacked. The girl had no boundaries.

"Sit." She popped a square into her mouth. "Eat. This stuff's good for the heart and mmm ..." She broke off into a low moan "... your heart needs some mending."

I nearly said that it didn't, but I bit back the retort because I felt like gosh-darn crying again, and I was so tired of that feeling that I didn't trust myself to open my mouth. Molly raised a brow and patted my bed.

I perched on the edge and picked out a square of chocolate that had a huge nut protruding from the side, then placed it in my mouth.

"You guys were so happy. What happened?"

"We weren't right together. It just wasn't working."

"Bullshit."

"Pardon?"

"I know a lie when I hear it, Olivia. It's got something to do with those dumb-arsed rumours doesn't it?"

"They're true." My voice came out tiny.

Molly reached across the bed and grabbed my hand, which had begun to shake. "If he dumped you because of that, he's a jerk that isn't worth mourning."

I choked back a sob. "He didn't."

"What the what, Olivia?"

"I can't be with him, Molly. Not with all the issues I have, it just … it isn't right. I can't sleep in the same bed as him and not do it. I have absolutely no control, and that sucks. It really sucks. But it's life, and I have to deal with it."

She never asked how, or even if I knew if it was real, and for that I was grateful. Instead she pinned me with a penetrating gaze. "Honey, I'm so sorry."

"Me too."

We finished off the entire block of Fruit and Nut, piece by merciful piece. People say chocolate causes the brain to release the same chemicals you experience in orgasm, which was kind of ironic really. But it didn't make me feel any better, especially when we were left staring at the empty wrapper and my tummy felt a little queasy.

"I wonder if it's something that's …" Molly glanced away "… curable. There might be something you can do to fix it. Not that I think it's a bad thing, I mean it's just ... it's natural, right?"

"Don't sugar-coat it. It's awful."

"But clearly you're not happy, Liv. I mean, lots of people probably percolate along just fine and don't care. It probably doesn't affect their lives. But you're not happy ... and you hate it. So I wonder ... maybe a doctor—"

"No way." I shuffled back on the bed and pulled my knees into my chest. "I'm not going to sit in a doctor's office with a total stranger, and talk about touching myself every night. They'll probably want to do a freaking sleep study or something."

"My brother had a sleep test before he had his adenoids out. It's not so bad—"

"You think? They'd watch me. All night."

Molly flopped back against the wall. "Have you talked to Logan about it?"

"No!" My cheeks flared with heat and I dropped my head into my hands. That would be worse than talking to a doctor.

"Oh, honey." Molly's hand curled around my knee. "I think he'd understand."

"I will not tell him about it." I clenched my jaw to hold back the building tears. I missed Logan so much, but everything I'd said was true. It would be selfish to expect him to understand.

Molly jumped up and tugged on my hand until I stood too, then she threw her arms around me in the tightest hug. "Whatever you do, I'm here for you."

She was way too nice. The burning in my eyes overflowed into tears and I rasped out, "I just have to find a way to live with it."

It was late and we were both tired, so it wasn't long after that that she went back to her own room. Sometimes I was jealous of Molly and Savvy living in the same block, on the same floor. It would be nice to just walk out my door and knock on either of theirs whenever I felt like a chat, but then if they heard me during the night …

I slipped into my PJs, turned out the lights and climbed into bed. Today had been another long one. It wasn't the lectures or the assignments, or even the lack of trusted friends that made it drag on, but rather the fear of the night. Fear of where I was right now, lying in my bed, not knowing for certain what sleep would bring. Whether tonight would be the one I'd wake to find people huddled around my door, listening, laughing.

I tossed over onto my back and the sheets rustled. Whatever they did to the laundry here made the things so gosh-darn stiff.

Don't let it happen.

I rolled onto my tummy and shoved my hands up under the pillow, jamming them as tightly beneath my head as I could. Maybe that would help.

Don't do it.

My fingers went a little numb.

Just sleep.

In the morning I'd have no idea if I did or didn't. That was the worst part.

Please, sleep.

And there was no cure.

Only …

Sleep.

Chapter 22

THE NEXT few weeks were long. Not sleeping made some days feel like weeks, then crashing from exhaustion made others pass in the blink of an eye. Thankfully the times I did sleep, I was so dog-tired that I passed out cold. There was no other option—even the fear that I was making noises for everyone to hear couldn't fight fatigue.

I went to classes; I went to tutorials; I even submitted assignments. It wasn't my best work, but it was the best I could manage. Socio was particularly difficult. The first time I snuck in late and sat up the back of the room, but I needn't have bothered.

Logan never showed.

He didn't contact me either. Not a single text nor email, not even another wordless message pinned to my door. So why was I so miserable? This was exactly the way I'd wanted it to end, without actually having the talk about that night. But him giving in so easily twisted a pain inside me. It was wrong of me to want him to fight for us when I knew it wouldn't make a difference, but I still did.

I didn't spend a lot of time with Savvy or Molly either, despite Molly's constant drop ins. I was always too busy studying. Grades were of utmost importance. So much so that I planned to stay back during term break to work right through it. I needed to throw everything into my study if I was going to pull the results I needed. Even if I couldn't get into Deakin Parry anymore, I needed good grades to get a job somewhere.

With a whole afternoon ahead of me I left class, intending to study in the library. I had a major assignment due next week and needed access to the university database. The Law library had been crowded so I bypassed it for Dixon, planning to lose myself in one of the lower, more abandoned levels. As I walked under the bare trees, I stopped.

Sitting on the wall outside the library was Logan. The tall brunette I'd seen him with before was draped over his shoulder like some kind of human mink. He had his grandpa cap pulled low on his head, and his vintage jacket hung open over a black t-shirt. Dark glasses shaded his eyes, so I had no idea if he saw me. I quickly veered off-track and turned back toward the Law building. It was the way I'd come, not the way I needed to go, but the burning pain in my chest was more than I could bear and he hadn't seen me, so I'd just sneak home the other way and come back to the library tomorrow.

"Liv!"

I guess he had. I gulped a lungful of calming air and squeezed my eyes closed as I kept walking. His feet thudded against the pavement.

"Olivia." His hand closed around my arm. Thank gosh for the shield of my thick trench coat. "I know you heard me."

I drew in a shaky breath and turned to meet the guy I still held far too many feelings for. It was one of those stupid movie moments where we both stood, motionless, staring at each other, as if neither one of us could find the right words. Or any words at all.

Logan pushed the glasses up onto his head, and his gaze wandered over me slowly, making me hyper aware of each passing second. My breath caught until his eyes moved back to mine. Boring into me with a steady intensity, they were more bloodshot than a three-day hangover. What in the world had he been doing?

"Liv." He grimaced, as if I was the most disgusting thing he'd ever seen. "I want to be better."

My fingers twisted the hem of my sweater. That didn't make any sense. He didn't need to be better; he was already better than I could ever hope for. It was me who needed to improve, needed to be normal. Logan looked me right in the eyes with such desperation I almost flung my arms around him, but I had problems, and that was enough to keep those same arms pinned to my sides.

His Adam's apple bobbed, and he said, "Not again ... not like her."

Inwardly, I winced. "Is this about Kayla?"

Recognition flicked in his expression and hurt stabbed at my chest. This wasn't about me at all. It was about some other girl in his past. And I was tired of hearing her name.

"Liv, I can change. I'm not like that. I'm not like him."

A rip tore my hem, the force of my fingers unabated as I forced out the clichéd words that in this case were undeniably true, and we both knew it. "This isn't about you, Logan. It's about me."

"I just want you to be happy."

"It was never you that made me unhappy."

His hand hovered like he wanted to touch my face, but it fell away without contact. "Then why are you so goddamn unhappy?"

Couldn't he see? Didn't he know about my nocturnal condition? I dropped my gaze because I couldn't stand seeing the sympathy in his eyes any more than I could tell him. "Don't feel sorry for me."

Over his shoulder, the brunette hung around the library, waiting for him to come back. She looked slightly peeved, twirling her hair around her finger while glaring in our direction which just made me annoyed because I wanted to be normal too.

"You better get back to your friend." I turned and walked away, tamping down the ache that consumed me.

I ENJOYED Sociology far more than any of my Law subjects, which was probably why I worked on the essay rather than my major Law assignment I should have been doing. The essay wasn't due for another two weeks. The assignment, however, had a submission date of next Friday. Writing about the human condition, and the way we worked, was something fascinating that I could throw myself into without thinking about anything that related to me personally. Law just didn't offer that escape. My mind constantly wandered. The only problem with Socio was that I always had too much to say. My word count was at five thousand and the limit was three, so I had to cut out the waffle.

Staring at the screen with my chin propped on my hand achieved nothing, so I pulled myself away and grabbed my coffee mug, then shuffled down the hall to our kitchen, and flicked the kettle on. The concrete wall was cool against my back as I leaned against it and pressed the heels of my palms into my eyes.

"Olivia?" Molly's voice questioned from down the hall.

"In the kitchen," I yelled back.

She appeared in the doorway and nodded toward the kettle. "Yes, please."

I grabbed a spare mug from the drying rack, topped it with a tea bag and sugar then sat it beside mine.

"What's happening?" she said.

"Nothing. Just study."

She rolled her eyes. "When did you get so boring?"

"Ha!" I cringed at the sound of Ella's laugh. "She's always been boring. In high school she used to spend all lunch in the library studying. Move over." Ella pushed past Molly and into the tiny kitchenette that really couldn't fit three people. With a flourish, she snatched the mug I'd prepared for Molly off the bench. "This for me? Thanks."

"Speaking of high school," Molly said, "some people act like they're still there."

Ella's gaze rolled over my friend's classic Molly ensemble of a denim miniskirt and pink tights, topped off with a black jumper that sported a giant silver love heart. "And some dress like they're still five."

I plucked the cup out of Ella's hand and filled it with boiling water.

She opened the fridge, grabbed a can of soda and waltzed back down the hall, then stopped suddenly and turned over her shoulder. A smirk worthy of the twelve-year-old her I used to know played across her lips. "What did your parents think of lover boy?"

I frowned, trying to puzzle out what she meant, but before I could she laughed and disappeared into her room.

"She's a bitch," Molly said, passing me the made tea.

"Flipping, flapping, freaking ... yes! She told my parents about Logan. That day on the phone ..." And I was right "... Mum had threatened to cut me off if I didn't pull through on grades, and blamed it on *that boy*. It's the only way she could have known. I bet Ella told her mother knowing, no, expecting the gossip mill would take it straight back to my mother." Honestly, I was surprised Mum hadn't mentioned the sleeping thing.

"Like I said ..."

I stood aside to let Molly pass through into my room first, then pulled the door closed behind us. Molly was right. Ella was a right royal pain in the rear who had deliberately caused another problem for me, just like she'd done all year.

Molly took her favourite spot on my desk and sipped her tea while I moved toward the swivel chair and carefully sat down. Just as I was raising the cup to my lips, I noticed the empty space on my desk. The cup fell from my numb fingers.

My computer was gone.

ACCORDING TO the dean there wasn't a lot we could do. My room had been wide open, so there was no point calling for the cops to print the door. Our dorm was home to more than two hundred people, and there were often more than that onsite because people had visitors, and then there were all the other dorms nearby.

Unless I suspected someone in particular it would be near impossible to locate the thief. Of course, he logged the theft and reported it anyway. The best I could do though, was keep my eyes open in the hope whoever took it would be stupid enough to let me catch a glimpse of them with it. Not exactly easy when it was a black HP, just like so many others. My tablet, a wad of cash and some jewellery also went missing. But it was my computer's absence that hurt most. I'd need to start from scratch on that essay, and the Law assignment too, and I had next to no notes, since I'd always used my tablet in lectures. I was doomed to fail again.

I felt sick at the amount of work I'd have to catch up on. The dean promised to write my lecturers to support my plea for extensions, and exemptions, and all sorts of 'sions. It didn't make me feel any better though. Nor did the fact I was working out of Oxley's computer lab. It wasn't a place I'd ever visited before, but I had no option. The computers lining the walls of the ample-sized room weren't bad, and I could work all right if the other people there worked quietly, which thankfully they were.

I logged into my emails, and there was a reminder from Bethanie that I needed to RSVP, so I flicked back a quick message telling her I'd be there with bells on, but I was passing on the plus one.

The door squeaked as some other poor soul, probably pulling an all-nighter, entered. Anyone that was coming down this late would surely be here until sunrise. Like I would be, just to get this Socio essay rewritten.

A waft of disturbed air hit me with someone plonking into the next spot, and Molly whispered, "I ordered pizza. Come wait with me. I'm sure you could use the break."

A huge sigh wound its way from me. I stretched my arms above my head. "Only if you intend to share, because I need sustenance to stay awake."

"I ordered Ham and Pineapple." Molly winked, and pushed up out of her chair. I clicked through to save my work to the flash drive which I ejected and popped in my jeans pocket. There was no way I'd lose this essay again.

"What time's it coming?" I asked, pushing the heavy glass door open.

"Any minute," Molly said.

We walked through the dark, deserted courtyard, and our shoes echoed off the mini bridge as we went to wait in the front car park. It didn't look like we'd be waiting long though, because the beam of headlights swung into the parking lot just as we arrived. The car skidded to a halt right in front of us, and my heart just about jumped through my throat. It wasn't at nearly being run over, either.

Logan's red Corolla idled there, and I took a step back, cursing my traitorous friend.

Molly grabbed my arm. "I swear ... it's not ... I just ordered pizza."

I wasn't sure I believed her. My heart sped up and slowed down all at the same time. I wanted to see him, but I didn't too. I gulped, my mind a swirl of confusing mixed emotions. Then a familiar dark head popped up from the driver's side door, and I could breathe again.

"Hey." Jordan beamed.

I swallowed down the ridiculous fear that had clawed its way into my throat. It was okay; it was just Jordan. No. Big. Deal. "Since when are you a delivery boy?"

"Since the other dude's sick, and I begged Logan to borrow the Corolla to pick up an extra shift." He lopped around the front of the car, tapping his hand off the hood, then yanked open the passenger door and pulled out a heat-proof red pizza bag.

"How've you been?" he asked, pulling out the square box.

"She's been terrible," Molly answered.

I positioned my foot over hers and pressed down. Hard.

"Good. I've been good, Jordan. How about you?"

"Miserable. I miss you. Sergeant Logan's making me exercise and clean up and study. It's like boot camp gone bad."

I forced a laugh, and took the proffered box from him. "Sounds good for you."

"Yeah, well, it reminds me of Kayla, and I don't need

that shit." Jordan took the twenty Molly held out and bounced off the hood again on his way back around. "Good to see you, Liv."

He ducked in behind the wheel and took off. Kayla... there was that name again. Logan didn't want it to be like it was with her; Jordan didn't want to be reminded of her. The girl must have been some kind of perfect. She must have been Logan's world. What had happened, though? Why had she left him, and why was I anything like her?

The weight of the pizza lifted from my hands. "Wake up, girl. Our midnight snack is getting cold."

I shook my head to free it of the thoughts of Logan and Jordan and ... who the heck was Kayla?

"You coming?" Molly yelled.

I stalked up to her side, my blood boiling near the surface in a way that prevented me from thinking before speaking. "Who in heaven's name is Kayla? Some ex-girlfriend everyone's completely in love with. Still. And no one ever the flip talks about, unless it's something ambiguous that's left hanging with absolutely no freaking explanation."

Molly stopping walking. "He hasn't told you?"

"Told me what?" I demanded.

"Look, I don't know ... I wasn't really friends with him back in our first year, but I'm pretty sure he took the next year off because ... there were rumours."

"For crying out loud. If he's still in love with his ex just tell me."

"Sometimes you sound like such an old lady." Molly's voice rose to a screeching octave in mimic of my own. "*For crying out loud.*"

I hit her, smack in the arm with my fist.

Molly chuckled, but it was tight and edged with something I couldn't quite place. "I thought you broke up with him, and you know ..." She sliced me an I-can-see-into-your-soul look. "... you don't care."

"I don't." Darn it, she was right. I had no place to care who the bejeebers Kayla was, or what she meant to Logan. In fact, I had no place to even be thinking about him, or her, or any of it.

Molly ducked up the stairs toward her room and I followed, trying to push the unwelcome coil of hatred away. When we reached our destination, she slid the key in her lock and held open the door. I threw myself onto her tartan blanket covered bed, and Molly started speaking before she'd even set down the box.

"Logan up and left toward the end of our first year. He'd been a pretty big partier, slept around a bit, had lots of friends, but he just up and drove out of here early one morning without even packing up his room or saying goodbye. A rumour went around ... hell, a dozen rumours went around. But a few weeks later, when Dane came back from dropping all Logan's stuff to him, he said Logan's sister had died, and he wasn't coming back."

It felt as if my heart abandoned my chest, leaving behind nothing but a gaping ache.

I'd never had a sibling, so I could barely begin to imagine the pain he'd been through. It must have been horrific. Worse. It must have shattered their world and continued to do so every single day. I was such a jerk for worrying about grades and careers and futures, and my stupid reputation, while Logan supported me through it all when he'd lost his sister. My problems were nothing compared to that.

Chapter 23

MY **LAPTOP** had been gone for two days and I felt lost without it, but I tried to keep perspective. Even if I relied on that thing heavily for schoolwork, for music, for keeping up with the rest of the world, it was only a computer.

I was stuck in Oxley's computer lab and it sucked worse than chilli chocolate. Law was a hard enough subject as it was without the thump of some dude's rap music in the background, the constant chatter of the two fresher girls on the computer next to me, and the continual opening and closing of the door. Not to mention it was darn stuffy that I'd peeled off both my jacket and sweater then slung them over the back of the chair. Heaving a frustrated sigh, I ground my molars together and tried to focus through the cacophony of noise.

Noise wasn't the only barrier to my focus. It had been

twenty-eight days since I'd run out on Logan. Five days since I'd seen him up at uni. One day since I'd learned the truth about Kayla. Even though she'd died almost two years ago, it must still hurt every day. He must still think about her constantly. For him and Jordan to rarely mention her—they both had to be carrying the pain of death close to their hearts. It made me want to hug them both, tell them how sorry I was that life sometimes sucks.

Focus. It had been twenty minutes and my cursor still hadn't moved. Nor had the volume in the room faded. I needed a computer in my room. Desperately. Pity I hadn't told my parents about my stuff being stolen yet. I knew it wasn't my fault, but I just wasn't in the right frame of mind for the lecture my mother would surely deliver. So as usual, I was procrastinating until I had no choice but to tell her or until I blurted it out. I had a long history of both.

The door opened again, and whispers hissed on the air for a few seconds before the room fell to deathly silence for thirty seconds. Outrageous laughter erupted on the other side of the computer lab.

I spun around. "Shut the hell up! Some of us are trying to study here."

The dude whose music had been irritating me for the better part of the last two hours spun in his chair and laughed even harder. There was a guy crouched beside him who wasn't there before. His gaze flicked back and forth between me and the screen.

Music-man looked right at me and said, "Go screw yourself. Oh, wait ..." He turned back to the computer, pointing to the screen. "... you already did that. Didn't you?"

Before I drew another breath, I'd darted across the room and was peering at his computer. The blue stripe of a popular social media site spanned the top of his screen and smack in the centre was a video clip. Before he even hit play I knew what it was, and the world dropped out from underneath me. My chest tingled with dread.

The infrared image I'd recorded weeks ago played on-screen.

The room was deathly silent except for the the undeniable rustling of sheets coming from the video.

My heart slowed to a sluggish beat, and my mouth soured. Someone slapped me on the back. Laughter filled the room. Then the image froze on me reaching to stop the recording.

Likes, shares, comments ... there were dozens of them.

This wasn't happening. Why did I ever record myself sleeping, and why, good lord, why didn't I delete it the moment I'd seen the truth? My palms slammed into the door but it didn't budge. I rattled the handle, but couldn't get out. I needed out of here, now. Why was the freaking door not letting me out?

The auto lock.

I flicked it, pulled the handle down and barged my shoulder against the glass. The door gave way, allowing me to burst into the cool afternoon air of Front Courtyard. Humiliation pounded through my veins and pumped my legs forward all the way out of Front, over the bridge, through the car park, and the hell away from there.

Once I was out I didn't stop.

That video would go viral.

Everyone in college, on campus, would see it. Heck, Ella had probably seen it and already emailed her mother, who'd ring my mother. And there was no getting it back. This would be worse than first semester. That moment in the dining hall would be multiplied by a billion. I'd never be able to show my face again.

I choked back the noise that tried to break free from my throat and kept running. This couldn't be undone. It wouldn't be forgotten.

I ran down the road and turned off campus toward town. I ran uphill, along roads, past houses. I ran and ran, and didn't even stop when the pain seared my lungs.

The image was scorched in my mind; the video on a continual loop of dancing blankets, soft moans, groans of pleasure, and my sleepy face paused at the very end.

Eventually, I collapsed on the ground, and everything was blurred pain. Each ragged breath in struggled to pull past the lump in my throat. A lump that represented the end of my dignity. I bit it down and erupted into sobs, huge heaves that tightened my chest until it would surely burst.

SOMETIME LATER, a warm hand brushed mine. I somehow knew that I was at the lookout, the lights of Armidale twinkling in the darkness below.

"Liv?"

I closed my eyes and swallowed. Everything felt numb; my fingers, my toes, my chest, even my thoughts. In the next instant I was moving, cradled against a hard chest and I melted into it, letting the horror of the afternoon carry me away.

I was in a car, then I wasn't; I was in Logan's arms as he carried me inside. The door snicked closed behind us and Logan placed me on his lounge, laying me along its entire length. It was far warmer than the hard ground had been. He walked away and returned with a brown blanket that he tossed over my legs and pulled up around me, tucking it into the side of the chair. He disappeared again and I started to shiver.

Trembles raked through my entire body in waves. I wasn't sure when it had gotten so freezing, but I was icy to the core. The shivers felt as if they came from my very bones, and now they'd started they couldn't stop, the coldness suddenly hitting me.

Logan appeared again and bent by my head. "Sit up a little," he urged, placing a pillow behind my back.

I did as instructed, and he pressed a steaming mug into my hands. I curled them around it, my numb fingers tingling with the sudden warmth, and lifted it to my face to inhale the balmy steam. Then he sat on the floor, his arm slung over his knee which was propped up. He focused on my face while I stared into the mug, coaxing the steam into my cold soul.

"Logan," I said his name softly, like a prayer. A prayer that once he heard the truth, he wouldn't send me away. I couldn't face college.

"Liv ..." He shook his head. "You were lying on the icy ground with no jacket, trying to freeze yourself to death."

A violent shiver tore through me, attempting to prove

his words true. I sipped the tea, but still I couldn't get warm. Something had frozen inside me and there was no hope. My world had fallen apart, and there was no way I could pull it back together. This time it was too much. The illusion of perfection was shattered. Everyone would know that I wasn't the person I needed to be for the life I was born into. My career, my reputation, me ... it was all lost.

Logan's hand smoothed the loose hair back from my eyes, his finger trailing over my forehead, down the side of my face. I closed my eyes slowly and leaned into his touch.

"Dane rang. Molly thought you might have come here."

My eyes sprung open, and I sucked in a sharp breath, remembering the reason I'd run. There was no way in heaven's name I could have come here.

The cold still wasn't fading. Another quake rocked my body as it tried to warm itself. Frowning, Logan took the cup from my hands and stood. He placed it on the floor, shrugged off his jacket, then edged his bare foot into the space between me and the back of the lounge, wriggling his way into the tiny gap behind me. There wasn't much room, but he lay on his side and pulled me back into him. My back pressed against his front, and my legs bent to curl around his knees. His arm fit over my waist and his hand tucked underneath my tummy while his breath warmed the back of my neck. The shivers faded as I thawed with the borrowed heat.

Logan sighed. "I'm sorry. I saw it, and I'm so damn sorry. People are assholes."

He tightened his arms around me, and my eyes stung

with unshed tears. My body wanted to relax into his embrace, but I knew that I couldn't. That was an understatement. People were downright cruel. The way we found humour in other people's pain was just so wrong. Everybody did it; we were all guilty, and I had to share the truth with him so that he understood what he saw.

"It's real." I dragged the words out through a tight throat. "I have this thing called sexomnia and it means I ... I masturbate while I'm asleep. I don't mean to do it, and I don't want to. I fall asleep every night telling myself not to do it; *don't let it happen.* But I wake in the morning not knowing if I did or if I didn't, and it's so flipping scary that I can do something and have absolutely no control or recollection. I hate it. And everyone knows ... I mean, they knew before, thanks to Christian, but they know it's real, because they've seen for themselves and I can't ..." My voice cracked. I held my body rigid, bracing myself for Logan to push me away. "I can't ever be normal."

He slid his hand out from under my side and pulled it through my hair, pressing soft fingers to my forehead, tracing the lines of my ear, my cheek, my throat. His lips pressed against the back of my neck and my heart paused, anxiously waiting, hoping, fearing.

"I'm broken. You don't need—"

"I need you, Liv."

"I'm not—"

"Shh ..." He pressed another kiss to my neck, and followed it with a second one right below my ear, awakening the warm buzz in my belly his touch always caused. "I need you, and I don't care about what you do or don't do in your sleep."

I sucked my bottom lip, pressing my teeth into it. He didn't get it at all.

"You've always been perfect."

My throat clogged with unshed tears. I was tired of fighting. I needed Logan as much as he needed me. He loved me regardless of my faults, my flaws, all the tiny imperfections, and there was something about that which made me feel as if I were falling, but it was okay—I had a safety net, and that net was him. He didn't understand though, and I couldn't allow myself to fall without him knowing exactly what it meant.

"You wouldn't be able to sleep in the same bed as me. I'd keep you awake at night, and you'd wind up hating me. It's no way to live, Logan."

His lips then his tongue flicked over the place where my ear met my jaw and he whispered, "I don't care. I love you and we'll make it work. Just don't try to block me out again. You've made me feel alive for the first time in years, and I'm not letting you go. I will be a better person. I promise you; I'll be the best that I can and we'll be okay."

I rolled over to look in his eyes. The couch was so narrow that our bodies pressed together, and Logan's face was a mere inch from mine, his nose almost touching my cheek. Despite the clenching of my chest and the thickness in my throat, there was a conflicting tingle running through my whole body. One that wanted to pull his mouth to mine.

But what he said was wrong.

"Stop putting yourself down. You're honest and kind and understanding. You're the best person there ever was, and don't you dare go changing. Not for anyone."

Logan's gaze dropped, his brow furrowed, and I knew he was thinking of her; of Kayla. I studied his creased brow, his long lashes fanned against his bronze cheeks, the golden stubble flecked with red along his jaw. I shouldn't have said it when he hadn't told me about her, but I wanted to ease his pain. "Whatever happened with Kayla wasn't your fault."

"And what's happening to you isn't your fault."

That was my breaking point.

I couldn't fight that darn ache for him any longer. I closed the miniscule distance between us, placing my mouth on his and kissing his soft bottom lip.

Instantly, Logan deepened the pressure. His lips moved hard and fast against mine as if this were the last kiss he'd ever give. His tongue traced the seam of my lips and I gave, tasting his breath as my mouth opened, sweet and familiar and *home*.

My hand found its way to his chest, trailed down to the hem of his shirt with my insatiable need to feel his bare skin. Good lord, I needed him. My fingers slid underneath and found his hard abs, just as perfect as always. Logan purred against my kiss and his hand slammed into my lower back, pressing my hips against him. All this time I'd thought he would reject me once he found out the truth. That he'd hate me the same way Christian had hated. But I should have known Logan was different. He was sweet and caring, and more special than anyone who'd come before him.

My heart felt like it expanded to fill my entire chest, leaking down into my arms, my legs, my everywhere.

Suddenly, one hand on his bare skin wasn't enough,

but lying on my side, the other was trapped underneath me. So without breaking our connection, I rolled onto his chest, my knee pushing between his. The movement freed my other hand and I brought it to his face, my fingers playing along the scruff at his jaw. Every inch where Logan touched me thrummed with anticipation. If I felt as if I were falling before, now I felt as if I'd been caught. And I knew with a certain surety that my net wouldn't break.

Desperate for breath, I pulled away just enough to draw in a lungful of air. "Logan—"

"I don't care, Liv."

He hooked his arm under my rear and stood, walking us to his bedroom. Finally, I was warmed with the heat flaring through every part of me. He flopped backwards onto the mattress and pulled me down with him.

I had no intention of ever letting go.

Chapter 24

I **DREW IN** a deep breath, as I did every morning when I first woke, and was filled with the heady scent of Logan. I wasn't perfect and nor was he, but I felt more confident to face what today would bring knowing I had him on my side. Snuggling further into his warm chest, it hit me that we were still in the exact same position we'd fallen asleep in—my cheek resting on his chest, his arm wrapped around me, and my leg hoicked over both of his. The implications of that were undeniable, and filled me with a ray of hope.

Surely I couldn't have partaken in any risqué behaviour without moving. Logan stirred, his hand roaming along my side to rest just shy of my rear.

"Mmm, morning," he mumbled.

"Hi there." I pushed my hips forward, pressing myself against his thigh. Logan moaned and his fingers moved sluggishly to cradle my chin which he tipped up, so he could place a none-too-sweet kiss on my lips. I could really get used to this sort of greeting. When he drew back, I whimpered, "Let's just stay in bed all day."

And that's what we did until Jordan came knocking at the door. "Hoi," he called through the timber. "You guys have company. Drag your arses out of bed."

Groaning, Logan broke the trail of kisses he was leaving across my collarbone. "Whoever it is, tell them to get lost."

"No can do, bro."

"Olivia Dean, get that tush of yours dressed and come talk to me." Savvy's voice screeched through the door.

I couldn't help but smile. It quickly fell though, as I recalled the events of yesterday. I'd been so wrapped up in Logan, I hadn't thought about what would happen when I faced everyone else. Molly knew about the sleep sex thing, but Savvy didn't. My tummy felt kind of weird in a rock-hard way.

Logan dragged himself out of bed and went to his cupboard where he pulled on his sweats and rifled through for a few seconds before tossing a t-shirt at me. "Put this on."

"It's cool. I'll just wear my clothes from yesterday."

Logan raised his eyebrow and said, "Wear the shirt."

"Why?" I asked.

"Just do it."

Shrugging, I pulled it over my head, and good heavens it smelt divine, like Logan, just after he'd showered—all fresh and crisp and clean, and with that oceany smell that must be his washing detergent. The black tee hung too long, hitting me mid-thigh, but Logan didn't seem to care. A slow smile spread across his face and he said, "Now, isn't that better than a thin shirt that smells like day-old sweat?"

"Hey!" I snatched a pillow from the bed and tossed it at him. Logan caught it out of the air and set it on the quilt. "That's my favourite blouse you're talking about." It was a long-sleeved Espirit shirt, and although I did love it, he was right.

I retrieved my jeans from the floor and tugged them on, then smoothed my hair into a ponytail. I probably looked as if I'd been doing, well, exactly what I had been doing all day. But there wasn't much to be done about that, so I switched to a messy bun, hoping that would help.

"What are you guys doing in there? Hurry up," Savvy yelled.

"Dumbass question, Savannah." Molly was there too.

My chest swelled and constricted wondering how they would react once I got out there. Just how bad things were back at Oxley?

Molly laughed. "What would you be doing if you were locked up in a bedroom with Logan Hays?"

"Not making my friends wait outside," Savvy answered.

"Whoa," Molly said. "Too much info. Didn't know you were into sharing."

Good lord, those two were out of control together. I reefed the door open just as Jordan broke into a deep laugh worthy of a whole pack of hyenas. My face burned in what I was sure was a ghastly shade of red.

Savvy flew at me before I was even out of the door, her arms pulling me into a tight hug. "Honey, I saw it."

She squeezed me tight, and I caught Molly's gaze over Savvy's shoulder. The other girl smiled wistfully as her shoulders rose on a sigh.

"We tried to get rid of it," Savvy continued. "Molly reported it to the dean, but ..."

She didn't need to say it. That damn clip would never be gone, and it was my own fault. Once things like that were on social media there was no getting them back, and no stopping them spreading like fire. We all knew that's exactly what would have happened in the first two minutes it was up. Just thinking about it made me feel sick. It was a wonder my mother hadn't blown up my phone with messages.

Savvy finally let me go and glanced around looking for somewhere to sit. She plopped herself on the floor. Molly's smile fell, and she said, "How are you?"

I shrugged, pinching my lip between my teeth to hold in the emotion. I couldn't look her in the eye when I said, "All right, I guess."

Savvy had found a spot on the lounge and patted the seat beside her. I glanced behind me, looking for Logan, and he threw me a lopsided smile as he walked across the room and snaked his arms around my middle, resting his chin on my head.

"You got any more tea?" I asked.

"Sure."

"Water for me, please," Savvy said from the couch. "And nice attire there, Livia. Makes you look like he owns you."

Grumbling under his breath, the words "that's the point", barely audible, Logan retreated to the kitchen and

I sat my butt on the floor facing Savvy. Being owned by Logan wasn't a bad thing at all, and truth be told, he'd probably owned my heart since the day he took me to the falls.

"Any clue as to who took the footage? It might help track the lowlife down," Savvy said.

"Really, Savannah?" Molly plonked beside me on the floor, crossing her legs grade-school style. "Think about that for a minute."

"What?" Savvy said, totally clueless to the obvious answer.

Glancing at my jeans, I tucked my hair behind my ear. "I took it. It was on my laptop, and it was the stupidest thing I ever did. That's why the final frame is me leaning toward the camera to turn it off."

Savvy's mouth dropped slightly open. "Oh. But why would you—"

Molly cut her off. "Doesn't matter. Look, Liv, I know you probably don't want to face Oxley, but you have to march back in there with your head high, because if you don't, they'll only keep talking and it'll get worse. It'll get worse in your head as well. The sooner you face this, the easier it's going to be."

My throat constricted as I said, "It won't be easy at all."

"No, it won't be easy, but we'll be there with you."

"Me too." Logan passed me a steaming mug, gave the second one to Savvy, and dropped to the floor beside me so I was flanked by him and Molly. I swallowed against the sudden dryness in my mouth. I really didn't want to go back there. I'd be happy never to set foot in the dorm again, but Molly was right. Although it made me feel like throwing up, I had to face reality.

"So, we hitting the dining hall for dinner?" she said brightly.

"Okay."

A STEADY stream of people trickled past where we stood in Front Courtyard. It was smack on six o'clock, and apparently everyone in the entire dorm was hungry. Except me. My stomach churned worse than a washing machine on a wonky spin cycle, and I'd be happy to never eat in public again. But Molly was right; I had to do this, and it had to happen today.

Logan's hand rested against mine. Our entwined fingers reminded me I was far from alone. Molly stood with us, blowing warm air into her hands. Snow wasn't something that happened here often, but occasionally it did, and today was one of those days when it might. The air was certainly cold enough.

A small group of girls walked past, their conversation ceasing as they stared at us. Looking away, I edged a little closer into my circle of friends. But Molly threw back her head and laughed, then jabbed me in the arm with her fist as she said, "That's so funny."

The girls kept walking, and I breathed a sigh of thanks to my friend for the diversion.

"Well, well, well ..." *Ella. Great.* She walked toward us out from the direction of Back Courtyard.

"What do you want, Ella?" Molly snapped.

Ella eyed Logan over then turned a fake smile on me. "You missed social committee. Again."

"You know what?" I said. "I missed it because you keep stuffing me around with the dates and times, and I'm over your crap, Ella. I quit." I returned her plastic smile. "You can go tattle on me now. I'm sure my mother will be excited to hear from you."

Ella's mouth dropped open. I'd never really seen someone's mouth form a wide *O* like the surprised face actors always pull, but there it was, right on Ella's lips for at least a minute.

I blatantly stared at her, and finally she shook her head, snapping out of her trance.

"Shove off then," Molly said, super sweetly.

Logan chuckled.

Ella pulled her coat closed and tottered away.

Molly directed a grin my way, and her laughter joined Logan's. Ella had been such a cow to me all year, it felt mighty good to tell her where to go. There was no room for people like her in my life, and I wasn't going to let them control it any longer. I wasn't exactly free from caring, but she'd pushed me so far that she was one person I didn't give a single hoot about keeping happy.

"Hey." My shoulders tensed at the male voice, but Logan's closed hand shot out and Dane fist bumped it. Then Dane dropped his arm over my shoulders and pulled me into his side, dwarfing me under his arm. "Hey, Liv. We going to show these losers what you're made of?"

"Let's eat," Savvy said, appearing between Logan and Molly.

I glanced around our tight circle and felt like crying.

Again. Never in a million years would I have imagined feeling so loved by friends—true friends—who stood by my side, regardless of what other people would think.

Molly led the way into the dining hall while me, Logan, Savvy and Dane followed. The dinner line coiled around the edge of the room, but I could tell only about half the Oxley kids were already here. That meant we'd be smack in the middle of the line, so everyone would see us here tonight whether they came to dinner early or late. The whispers and glances started immediately, and I felt Logan's grip on my hand tighten. Molly and Savvy talked around us, and even though I was so distracted that I had no idea what they were saying, I nodded and smiled.

We stood in line, and unlike the other times I'd faced this—the hub of college life, alone—no one approached me. People nodded and greeted my friends, and I smiled when I should have, until we were almost at the front of the line. Molly and Savvy had already swiped their cards and moved through the servery. With a quick nod to Dane, Logan moved to wait just outside; since he didn't live here, he couldn't eat here, nor could he enter the servery.

The voices came from behind us.

A guy and a girl. "Heard Oliva Dean did it in the court-yard, totally naked and not caring who saw …"

Swallowing, I blocked them out and concentrated on the feel of Dane's hand on my shoulder. I could do this. People were going to talk, and they sure as heck were going to exaggerate. I had to face that truth and live with it. Dane's hand suddenly dropped and I tensed.

"Shut the hell up," he growled.

This was ridiculous. What would happen when I was

alone, as I surely would be at some point? I spun around and looked directly at the girl. "I never did it in the court-yard, but I was thinking about putting on a show tonight if you want to spread the word. Dane, here, will be selling tickets. Five bucks a pop."

The girl looked back at me blankly, her eyes unblinking and the guy, her boyfriend I was pretty sure, started laughing. I turned around, grabbed a plate of roast dinner and moved through the servery, slamming cutlery, des-sert, and a drink onto my tray.

As I came through the 'out' door, Molly's amused smile greeted me, and in response the anger melted and my lips tugged. I'd actually faced the gossipers head on without letting them get to me too much. Unable to suppress the smile, I met Logan's gaze next; he nodded toward the ta-bles. His hand fell to the small of my back and I felt strong.

I was strong.

Keeping a steady, raised gaze, I walked to a free table in the centre of the room and took a seat. My friends filled in the spaces around me.

"What the hell happened in there?" Savvy asked.

Dane slapped his tray down on the table. "Our girl here just put some assholes in their place, right, Liv?"

"Right."

It felt kind of good and awful at the same time. Those people had seen footage of me in my most embarrassing moment, and my dignity was shot to threads, but I'd been the focal point of conversation for long enough. It was time that it ended, and I was the only one who could make my life somewhat normal.

My friends were pretty awesome, but if I wanted to be

treated normally, I had to act it. My thing was a thing, yet it didn't govern who I was or who we were as a group, so I changed the conversation back to them. "What are you all doing for term break?"

"Going home to research primary schools," Savvy said. "I've got prac placements coming up, and I need to figure out which school to request."

"Ooh, sounds fun," Molly chimed in. "I guess that's the real test to see if you like teaching, hey?"

Savvy grabbed the pepper, which she sprinkled generously on her food. "There's no test. I'll love it."

"I'm going home too," Molly said.

"Yup, same here," Dane chimed in. "I need a good dose of ocean air. That stuff is like medicine."

Everyone tucked into their dinner while I handed Logan the extra fork I'd snatched, and motioned for him to share off my plate. "Well, I'm staying here. I've got to catch up on a ton of work."

Logan looked at me sidelong. "Good. I'll have company."

Chapter 25

LOGAN AND I stood outside Belle Venue, watching the sun set over the expansive gardens while the bridal party posed for photographs below. I'd been dreading Bethanie's wedding for weeks.

It wasn't that I didn't like my cousin; I adored her. Growing up, she'd been just enough older that I'd always looked up to her with a kind of childlike envy. I'd thought she had it all—a brother, parents who doted on her, and a pony. All the things I'd always wanted. Her letting me change the RSVP to include the plus one I'd previously declined was super kind. I wasn't sure I would have made it through the occasion maintaining civility with my parents if it weren't for Logan's reassuring touch. Not after the painful phone call that ensued when she finally saw the video. Turns out you can't be tagged and not have everyone in your friends list witness the tagging. When we'd seen them from a distance at the church it hadn't been too bad. Sure, Mum gave Logan the onceover in the same way she'd eyed up my purse to make sure it matched my shoes, and the look in her eyes said she thought he didn't match, but I didn't care.

He looked mighty fine in suit pants and a dress shirt, especially with the top button undone to show off that tiny bit of skin at his collar that I couldn't resist touching. There was no one else I'd prefer to have as my plus one, regardless of how he or she looked. I would have preferred it if he didn't shave, though. His face seemed sadly bare.

"At the last wedding I went to, Kayla and Jordan decided to make chocolate-covered rose petals while everyone was distracted with cake cutting."

His hand moved in circles across my back.

"No way! Please tell me it wasn't from the bouquet."

He chuckled.

"Tell me about her."

Logan sighed, a heavy drawn-out noise that spoke of heartbreak. "She was beautiful, and sassy, and she was sixteen ..." His voice choked, and I hung my arms around his waist, resting them on his hips, feeling terrible for dredging up painful memories. She was a huge part of his life though, and I wanted to share it. Maybe in time ...

"I'm sorry. I shouldn't have asked. You don't have to tell me, I get—" Logan silenced me with a soft kiss.

"It's okay. I want to." He nestled my head in the space under his chin. "Kayla and Jordan were only a year apart, and they were close. I thought they'd both be all right if I left. But they were trouble. Together, apart, they were always up to no good, and I was forever bailing them out. Like at that wedding with the fondue fountain." Logan sighed. His voice had an almost wistful tone, but that changed when he continued.

"The bastard never actually hit any of us, but I guess I never realised how much I'd shielded them both from his constant attacks." Logan took a long breath and I rested my cheek on his chest, my fingers stroking the exposed *V* of skin. "He'd yell that we were worthless sacks of shit for stupid stuff like not putting a dirty dish in the sink, then he'd slam it into the wall so close I'd think he was trying to brain me. But that wasn't the worst; there were the times he'd go days without talking. He'd talk to everyone else, just not the person who he was pissed off with. Walk right past them, like they didn't exist. God, that made me feel like I was the worthless sack of shit he was always banging on about."

"Whatever happened, Logan, I'm so, so sorry. You have to believe, though, that it wasn't your fault."

"It was and it wasn't." His hand dropped from stroking my hair and his chest rose beneath my cheek. "It was that bastard's fault for the years of beating us all down with hurtful words until we thought we were no better than dirt under his feet. It was my mother's fault for being just as bad, but mostly … mostly … hell, Liv. I should never have left either of them. I'd thought I was doing the right thing. My parents laughed when I told them I was going to uni to get a degree. They thought I lied about my high school results, that there was no way I could have achieved the right grades to get in and that … that made me so damn determined to prove them wrong. I lost sight a little though, got wrapped up in the college life. I still studied, but I partied hard too. Then the night I got the call ..."

Logan scraped his cheek through my hair and I tightened my arms around him so my hands came together at his back.

"The second I woke to my phone buzzing, I knew. My stomach dropped, and I didn't know if it was Kayla or Jordan, but my gut told me there was something wrong. And it was with one of my siblings. Jordan was screaming down the line when I picked up. He couldn't wake her."

His voice cracked, and his chest heaved against my cheek. I held onto Logan while he let go, small sobs and sniffs that I could feel in my own heart, and I cried with him.

"Painkillers," he said. "Did you know that if you take enough of them you just fall asleep and never wake up?"

I released my squeezing hold and took his face in my hands, then gently placed a kiss on his mouth and followed it with another. I dropped a million tiny kisses all as soft as could be, and Logan's tears mixed with mine—salty, and wet, and oh-so broken. My heart bled for his loss. Not only the loss of his sister, but the loss of so many other things. Logan was a precious man who didn't deserve the cards he'd been dealt. He'd lost his sister, and here he was, raising his brother to save Jordan from a similar fate.

How dare my mother look at him as if he were anything less than saintly?

We stood in the fading light until the bridal party disappeared from their photo shoot, each of us quiet as we clung to each other. Logan had had a hard life, but he didn't let it knock him down, or taint his caring personality. More than any degree or job, that was something to be proud of.

I locked Logan's hand in mine and together we entered the reception hall, ready to face the evening, both of us a little more sombre.

Of course the seating plan had us at the same table as my parents. I hadn't really expected anything less, but I'd hoped it would be different. We walked into the room amidst a wave of guests, my arm around Logan's waist and his around mine. My heels clicked against the polished floorboards as I led us toward the table marked with a *four*.

They weren't there yet. Probably making connections, working the crowd, or one of those other terms my mother used for talking to people she barely knew, but from whose acquaintance could be a benefit. It was so fake.

Logan pulled the chair out and I snapped from my daze. "Sorry. I've been so lost in my own thoughts today."

"It'll be okay." His lips brushed over my forehead. What he didn't say then, but he had earlier was *Don't let them hurt you.* I concentrated on those words as we both sat then I reached for the wine in the centre of the table. "Want one?"

Logan shook his head and his hand settled on my leg which was jigging. I was so nervous, I even forgot he'd volunteered to drive tonight.

"Welcome ..." The MC had taken his place behind the microphone and gazed out over the assembled guests. "The bridal party will be with us shortly. But while we wait, let's go over a couple of house rules ..."

My attention was yanked away as my mother bustled up to our table and delicately slipped into the seat beside me. Dressed in a teal number that would have cost more than Logan's Corolla, she looked stunning, if somewhat thin. Dad was two steps behind her, his tie matching her dress. I hadn't seen them at the church as we'd snuck in a little late. Her elbow bumped into my chair as she took her napkin and laid it across her knee with a flourish.

Oops. I'd forgotten; I reached for the folded square of material on my plate. Logan squeezed my knee, and with a steady breath I dropped the napkin where it was and snuck my hand under the table to rest on his. It was a tiny act of defiance.

We sat through the MC's greeting and the welcoming of the bridal party without conversation. It wasn't until they were seated that my mother acknowledged my presence with a, "Hello, Olivia." Her gaze slid to Logan. "Is your friend a fellow Law student?"

"This is Logan, who I told you I was bringing, and no. He's not, which I also told you."

Logan reached across me, extending his hand. "Logan Hays. I'm majoring in psychology."

"Oh, lovely. There's a lot of money in the private sector. Will you open your own practice right away, or mentor under someone in one of the major clinics for a few years?"

Bam. Pleasantries were only for people she wanted to impress.

"Actually, I'm planning on working in schools, or somewhere I can help teens."

"Well, Olivia." My mother's attention had moved on from Logan already. "How is school? Are your grades high? I'd hope so after the debacle with that disgusting footage."

How dare she brush him off like that? Logan was a noble man who'd make a fine councillor for troubled kids. It was a career to be proud of, and one that would make a huge difference to many lives. Her questions were what were insignificant.

"Logan's darn good at what he does. He pulls the top grades in his classes, and he's got a knack for empathy and understanding."

"What about your grades, Olivia? I hope they've improved this semester."

"No," I snapped. "And actually ... I'm thinking about switching degrees."

Dad leaned across the table from his spot beside my mother. These huge round tables really weren't as conducive to conversation as people thought. "I beg your pardon?"

"We'll talk about it later." I nodded toward the head table where entrées were just being served. "This is Beth's wedding, after all."

"Absolutely not, young lady, we will talk about this right now." Mum tapped her red nails against her plate.

Logan leaned back in his chair and I felt his other hand press against my lower back, subtly letting me know he was there.

"Fine. Now it is. Law is never what I wanted to do. I don't enjoy it, I've pulled bad grades all year, and I refuse to devote my life to something I've grown to loathe. It was never my dream; it was yours."

"Then what do you propose to do?" Dad said, his tone tight.

I looked him right in the eye. "I don't know. Something I enjoy."

The breath my mother huffed out through her nose was so loud my aunt and uncle glanced at us from across the wide table.

"Where in the world did this preposterous idea come from?" Mum pinned Logan with an icy glare.

"Hardly," I said. "Logan has nothing to do with this decision."

Her lips pursed. "Totally out of the question," she said. "I won't have you disappointing your father any more than you already have."

"You can't choose my future."

"You're nineteen, Olivia, and we're supporting you. So yes, we can."

"Fine. Cut me off. I don't want your money."

My father cleared his throat and I realised the entire table—ten other people—were staring, but for once in my life I didn't care. Logan leaned in, his nose brushing my cheek as he whispered. "You okay?"

I nodded and gulped down a mouthful of wine.

"Need some air?" he asked.

"Sounds wonderful."

Logan took my hand and led me to our spot outside, where he pulled me into a hug which cooled some of my anger, making my legs feel a little weak with the brush of his lips against my forehead.

"Holy cow, that woman is impossible. She makes me

feel like an errant ten-year-old."

"Don't feel bad. Your whole life has been about them, Liv."

My hand rested on his chest. The steady rhythm of his heart beat beneath my palm, and I felt tired. I'd been fighting for so long; fighting to keep my grades high, fighting to maintain a pristine reputation, fighting for everything my parents said I wanted. Realising I wanted none of that had released so much tension. I felt like a sandbag with a hole.

"It's like I don't even know who I am. I mean, I know I enjoy hockey, planning stuff is kind of fun, and I love you. But I have no idea what I want to do with my forever ... and to be honest, I wasn't even sure of you until you made me realise that what I thought I wanted wasn't what I needed at all."

The corner of Logan's mouth tipped up and a blond wave flopped over his left eye, making him look totally mischievous and utterly adorable all at once. "What did you say?"

I frowned, replaying the words in my head, and the moment my thoughts snagged on the right one, I smirked up at him. Logan's hand moved to cradle the base of my head, and I grabbed the collar of his shirt, tugging his face down to meet mine.

"I love you, Stalker Boy."

The kiss he responded with was borderline inappropriate for being in such a public place, but I didn't care. Logan was my anchor in an unsteady future.

Epilogue

6 MONTHS LATER

I **PEERED OVER** Jordan's shoulder at the UAC guide flopped open under his hand. A huge red circle marked Bachelor of Engineering, and it was at UNE; our university, right here in Armidale. I hid the excitement from my voice, knowing it might sway his mind. Staying close was what Logan had hoped he'd do, but we both knew telling Jordan that would make him run in the opposite direction.

"Do you really want to be an engineer, or have you just heard all the rumours about them partying the hardest?"

"Bit of both," Jordan said, then flipped the pages forward. "It's so hard coming up with all these choices. What I really want to do is Medicine, but then ..."

"We'd have the same classes?" I teased.

"Oh man, we would? You'd totally cramp my style, Liv. Please tell me you aren't doing Sports Medicine when you go back. Please."

I chuckled. "Nah, fun as that would be, I'm leaning more toward Marketing. I loved Socio, and Marketing revolves around human reaction and perception, so Socio would be a subject I could continue through to four hundred level. Using that knowledge would be pretty awesome too, once I'm out in the work force."

"You'd be good at that—yellow sells more burgers and all that crap. Hey … I bet you'd get to organise shit too."

"Probably. What's your third choice?"

"Dunno." Jordan twirled the pen between his fingers.

He had months to submit his application yet. Good for him he wasn't like me, though. I must have switched choices a dozen times already. My life had changed so much, and moving out of Oxley was just the beginning. I still had my nocturnal issues, but Logan was so supportive. Turned out it wasn't every single night, and it wasn't all night long, as Christian had led me to believe. The sleep specialist had said it was stress related, so maybe that was why it wasn't too often now that everything had settled down.

"You ready, babe?" Logan's voice carried from the kitchen.

"Two minutes," I yelled, running back into the bathroom where I applied a final coat of gloss to my lips and stepped back into the living room, my tummy fluttering with nerves.

Logan gave me a huge smile from where he leaned against the couch, his long legs crossed at the ankles.

"I'm so darn nervous, Logan. Am I making the right choice?"

He pulled that errant lock of hair back from his face. "You're doing the right thing. Forget about what is right, or proper, or bloody pretentious, and remember that for once you're doing what's right for you. What makes you happy."

I drew in a deep breath. "Why are you always so right?"

"It's a talent." He smirked.

I grabbed my purse, and Logan's arm swooped around my back as I bent to retrieve my joggers. I stood up, swivelling around to face him, and Logan pulled me against him and planted a solid I'm-not-going-to-see-you-for-six-hours kiss on my lips, totally making the earlier gloss application pointless.

"Take it outside, bro. I don't need to see that shit."

I broke away from our kiss, just far enough to yell at Jordan, "So don't watch."

He groaned and Logan brushed his nose against mine. "Ready?"

"Ready."

Logan slung his backpack over his shoulder and held the front door open for me. The outside air was already warm and I could tell it was going to be a beautiful day.

We climbed in Logan's car and as the engine started I stared out the front window, and Logan's hand fell on my thigh. We were both headed to uni today, but for entirely different reasons.

This would be his final year of study.

But not mine. Taking a year off to figure out what I wanted to do with my life had seemed like a good idea, but I couldn't just sit around the apartment doing nothing. It took exactly two weeks for that to get boring, and I needed a solid income to pay my share of the rent. They'd offered me a job at the sports centre last year, but I'd knocked it back because it would have eaten into my precious study time. Since I had nothing but precious time to ponder my future, the job seemed perfect.

Not only was it something I'd enjoy, but it was at a convenient location. Since it was on campus, Logan could drop me off on his way to lectures, or I could walk. I was lucky they had a position when I hit them up. I'd be working four shifts a week in a mix of locations; the front desk, the shop, and during school breaks, they'd offered me full-time hours to help out with vacation care for primary school kids. That I was most nervous of, even though the idea of running sports for kids sounded like fun.

I took a deep breath and stepped out of the car, hoping that I actually did enjoy this.

"Liv." Logan dipped his head to look out the window. When our gazes met, he said, "What do you want for dinner?"

"Surprise me." Smiling at how domestic we'd become, I turned to the sports centre, but before I'd taken three steps Logan called my name again. I spun around and the grin spread across his face was so huge that the chunk of hair that often fell over his eye brushed his top lip. "Love you."

I grinned. "I love you, too."

I didn't know where my life was going, but I knew I had the friends in place to get where I needed to go.

If you loved *Shh!* read on for a
sneak peek of Stacey Nash's

Oxley College #2

SYNOPSIS:

Jordan Hays knows just how precious life is; that's why
he has his own mapped out. He'll work to pay his way
through university while he studies hard, regardless of
the constant distractions. Because when it comes to becoming a nurse, he's deadly serious. He won't fail to save
someone again.

But Hex Penton is way too similar to the sister he lost,
and even though the only thing more fun than stupid
dares is the crazy girl who sets them, Jordan needs to
make a choice. Hex believes every moment is important;
every opportunity must be taken, because you never
know when the world will be yanked out from underneath you. With the foundations he's based his life on
shaken, Jordan must discover what's more important:
making sure Hex's life isn't wasted, or remembering how
to live his.

It's time to play truth or dare.

Wait!

HEX

I POURED MYSELF a shot and mixed it with lemonade. Liquid courage, that's what this was, and I'd only need one more then I'd be right to head downstairs to the function that was rocking this joint tonight. I didn't bother with the stupid meet-and-greet the senior guy had said I 'had to attend'. Mum had only just left by the time five rolled around and I just wanted to sort my room out. From my window, I could see people filling the courtyard already. The music was loud, but the voices weren't. They all looked a little awkward, standing around, cradling plastic cups as if they were scared of each other. It wasn't hard to pick out the seniors. They were the ones rocking massive smiles and working the crowd. I tipped my head back and downed the drink in a single gulp. Well, only one way to make this shit downstairs bearable. *Eeesh*, the drink practically stole my breath. Might have made it a bit strong.

A quick look in the mirror and everything was in place—hair looked pretty decent, shorts weren't riding up my butt, and all the essentials were tucked away beneath my tank top. Everyone had said it was going to be freaking freezing up here in Armidale, but so far it was like living in a sauna. The air was thick and hot, and that sun had one heck of a bite. Good thing it was sinking now, so my shoulders wouldn't burn. Again. They already stung like a bitch from the little bit they'd seen while we lugged my stuff in from the car this morning.

Right. I drew in a deep breath, squared my shoulders. This would be a piece of cake. I tucked my room key into my bra and snuck one last look out the window at the courtyard below. People. Easy-peasy.

Before I could over-think the whole thing, I yanked open the thick wooden door and stumbled as it caught my heel on the way out. Good thing my Docs were solid. Those fashionable strappy sandals everyone wore this summer wouldn't have saved my bony ankle from certain destruction.

My dorm floor was dead empty. I swore I'd heard voices earlier this afternoon, but whoever it was must be in the throng of it already. The senior resident had said there were three first years on this floor, but there was no way of telling which rooms were occupied. I guessed the others would fill up later in the week, so I'd find out who lived where soon enough. Geez, I was still stalling— standing here staring at closed doors like a freaking lunatic. Before I could conjure any more time-wasting thoughts, I stepped out of the hall and into the stairwell. Music from the courtyard echoed all the way up the structure, bouncing off the concrete walls and tiled stairs as if they were made for just this purpose. The music wasn't too bad. Not top forty, but not golden oldies either. Good dance music.

As I emerged into the courtyard, I plastered on the

friendliest smile I could muster. I didn't need to seek out someone to make me look less alone. My block senior marched up to me right away with a mock scowl. "Where were you?"

I shrugged. "Sorry."

"Well you missed out on meeting the other freshers in our block."

"Oops." I needed to find a way out.

"Looks like you need a drink." And there it was.

"Ahh, yeah. That'd be great, thanks."

He disappeared. The crowd wasn't as thick as it had looked from my window. People were scattered around sparsely in small groups. Some girl caught my gaze across the way. Maybe she'd be a good one to start with, but a bouncy chick grabbed my arm like we were best buds. "I'm-Amber-and-you-have-awesome-hair."

It took me a second to make out what she was saying, she spoke so fast. I fingered the blue tips of brown hair. The colour freshly applied this morning. "Thanks."

With her arm hooked through mine, she piloted me toward the largest group of people. "Hey everyone," she cooed, "meet my new friend ..."

"Hex," I answered.

"Hex," she mimicked. "Where are you from?"

"Umm ..." it wasn't a trick question, so why was I stumbling. "North."

"Ahh, a coastie."

"Not quite, it's more inland—"

Just then Jason, that was his name, reappeared, passing me one of the plastic cups everyone else seemed to have. I shot him a grateful smile and downed it in two gulps. Holy crap the stuff stung on the way down. I spluttered.

Amber laughed.

Jason cheered. "Looks like you've been here before, Hex."

The evening wore on much the same—meeting new face after new face, with so many names I'd be lucky to remember two or three come morning. Amber remained glued to my side, and after only an hour in her company I was certain we'd wind up good friends. The girl sure was fun and seemed to draw in a crowd with just her bubbly voice. The drinks flowed steadily, but there wasn't so much that people got plastered.

The music lulled and a song I knew well blared to life. I grabbed Amber's hand and pulled her up onto one of the long wooden picnic tables in a corner of the courtyard. She squealed the second she realised what I was up to, and in three seconds flat had her hands above her head, her eyes closed, and was shimmying her body like a pro. I'd definitely found my long-lost twin. Someone wolf whistled below us, but I drowned them all out with singing.

When the music ended, all I could hear was a chant.

He-ex. He-ex. He-ex.

I grinned as I took the plastic cup some guy held up to me. Then Amber joined in the chant and I realised what it was they wanted me to do. I yelled out, "bottom's up," and tipped the entire contents of the cup into my mouth. Amber's name came next and she followed my lead, giving the people what they wanted.

She must have decided it was time to climb down, because she stumbled to the side, and almost fell. We both grabbed hold of each other at the same time and she laughed as if it were the funniest thing ever. Her laugh was amazingly contagious and I burst out too as we both stood there clutching each other by the arms.

When we'd finally pulled ourselves together, I stepped down off the table and right into the personal space of a six-foot-odd hunk of solid muscle. Dark eyes regarded me with a deadly seriousness that shouldn't be seen in a face that handsome. I held his stare for a long minute. There was no way I would back down to this guy who thought he was all that. His jaw clenched and my god, it was as chiselled as any A-grade movie star's. A peppering of jet-black stubble gave him a rugged edge, or maybe that came from his shaggy hair. But geez, he needed to give it up already. He was still staring like he was waiting for me to apologise. God only knew how I'd offended him. A quick check proved my feet weren't stomping his toes.

I raised my right eyebrow.

That made both of his dip.

I held out my hand. "I'm Hex."

"Hex?" His nose screwed up.

"Yes, Hex."

"Weird name."

"No weirder than your attitude."

"You should slow down."

"Excuse me?"

"With the drink. You should slow down."

"And you should piss off."

Who did this guy think he was? He was a tool, that's who. Probably some member of the anti-fun brigade, and that was too bad, because damn, his whole look was amazing.

A laugh burst from him so suddenly, I flinched, and re-alised our hands were still clasped. "Jordan," he said, like he'd only just remembered he hadn't told me his name.

"Well, the pleasure was all yours, Jordan." I retracted my hand. "Don't party too hard, now."

Acknowledgements

In many ways writing Shh! was a huge step out of my comfort zone, but I'm so glad I took that leap. There are many people I need to thank for pushing me into writing this book, into publishing, and most of all into believing I could do this.

As always, my family and in particular my hubby were my biggest supporters. Without their loving support I could never be the writer I am. So, thank you for the constant love and encouragement, and for being my first fans.

I need to send out a huge thank you to the ever patient Keely Crosbie. Thank you for answering my endless questions about life on campus today. It is true that I was once a college student, but you ensured all my knowledge was up to date. Good luck in this year's MB comp!

My twisted pea, ST Bende. If ever there was a born and bred cheerleader it is you. Thank you, thank you, thank you for urging me to write this book. When I said what about a girl with Sexomnia, you could have said no, write MORE JAX, but you didn't and because of that we got Logan. For encouraging me when I thought I couldn't write this story. Whenever I had a moment of doubt you were there telling me that I could, reading my terrible first draft and assuring me that it rocked.

The ever fabulous Anabel is always at the other end of

my phone. Whether it's for a brainstorming sessions, help naming a character, or just to chat about books. You encourage me in so many ways, and for that I am ever thankful. You always read and reread my stories, your generosity knows no bounds. I heart you.

Ah Lauren McKellar, guess what? Contemporary romance is my genre now too. I love you. Thank you for being there through all the yo-yos of will or won't I, which is the right publishing path for this book, oh-my-god have I made the right decision? You never once influenced me one way or another, but were always amazingly supportive. Then when I decided to bring Shh! into the world, you helped me every step of the way. I'd be lost without you.

Also huge a thank you to Suz and Kim for reading Logan and Olivia's story with a fine tooth comb. You ladies are the best. As is my support network; Aussie and Owned and Read, Hunter Romance Writers, thanks for keeping me on the straight and narrow with goals and deadlines, and just well, everything.

My talented cover artist, KA Last, of KILA Designs, you are one clever lady. The art you've created is perfect for Olivia's story. Max Effect did a wonderful job with the formatting, and even though I've already mentioned the wonderful Lauren McKellar it must also be noted that she is the best editor.

But the hugest thank you of all goes out to all my readers, the Nash-alohic street team, all the bloggers and readers who've supported me since Forget Me Not. You are the most important people in this whole process. I am so grateful for each and every person who takes time out of their busy schedules to read and enjoy my books. Readers rock!

About the Author

Stacey Nash calls the Hunter Valley of New South Wales, Australia home. An area nestled between mountains and vineyards, its history and culture have always called to her. Stacey has loved reading for as long as she can remember, so it's no wonder she finally opened a word document and wrote chapter one. Stacey made her publishing debut in 2014 with a young adult novel titled *Forget Me Not*. Writing for the young and new adult market, Stacey's books are all adventure filled stories with a lot of adventure, a good dose of danger, a smattering of romance, and plenty of KISSING!

You can connect with Stacey via

FACEBOOK:
https://www.facebook.com/StaceyLeeNash
TWITTER:
@staceynash
GOODREADS:
https://www.goodreads.com/author/show/
7150198.Stacey_Nash

To stay up to date with new releases and upcoming titles be sure to sign up for Stacey's newsletter at
www.stacey-nash.com

If you enjoyed Oxley College, you may also like

THE PROBLEM
WITH CRAZY

by Lauren K. McKellar

Read on for a sneak peek...

.

THE PROBLEM
WITH CRAZY
by Lauren K. McKellar

The problem with crazy is that crazy, by itself, has no context. It can be good crazy, bad crazy ... or crazy crazy—like it was when my ex-boyfriend sung about me on the radio.

Eighteen-year-old Kate couldn't be more excited about finishing high school and spending the summer on tour with her boyfriend's band. Her dad showing up drunk at graduation, however, is not exactly kicking things off on the right foot—and that's before she finds out about his mystery illness, certain to end in death.

A mystery illness that she could inherit.

Kate has to convince everyone around her that her father is sick, not crazy. But who will be harder to convince? Her friends? Or herself?

The Problem With Crazy *is a story about love and life; about overcoming obstacles, choosing to trust, and learning how to make the choices that will change your life forever.*

www.laurenkmckellar.com

THE PROBLEM WITH CRAZY

In books, people say that bad news can make you look older. I hadn't really seen evidence of that before, but looking at my parents, I could definitely see the toll of time wearing on their faces and bodies: slumped shoulders, crushed foreheads, tired eyes. My middle-aged parents had become old.

"Katie, I'm sorry." Dad raised his head and looked at me. His blue eyes were surrounded by fiery-red streaks from the tears he'd shed, little spidery veins of sadness.

"It's not your fault."

"Th … there's more."

I clutched the edge of my seat, my fingernails digging deep into the creamy suede material. What else could there possibly be? What could possibly be worse than a disease that was going to make him half a man?

"I'm … I'm going to die."

The words ricocheted through my body.

Die.

My dad was going to die.

"He doesn't mean in the 'everyone-is-going-to-die-one-day' way, sweetie, he means—"

"Mum, I know what he means." I snapped my lips together.

"H ... how long?"

"Prognosis is good. About fifteen to twenty years." Mum stared at her nails, unable to make eye contact.

"Wow." I thought about all the things that would happen in the next fifteen to twenty years. I'd move out. I'd have a tour management career. I'd get married. I'd have children. They'd grow up, and Dad would be there for some of it, but not all of it. One day, my dad was going to die, and my kids may not ever have known him except as a distant memory.

One day, I was going to have to face the world alone.

Without him.

Even more without him than I'd been for the last three-hundred and seventy-something days.

"This is just—it's a lot to take in." I bit my lip. "I'm sorry, Dad."

I stood from my seat and crossed the room, hovering over him with my arms extended in an awkward sort of way while Mum, reluctant to leave his side, extended one of her hands to my shoulder.

I felt myself still as time slowed down. My hand was on Dad's shoulder, and he wasn't hugging me back. It was surreal, this moment, seeing the drool as it pooled in the corner of my father's lip. Was this really happening?

"How sweet." I heard Dave before I saw him. He'd walked in the door without knocking. For the first time ever, I wished he were a tiny bit less familiar with my home.

"Hi." I quickly disentangled myself from our embrace and smoothed down my shirt, before walking to Dave's side. He gave me a quick peck on the cheek and handed me a weighted plastic bag.

"I bought ice cream," he smiled, "but only for three." The last sentence was directed with a cool gaze in Dad's direction. I elbowed Dave in the ribs. Couldn't he see that my father was upset?

"Deb, do you need me to remove any unwanted guests?" Dave took a step towards my parents. His knuckles were fisted, white bones showing through. Mum shook her head, no.

"Can you help me pop these in the freezer?" I grabbed the plastic bag from Dave's hands and walked to the kitchen. He followed.

The second we were alone, he cornered me against the bench, his arms on either side of mine so my body pressed hard up against his.

"Now I can give you a proper hello," he whispered in my ear and started nibbling against it.

"Dave." I sighed, and gave him a nudge. He ignored me, pressing closer still.

"Dave. Seriously." This time I gave him a shove, and he stumbled backward. I pushed away from the bench and opened the freezer to put the ice cream in.

"What's your problem?" His arms were folded and his face was grim.

"Dave, it's Dad," I whispered. "He's sick." Even as I said it, the words seemed surreal. How did I describe an illness I barely knew anything about myself?

"Like, a sick idiot who ruined graduation?" I punched Dave on the shoulder. How could he be so tactless when I was trying to tell him something important?

"Stop being such a shit," I hissed. "He has a disease. Something starting with *H*." The actual name escaped me.

I hadn't heard of it before today. There was no "day" or "month" to honour it, like there was with cancer or MS.

This disease was going to steal my father from me— and it wasn't like anything I'd ever heard of.

"What sort of disease?"

"It affects everything. He's going to lose control of his speech, his movement—and then he's going to die." I felt tears well in my eyes and forced them back. Dave put his arms around me and I collapsed into him. I breathed in his cologne as he stroked my hair.

"How long?"

"Mum said maybe fifteen to twenty years? He's going to die," I repeated the words, with little to no inflection. I was removed from myself, from this scene.

"You'll be okay."

His words were of no direct comfort to me, but feeling his arms take my weight and support my body helped. I stood there for a moment, losing myself in him, and let my thoughts fly. I was angry Dad hadn't told us, furious he'd run away, and devastated about the whole situation. I'd never felt so many emotions before: mad, upset, protective, confused, and hurt. Was this normal? To feel everything, all at once?

"I have to go back out there." I forced out the words. I pulled back to look at Dave's face, his pale skin, his electric-green eyes ... he looked so steady, so sure. I wanted to stay in his arms forever.

"We'll go together."

Dave placed his hand on the small of my back and led me back into the living room where my parents waited.

"Kate told me." Dave walked over to the couch. "And I'm sorry, man. That's really rough." He stretched his arm out and took Dad's hand, pumping twice before joining me on the opposite couch. Dad's forehead creased up.

"Paul." Dad nodded slowly.

"You've met Dave, dear, that's Kate's boyfriend."

"Dave," Dad repeated, stretching the word out on his tongue.

Everything my parents had said became somehow more real. Dad had met Dave before, many times. And yet, here he was, acting like he was being introduced to a total stranger. Memory loss.

Wow.

"Dude, you like, came to some of our concerts."

I gave a sharp kick to Dave's ankle.

"Kate, I know you must have a lot of questions," Mum said. "So feel free to ask us anything, anytime. I'm still— I'm still trying to take it all in myself."

"O … okay." I'd never stuttered so much in my life.

"And there is something else we need to tell you, dear."

"Deb, not now. Give 'er a rest," Dad interjected, his voice sounding ever more weary with each passing word.

"What? Tell me." My fingers clenched into tiny fists. "What could possibly be worse than what you've already said?" I felt Dave place his arm protectively around my shoulders.

"Maybe we should wait." Mum eyed Dave's hand.

"Anything you have to say, you can say in front of him." I shook my head. "He's family. You know that." Dave and I locked eyes, and he gave me a special little smile.

"Kate, it's not a good time." Mum's voice was shrill. My heart was beating like a jackhammer, *thud-thud-thud*, over and over in double-time.

"If you don't tell me now, I'll Google it. I'll just search

the disease and see what I can find. We both will."

Silence. Dave took my hand in his, clasping his other hand around it so I was protected entirely within his palms. Mum and Dad looked at each other, her lips pursed, his still loose.

"The disease your father has ..." Mum paused. I nodded at her. *Go on.*

Just tell me. Get it over with.

"It's hereditary."

I struggled to breathe as Dave's fingers slowly unlaced themselves from mine.